Hunter Killer
By
A P Bateman

Facebook: @authorapbateman

www.apbateman.com

Rockhopper Publishing

2021

The Alex King Series
The Contract Man
Lies and Retribution
Shadows of Good Friday
The Five
Reaper
Stormbound
Breakout
From the Shadows
Rogue
The Asset
Last Man Standing

The Rob Stone Series
The Ares Virus
The Town
The Island

Standalone Novels
Hell's Mouth
Unforgotten

Further details of these titles can be found at www.apbateman.com

To Clair
For your understanding, as well as your laughs
and love and friendship

To Summer and Lewis
For keeping me on my toes…

For Dad
For always being there

Chapter One

The Arctic Circle
Fifty miles southeast of Spitsbergen Island
Svalbard Archipelago

King looked at the pistol in the man's hand. He'd been there before, and he'd never got used to it. The impotence of being unarmed and staring down the wrong end of a gun. The man wore thick thermal gloves against the cold and his trigger finger was still nestled against the frame. The sign of a pro. Little chance of a negligent discharge, but given the cold, the thick gloves and the immediate proximity, King would have had his finger on the trigger. But then again, King did not have the gun and the man in front of him did.

The ship trundled onwards, its diesel engines thumping and droning lazily in the background, the steel hull striking occasional slabs of sea ice the size of a single bed. King could see the man's breath in front of him, almost frozen by the time it reached his own face. The breath crystalising slowly and falling to the deck like a snow globe that had been given only a lacklustre shake.

"They warned me about you in Moscow…"

King shrugged. "Whereas I don't even know who you are."

"That makes for the better operative, don't you think?"

King looked at the man's gloves. They seemed thick and cumbersome and half an inch in diameter too big for the trigger guard of the Makarov pistol. But then again, the man was a Russian and they tended to be at home in the cold. Although as he felt the sharp, icy chill on his face, he seriously doubted anyone could get used to this. But King knew that if the tables had been turned, he would have taken off the gloves before he had reached for the gun. Experience counted for so much in this game, and the thought that his opponent hadn't thought this through as thoroughly as he would have, gave him some hope at the very least.

"What do you want?" asked King.

"The same thing as you do."

"I seriously doubt that."

"Well, I suppose I want what's ours, and you want to make sure the world never finds it." He paused, his breath all around him and falling steadily to the frozen deck. "But essentially, we're after the same thing. We both want something and are prepared to kill to stop the enemy getting their hands on it."

King glanced at the ice under the man's feet. Behind him, the rail was heavy with a build-up of icicles, large stalactites hanging down several inches. Eight inches or more in the darker recesses behind the lifeboats. King had the advantage of standing on galvanised steel grating, his footing feeling both firm and secure under him. He realised he was still holding the mug of tea. He looked around for somewhere to put it, then simply dropped it on the deck between them, the tea flooding around the man's feet, the tin mug clattering across the deck towards the lifeboats. "There's a manifest," he said. "If you kill me, they'll know in no time." He nodded at the gun in the man's hand. "And you certainly can't kill me with that, or they'll be looking for a murderer."

The man shrugged like it was nothing. "People have accidents all the time. They slip on ice, fall overboard. It happens."

"Not with nine-millimetre holes in them."

The man waved the pistol to the port side. "Step this way…"

King smiled and shook his head belligerently. "Not in a thousand lifetimes, sunshine," he said. He watched the hesitation in the younger man's eyes. "You shoot me, and there'll be an investigation. People will recall conversations, they'll have alibis. But where were you? As soon as we dock, you'll be the number one suspect."

"I'll be gone way before then," he said, looking at the inflatable tender with its forty-horsepower engine.

"There will be a reception committee at the rigs. You're going nowhere before the ship gets there." He paused, glancing down, and watching the spilt tea freezing around the man's feet. "You made your move too soon, son. Inexperience, that's all."

"Don't you dare patronise me!" He stepped closer. King noticed the finger was inside the trigger guard now, the material of the glove had bunched up. He could see that the Makarov's hammer was not cocked. The trigger could still be pulled, but the weight of the pull on the double-action Makarov was up there with gym equipment. Twice that of a Glock, at around fourteen pounds.

"That RIB won't do you any good out here."

"Let me worry about that. You should worry about yourself. The water will be cold, but it will make your death swift. Give into it, you'll know next to nothing about it…"

King moved quickly, grabbing the pistol, and pushing it back towards the man as he kicked him in the shin with all the force he could muster. Not to cause pain – which it invariably did – but to shove him backwards in the ice formed from the tea he had intentionally spilt. The man had pulled the trigger, but King's grip had eased the slide of the weapon back just enough to disengage the striker and as long as he kept up the pressure, the weapon was useless. The man slipped and tried to regain his balance, but King kicked out again, and followed up with a headbutt onto the bridge of the man's nose. The younger man recoiled, his eyes closed, the pain excruciating, but King gripped him by the windpipe, adding a further dimension for the man's instincts to wrestle with – three different areas for the pain receptors to signal the brain and for the brain to become confused how to deal with each - and pushed him back against the railing. King had the weight and strength advantage, and the man was struggling for traction on the ship's slippery deck. Then King changed tactics and instead of kicking the man's shin again, he hooked his foot behind the man's heel and pulled his leg towards him as he pushed hard on his throat, forcing him backwards against the railing. Momentum, inertia, and gravity came together like the independent notes of a symphony and the man pirouetted over the railing and fell silently twenty feet or so into the icy water. Not even a grunt, let alone a scream, as the man's instincts were to take a deep breath in mid-air, nothing more.

King did not hear the splash above the monotonous thump of the engines. He had the Makarov in his hand, and he tucked it into his pocket as he walked the length of the railing and searched for him in the water. There was plenty of ice, but no yellow and red flashes of colour of the man's ski jacket. King realised he had underestimated the ship's speed, and he looked further out to the stern and saw the man floundering in the water. He turned around and watched the bridge. Above him he thought he saw movement on the upper deck, somebody stepping into a doorway. The light was dim and grey, and it was difficult to judge both distance and movement. But no alarm sounded and nobody else appeared. King turned and looked back at the water for his would-be killer, but the man had gone. Succumbed to the cold and the inevitability of death in such a hostile, merciless environment. Perhaps he had remembered his own hollow words and simply given up the struggle in favour of a swift end. A lungful of water and short struggle under the surface to end the searing pain of the cold. Whatever the scenario, the wake of the ship rolled on, there was no colour in the grey water and King's mission was unimpeded.

For now.

Chapter Two

Three days earlier
Dorset, England

"I really do wish there was another way."

"There is. You're just not looking at the other options. There's always another way." King paused. "The easy way, and the right way. It doesn't sound like either way is going to do us any good here."

"We need you to try."

"We?"

"The service." Mereweather paused. "Very well, I need you. The ramifications of this are far-reaching."

"You were giving me time to help with Caroline's recuperation."

"To act as a mere nursemaid? Caroline is mending well. I spoke to her before I left town." Town. King smirked. Mereweather came from a class of people who probably still thought London had a season. "The point is, and don't think for a moment that this can reflect in your salary, but I can't think of anyone who is more capable."

King smiled wryly. "Bullshit. You can't find anybody crazy enough to take it on. That's usually how these things work."

"You are the first person I've spoken to."

"But that is only because you already know the answer the others will give you." King turned to Dave Lomu sitting at the neighbouring table, a tabloid newspaper open, his eyes flicking up every now and then to the entrance of the café. "Would you have a crack at this, Dave?"

"Shit, no," the big Fijian said without looking up. He took a bite out of his roll and said through a mouthful of bread, bacon, and brown sauce. "Black people don't swim well enough. And with a cover as a marine dive engineer, I'm betting there's a bit more than paddling involved."

"But you're from Fiji," King retorted. "Don't give me all that white men can't jump, black men don't swim, shit. You used to dive for your bloody breakfast."

"Well, okay. But I doubt I would find a wetsuit that fits."

King shook his head. "Just as well. You mean a thermal dry suit. You'd most likely die of cold inside thirty minutes in a wetsuit in those temperatures…" He looked back at Simon Mereweather, acting director of MI5. "What about Rashid?"

"Nah, he has a firm sense of his own mortality," Big Dave interrupted. "Besides, he hates the cold as much as I do, and doesn't like getting wet either."

"He's on assignment anyway," Mereweather replied tiresomely.

"There's the SBS. If this isn't what they do, then I don't know what is." King had worked with the Special Boat Service before on an operation to rescue civilians, including intelligence officers in West Africa. It was a long time ago, but he had always held them in high esteem.

"No, he wants the crazy motherfucker who jumps between aircraft without a parachute…" Big Dave jeered through another mouthful. He looked at Simon Mereweather and shrugged. "Tell it how it is, boss. This mission is so bullshit that you know that nobody, but our man here will rise to the challenge. Damned fool doesn't know when he's beat, or when he shouldn't even step into the ring." He looked at King and said, "Stay away from this one, mate.

Spend some time with the missus. How is she, by the way?"

"Recovering. Still needs the crutches for prolonged periods on her feet, but slowly getting there." King paused. He wouldn't mention the tragedy of the miscarriage. That was their business only. "There's the mental scars as well," he added, thinking of her ordeal.

Big Dave nodded. "Understandable. That mental shit is the worst. Glad she's getting there. Send her my love…"

"Do you mind?" Mereweather stared at him, perplexed. "Perhaps you should wait outside?"

King looked at the window, the rain lashing against the pane. Beyond, the sea was angry and taking its mood out on the shingle beach. Sea spray showered the cars parked outside. "That won't be necessary. He's got my back, that's all." He paused, took a mouthful of tea and said, "I don't think I'm reading this right. Give it to me. And don't hold back." He looked up as Neil Ramsay returned to the table with four more cups of tea and another bacon roll for Big Dave.

"Don't hold back on what?" the MI5

liaison officer said as he put the tray down on the table.

"The mission. The parameters and the objectives," Mereweather replied tersely. "For goodness' sake, I knew that we should have done this at Thames House."

"But we couldn't," Ramsay protested somewhat pointedly. "It's a deniable operation. No records, no trail."

"A black-ops mission, then," Big Dave added looking at Ramsay.

"Shut up," Ramsay replied.

"Something we should know about?" Mereweather asked.

"Private joke," said Big Dave. A black Fijian, he was always poking fun at Ramsay's middle-class sensibilities, or general ignorance thereof, on people of colour. When Ramsay used something innocent that could have connotations, Big Dave loved to twist his words or bait him into an awkward situation.

"The point is…" said Ramsay, ignoring his colleague. "… this is deniable and worse than that, it's practically suicidal. MI6 wouldn't come up with something like this, and we all know the egos on that lot. The SAS or SBS wouldn't condone a mission like it if they had the full facts, and something like this is not even within MI5's remit."

"There's a great deal we do that's nothing near our remit," said King.

Ramsay shook his head despairingly. "True. And this is a vitally important operation, but I can't in good conscience recommend you take it on, Alex."

Mereweather sighed. "Oh, for God's sake!" he exclaimed in exasperation. "Okay. It's an unfortunate situation, and a difficult mission. But let's not forget that it was King who put the asset on the submarine, and it was King who did not check whether she was infected in the first place when he met her. In effect, losing a Royal Navy submarine and its entire crew…"

"Don't pull your punches, Simon," said King coldly.

"You asked me to give it to you straight and not to hold back. Well, here it is…" Mereweather replied testily. "You got a Russian asset out of a Russian biological weapons research facility through Lapland, Finland and Norway. In doing so, we retrieved the information that we required on a stolen USB. Not to manufacture, but to keep Russia from doing so. The formula was incomplete. No harm, no foul. A team from the SAS later destroyed the laboratory, making it look like its hydroelectric turbines had overheated during the spring thaws and rising water levels and the regenerator had failed and caught fire. The laboratory was vaporised. So, we didn't have the genetic building blocks for the virus to procure a vaccine, and the Russians didn't have them either, so couldn't finish making its weapon. That wasn't the perfect outcome, but it was about as near to bloody perfect as anyone could wish for."

"But Natalia Grekov became infected getting the evidence out. How was I meant to know?"

"You should have anticipated it."

"What, strip her naked and use my non-existent training in medicine and biological pathogen research to perform a relevant examination?" King scoffed. "It's worth noting that I would have travelled with her on that submarine, but when I got her to her ride at the exfil under fire, I bailed on the escape plan and remained so that I could ensure the sub got away safely out of the fjord. It was coming under fire from an RPG."

"Luckily for you," Big Dave commented flatly, then shrugged. "The submarine ride home, that is. Not the RPG, obviously."

Mereweather nodded. "Indeed. That submarine subsequently went missing. I've seen the footage, the pictures of the animals in the laboratory. I've been briefed by the scientists and can't truly bring myself to imagine the full horrors of what the poor crew must have endured before they died. Or of what happened onboard for it to disappear. But it doesn't take a stretch of the imagination. The virus was cultivated and designed as a unique weapon. To be released upon unsuspecting nations and render the population inhuman. To lose all inhibitions and morality, to have them attack each other in rage…"

"Like zombies?" Big Dave asked. He hadn't been with the team during the time of this operation, having later come in as a military contractor before being officially signed up to MI5.

"No," Mereweather said sharply. "The scientists were both abundantly and adamantly clear on that. And we can't trivialise this bioweapon by throwing the Z word out there. It's too fantastical. There are similar drugs that affect people in such a way. PCP, for instance. That stops people feeling pain or fatigue. And spice makes people function comatose, zombie-like. The world moves around them, and they are unaware. Anabolic steroids can create anger issues." He paused. "These attributes are all found within this virus."

"Dialled up to eleven by the sounds of it," said Big Dave.

King remained silent. He hadn't known that the asset had become infected and having been pursued by a Spetsnaz hit-team, things had been rolling along quickly. He had been lucky to get the asset to the exfiltration point. Lucky to have made it out of the frozen fjord and get away to safety.

"You will, of course, have heard that the submarine has been found," said Ramsay.

King had seen the news. "I heard," he said quietly.

"Quite a feat," said Mereweather. "Considering a nuclear-powered attack submarine is designed to remain undetected. The Admiralty were not aware of the exact route the captain would be taking back, but it was safe to assume that it would be the Norwegian Sea and Atlantic Ocean, as it's the only practical way back." He paused. "Now, all we know is the submarine went dark. No communications, no distress signal, and no emergency beacon. All we can assume is that Natalia Grekov infected others onboard and you can insert your own apocalyptic, horror scenario here."

"The news said a Norwegian salvage team found it by chance," said King. "But as the wreckage is in something called a green sanctuary, maritime engineers will raise it and tow it to the Faroe Islands. I thought they belonged to Denmark?"

"They do, but it's not as simple as that." Mereweather paused. "The green sanctuary is an area the size of France. It's a UNESCO World Heritage Site. Now, a consortium of nations, including the United Kingdom I may add, operate a series of experimental environmental projects inside the green sanctuary. Within this area, Aurora, a green energy think tank and alternative energy power company are conducting hydroelectric non-profit research. It is a similar setup to the accord in Antarctica, in that there can be no military presence from any nation. Which is why a team of marine engineers from various countries within the consortium will be handling the salvaging of the submarine and basing themselves at Aurora's site. Once raised it will be towed to the Faroe Islands, for safety reasons. Once there, the Royal Navy can take over command and retrieve their submarine."

"What's safer about the Faroe Islands?" Big Dave asked, having finished his second bacon roll.

"The marine engineers will have flotation devices around it and they feel any handover should be done at a port," Ramsay replied. "The Faroe Islands have a more suitable port, as well as being substantially closer to Britain than Spitsbergen. Also, Denmark is not a part of the green sanctuary consortium, so is therefore a neutral party."

"And you want me to see that whatever is inside that sub remains inside until the Royal Navy collect it?" asked King. "There'll be Russian interference, of course. So, among the marine biologists, oceanographers and engineers, there'll be plenty of opportunity for an agent to hide and integrate. You want me to defend the submarine and its secrets, while still blending in and not giving my cover away."

"Heavens, no," Mereweather said, shaking his head. "That would be all too simple. No, I want you to destroy it and see that it never again sees the light of day…"

Chapter Three

They had taken over the corner of the beach café. King supposed the place would have once been a seasonal business making enough for the owner from busy summer seasons, but lockdowns, trading restrictions and loss of trade in general had changed things for most people and the tiny beach café was no different, now opening throughout the winter and on dismal early spring days like today, where it felt cold and wet and isolated. They were not being the best customers as they hunkered down over cups of cheap breakfast tea and spoke in little more than whispers, but Big Dave was slowly working his way through the menu and they were now on their third round of teas and coffees, with the big Fijian tucking into a large slab of millionaire shortbread. Nobody else had entered the café since they had been there and when the man stepped inside out of the rain and brushed the water from his coat and shook out his umbrella, King studied him curiously. Sixty years old, fit-looking and with a well-tended white-grey handlebar moustache. He wore a tan trench coat, pinstripe navy-coloured suit, highly polished tan oxfords and carried an umbrella with an ornate silver handle in the shape of a fox's head. The briefcase he carried had an ornate crest stamped on it, the leather looking thick and polished and well-cared for. The man made his way over to them, and Mereweather stood and greeted him warmly.

"This is Galahad Mereweather," he said, rather stunted, perhaps a trifle embarrassed. "My father…"

There were a few murmurs of both greeting and surprise all round and the man said, "Thank you, Segwarides."

Mereweather nodded, flushing red in his cheeks. "Please sit, father. Would you care for some tea?"

"Yes. Earl Grey."

"I'll see what I can do." Simon Mereweather stood up and walked to the counter. King watched him go and smiled at the older man. "Segwarides?"

The older man smiled wryly, but there was a youthful twinkle in his eyes. "Many, many generations ago, the men in my family started a tradition of being named after the Knights of the Round Table. My father was Gawain, my uncle was named Galehaut. Naturally, the dozen or so names in common literature and film have long been used up, but there were indeed over one-hundred and fifty knights of legend and still a few names left. Segwarides' son is Daniel, although that was chosen as a compromise. I suspect my son was pleased that some names work well enough today."

"So, who was Lancelot?" asked Big Dave.

"A second cousin. Bit of a black sheep. Had a few marriages and many more affairs."

"The truth's in the name, then," Big Dave commented with a grin. He looked up as Simon Mereweather returned with his father's Earl Grey and placed it in front of him. "Ah, Segwarides…"

"I really should have asked you to go outside," Mereweather replied without looking at him. "I took the name Simon at university," he explained somewhat reluctantly. "I wanted to at least stand a little chance with the opposite sex. I figured I could still sign my cheques with an S…"

"What kind of girls were you dating? I've never known any chicks who take a cheque." Big Dave laughed and stood up, swilling the last of his tea down. "Right, I'll get my coat…"

"For the best, I think," Mereweather replied curtly. "Don't steam up the car while you wait in the cold."

Galahad Mereweather watched the man-mountain leave and said, "Interesting fellow, Segwarides. An interesting fellow indeed..."

Simon Mereweather nodded. "No respect for authority. But he's a good man."

"One supposes when you're that size, nothing and nobody appears to be a threat."

"He's never going to be a front man for the Security Service. And he'll never have his name on an office doorplate." King nodded. "But you'll never regret having him by your side in a pinch."

"Well, that makes two of you," Galahad Mereweather replied. "I can see that you are a behind the scenes man, too."

"Father served in the service and later at GCHQ after a career in naval intelligence. He's retired now," Simon Mereweather explained.

"But not today," King commented.

"Not today, no," Galahad Mereweather replied. He placed the briefcase on the table, then using his signet ring on his right hand, unclipped the locks. "Magnetic," he said quietly. "The magnet is the same size as the opposable magnets within the locks."

"You see, Simon, this is what we need; a few gadgets to make the job more exciting," King said humorously.

"And jumping out of helicopters isn't exciting enough for you?"

Galahad Mereweather smiled as he took out several sets of plans on thick, folded paper. "That certainly doesn't sound like the Security Service I knew."

"We broadened our parameters and played a little faster and looser with our remit," replied his son.

"We always had those slippery buggers across the river for that sort of thing. I was previously up at Oxford with half of the men and women who later went to work over at Six when I was in the service. Most of my peers thought I should have gone into bat for them, but I saw something a little less disingenuous about the Security Service. A little less self-serving and a little more tasteful." Galahad Mereweather paused. "Do make sure you don't go in for all the theatrics over substance, Segwarides. The games of cowboys and Indians will only do so much. Solid detective work is generally the best approach. Dogged, but inadmissible within the legal system when uncontrived and honestly sought."

"We've just taken on a former detective with the Met to keep things the right side of legal," Neil Ramsay ventured, seeing his boss looking at his father as awkwardly as a teenager would having the facts of life explained to them. "In the field, that is. God knows the lawyers are always there to tell you what you're doing wrong. So far, we're finding it's been invaluable."

Galahad Mereweather spread out the plans in front of him. They were of a British Astute class submarine and some of the sheets showed a dissected view. "I can see that this detective has a lot of work in front of him…"

"Her," Ramsay corrected him quickly.

"…Her, then." The older man paused. "Because showing you these plans… which I procured through a contact in the Admiralty… with a view of where to place explosive charges to make this boat unsalvageable, while keeping its nuclear reactor intact, and making sure that the crew… God rest their souls… are sucked out in the shockwave, isn't exactly keeping one's nose clean and flying straight and true before the law of the land."

"Well, we're a work in progress," said King.

"I can see that. Far different in my day."

Ramsay looked at the plans and said, "If the crew are sucked out, then surely they will float to the surface?"

"No," replied Simon Mereweather. "I have it on excellent authority that if the vessel was intact, or at least watertight, then the air in their bodies would have vented by now. Decomposition would be slow, given the extreme cold temperature, but nevertheless, it would be a factor."

King thought of the Russian woman. She had been brave and conscientious. She had been a good person, and he couldn't bear to think about the horrific end she would have had, nor how her body would have reacted to time and temperature and environment. Clinical terms like venting and decomposition didn't fit with the bright and vivacious young scientist who had been chased through a polar vortex by a Russian Spetsnaz hit team to get to her rendezvous.

"That's quite right," said Galahad Mereweather. "Also, the saline level at that depth and the water temperature is a sure way for bodies to sink, rather than float. From there, well predators and bottom feeders will clean things up in no time. From a practical point. From a moral point, it's reprehensible. May they rest in peace. The poor, unfortunate buggers..." He paused, looking at King, then pointed at the charts. "The charges will need to yield a minimum of eight thousand metres a second detonation rate per kilo with a force value more than four-point-seven kilos per charge. That's standard PE-four. Here, here, here, and here. Four points, all crucial for the submarine to shift off the bottom, then two charges, here and here, for her to break apart and expunge its... er... contents."

"From a practical point, Semtex could mean smaller charges," said King. "Around three-point-five-kilos by my reckoning."

"EPX-One would have an edge further still. Three kilos, dead," replied Galahad Mereweather. "But it's still developmental. Personally, I'd stick with the PE-Four or C-Four. It's less volatile than that Czech stuff, anyway. That's the thing with Semtex, at least it blew a few of the Paddies up for us while they were making their homemade bombs during the Troubles."

"That's still getting thirty kilos or so of explosive, another six kilos of blasting caps and say, around five kilos of detonation cord down there. What's the depth?"

"The central charges will need to be closer to ten kilos each." Galahad Mereweather paused. "So, work on forty kilos, or ninety pounds in full fat, full cream imperial."

"Depth?" King asked again.

Simon Mereweather coughed to clear his throat, then said, "The submarine is on a ridge, rather like the top of a mountain. Each side of that ridge drops down close to three-thousand metres. Now, with a Rolls-Royce nuclear reactor, or more accurately a PWS2, pressurised water reactor on board, as well as Tomahawk cruise missiles and the Spearfish heavy torpedoes it was carrying, the plan with the charges is to shift the vessel off the ridge with the first series of charges, while two secondary explosions do the required damage on its descent into the deep."

"What's the depth?" King repeated.

"The ridge is three hundred metres across, but HMS Armageddon is on the very edge…"

"But, what's the depth, Simon?" King asked, staring at him curiously.

"It's seven-hundred and eighty metres..."

"For fuck's sake!" King sat back in his chair and shook his head. "I can't dive that deep!"

"You've got a PADI certificate," Ramsay said quite seriously.

"What?" King snorted. "Pay And Die Immediately? That's okay for holidays in the Red sea or the Mediterranean. I do have rather more than that, but I'm still only certified to two-hundred metres. And that took specialised air, a dive buddy, boat crew and a detailed ascent plan with decompression chamber on standby. No, it can't be done."

"No, it can't. Not practically, at least," Simon Mereweather conceded.

"Just as well, really," replied Galahad Mereweather. "Because this entire plan can only be done from inside the submarine." He paused. "And the team operating the salvage recovery program have a mini-submersible quite capable of reaching that depth and getting someone inside via a rescue hatch."

"Is that all?" King replied sarcastically.

"Well, there is the question of initiating the self-destruct sequence on the missiles and torpedoes," Galahad said nonchalantly. "Can't have them lying about for any Tom, Dick or Harry to salvage. Oh, and bringing up the data-logger for inspection. That's like the black box on an airliner."

His son nodded. Two decades younger, but essentially a facsimile of his father without the grey hair or moustache. "So, time is of the essence. We need to get you up there and embedded in that team before they make a move without you." He glanced at his watch, then said, "Finish your tea first…"

Chapter Four

Caroline stood with her back to King, watching the angry sea beyond the edge of the cliff half a mile away. Directly in front of her on the driveway below, Ramsay and Simon Mereweather waited awkwardly in the black Jaguar saloon. Big Dave sat behind the wheel of an identical vehicle, parked nose out and looking unbothered, unhurried, and completely at ease. He'd waved at her through the window, and she'd waved back, but ignored the other two. Dave Lomu was a foot soldier and was here as security for the acting director of MI5.

"It won't be long," said King. "And besides, you've made it pretty clear that I've been getting under your feet lately."

"Do you want to go?" she asked incredulously.

He shrugged. "It's important…"

"I get it," she said, turning around and looking at him. Her eyes were moist, glistening with tears. "You've been couped up for a few months and you need the action." She shrugged. "You've been great helping me get back to health and planning our escape has really helped me heal mentally." She pointed at a world atlas on the wall. It was torn, had been well-folded and was busy with drawing pins and handwritten notes, dates and destinations circled in red pen. "That is what's important. Buying that yacht and heading out for an adventure at the end of this summer."

King nodded as she walked from the bay window to an upright leather chair. She favoured her right leg, but she was managing inside without the crutches, which were propped up against the wall behind her. He went to help her but stopped because the action seemed ridiculous considering he was about to ship out and leave her on her own. Since Caroline had been involved in a traffic collision three months ago, caused by a man chasing her to get to King, she had undergone daily physio and had various follow up appointments with surgeons. She had ditched using the crutches a month before they thought she would, for all but the walks outside that she took every couple of days, such was her dedication to her physiotherapy and well-being. The trip they had planned over the past weeks and months had helped her to reset mentally, enabling her to deal with the PTSD from her experience, as well as previous missions, tragedies, and misadventures. They had both been learning and training online in the theory of seamanship and sailing and they had a series of intensive courses booked throughout the summer at a local sailing club. Caroline had sailed as a child, and King had used a few powerboats and RIBs over the years. It was a crazy plan, but like most things they did, they would bluff through with determination and fluidity, changing the plan along the way to suit them best.

"It's a matter of closing the circle," he replied eventually, the silence between them uncomfortable. "I put that poor woman on that submarine and ninety-eight submariners did not come home to their families."

"And bringing their bodies home will heal a wound inside you?"

King hadn't gotten as far as the specifics of the operation. He would have loved for the bodies of the crew to be returned to the grieving families, but it wasn't going to be the right time to tell Caroline he would be attempting to blow up their underwater grave and release them to the deep instead. He settled on, "Seeing that the Russians don't get something usable out of this will," he replied truthfully. "A tissue sample or biopsy could change everything."

Caroline nodded. She had served in army intelligence before becoming a field operative with the Security Service, so she knew that Britain had its enemies and what lengths they would go to strike at them as well as their allies. "Since we've been working together, I worry when you go into the field alone," she said quietly. "You need someone to have your back." She shrugged. "And it can't very well be me, because I'm still not fit enough…" She trailed off and King knew it was because she had recently voiced that she wasn't sure that she ever truly would be again.

"I'll be okay," he said a little lamely. "It's not a tough job," he lied. "Just room for one, by the sounds of it. I'll be back before you know it."

"Kiss me," she said quietly. She smiled as he made his way over and kissed her tenderly. She rubbed his shoulders and said, "Just bugger off and get it done. I'm not going to jinx it by wishing you good luck and nonsense like that. So, don't trust anybody, give the other guy hell and get your retaliation in first." She broke away first, leaning back in the leather chair. "And you were right, you were getting under my feet. Sorry I didn't hide it well enough." She paused, blinking a tear away. "Now, get out of here. Go and get the job done."

Chapter Five

Longyearbyen, Spitsbergen Island
Svalbard Archipelago
800 miles from the North Pole

King stepped out onto the runway, his boots crunching on the loose sand and salt chippings that had recently been spread, keeping the ice at bay. Except it was failing. The ground felt like a skate rink underfoot, with a layer of compacted frozen snow over what he guessed was once a tarmacked runway. He did a temperature test, sniffing hard through his nose, the moisture freezing and sticking his nostrils together. The air had felt sharp, and clean and salty. He figured it was – 16°c and the digital sign near the airport terminal, which relayed temperature and time alternately, confirmed it as – 18°c. In the bay, icebergs bobbed and dipped on the gentle swell. It was early April, just out of winter.

There was no passport control or customs check. That had been taken care of in Oslo. But he hadn't been able to get by with just a carry-on because of all the bulky thermal clothes he would require, and so needed to collect his bags from the terminal. He also needed to change, the cold biting viciously at him, so he couldn't simply make his way out of the unfenced airport. Besides, he had been warned about polar bears back in Oslo. Regularly scared off from town, it was a different matter outside the town limits where it was illegal to either travel without a weapon, or a person who was carrying one. Polar bears outnumbered the population of the island by three to one.

Inside the terminal, the warm air felt heavy and thick. King headed for the lone carousel. The flight had mainly consisted of Svalbard residents who had been shopping on the mainland, but among them had been people like King. Or at least the cover King had taken. He looked up from the carousel, nodded at the young Swedish marine biologist he had helped with her luggage back at Oslo. She had her diving equipment with her, including two tanks which had been emptied and the valves removed for inspection before the flight. She was young and keen and inexperienced. King also had diving equipment with him but knew enough to figure he'd get his tanks on location, and that he would prefer them freshly filled in his presence anyway, so couldn't see the point of her travelling with them in the first place, but he at least needed the kit to back up his cover story. The young woman had introduced herself as Madeleine but must have become well-acquainted with a fellow passenger during the flight. He looked a decade younger than King and spent more on grooming products in a week than King would have in a year. He could already see from the dynamic that she thought she had struck up a genuine friendship, but the young man was on the hunt for more than friendship and looked to be going in for the kill. She had mentioned that she would be spending the night in a local hotel in Longyearbyen before boarding her ship – he suspected they all would be – but he already foresaw the young man upping his game further in the hotel bar.

He wondered how many of the passengers would be travelling with him. But he supposed he'd know soon enough. He tried to work out what marine engineers, oceanographers and marine biologists looked like. Madeleine was in her mid-twenties, sported a discreet nose piercing and had a few braids in her wavy shoulder-length blonde hair. She looked like a surfer to King. He looked around the carousel. A few of the men looked casual, a little unkempt. He realised he was stereotyping now and gave up. The carousel started and the first of the luggage came out. Everybody stepped forward, but King remained where he was, studying the passengers and assessing who, if anybody, he was up against. And then he found him from the other side of the luggage carousel. Staring back at him, relaxed and the only other passenger not to have moved when the luggage belt started. King wasn't one to back away from a staring contest, and besides, it was too late now. The man was the physical image of King. Six foot - perhaps a shade under – and broad at the shoulders and narrow at the waist. King estimated him to be thirteen or fourteen stone and from the way the fabric of his sweater pulled at his arms, he knew he would be well-muscled. The man's face was craggy, his dark eyes resembled a shark's, and he wasn't bothered about what could have been an awkward situation. Still King's glacier blue eyes bored into him, cold and detached. Eventually, the man smirked and stepped forward to the carousel, breaking the stare and hoisting a large bag with an empty dive tank attached to it easily into the air. King could see from the way the straps strained that it was heavy, but the man had made light work of it. King saw his bags, but when he looked back, the man had gone.

Outside, taxis and guides took the passengers to their boarding houses or hotels, or back to their homes. King had hired a car from the desk in Oslo and collected the keys at the Arctic Autorent desk. He'd chosen a Toyota Hi-Lux pick-up truck, for no other reason than in every war-torn country he'd ever operated in, it was the one vehicle that seemed to keep going. He'd seen them fuelled on nothing more than cooking oil and a splash of white spirit in place of diesel and run for half a million miles without a service. Just fuel, oil and water, and air in the tyres.

King found the truck outside, parked nose in and close to the terminal. The locks had been de-iced and as he slung his bags onto the back seat and got inside, he saw that a can of de-icer had been left for him on the passenger seat.

Svalbard had been in Arctic winter until just six weeks ago, meaning that it had been in complete darkness for months. Now the archipelago was experiencing short days and long nights, but within a month it would switch around, and after another month it would be perpetual daylight until August. So, as he drove past the stretch of coast, then turned off towards

Longyearbyen, he reflected with some bewilderment that it was close to summer, despite seeing floating ice the size of buses in his rear-view mirror. Despite the cold, and the snow-covered mountains that seemed to spring up from the edge of town, much of the road was clear with patches of green showing in the snow. King drove steadily, the truck gliding over the ice without drama or incident. He checked his phone as he drove, opened the Google Maps app, and followed the road to the heading he'd put in as they taxied on the runway in Oslo. He needn't have bothered – there seemed to only be one road and it looped into cul-de-sacs of brightly painted wooden houses. Many of his fellow passengers were checking into the small number of hotels and boarding houses, taking their luggage from the taxis, and coping well with the ice underfoot. Most of the people on his flight had been Scandinavian, but there were a few adventurous tourists as well. He figured that the majority were Svalbard residents in need of some mainland sanity and comfort.

King pulled up outside the gun shop. With just three-thousand residents on the island a gun shop wouldn't have seemed an ideal business model, but with eight thousand polar bears at the last count and it being law not to leave town without a firearm or an armed guide, it made a little more sense. The small university even employed polar bear guards and ran courses on handling a rifle safely. King had been hastily issued with a UK firearms certificate, which negated the month-long pre-travel permission form process and firearms handling lesson. Of course, the gun shop was as much an outdoor pursuit store as the former, and King would stock up on a few things while he was here. He got out of the truck, the cold biting him and reminding him that he was well within the Arctic Circle. His coat was a thermal ski jacket, but his legs were already stinging from the cold air. His desert boots were tough and hardy, but his toes were already numb by the time he walked the short path and took the four steps to the shop.

Inside, King was blasted with heat and his face burned as the feeling slowly and painfully came back to his cheeks. He peeled off his thermal gloves and made his way to the counter, where a Viking who had clearly found himself in the wrong century was tending a till. He nodded a silent greeting as King fumbled with the two loose pages comprising his firearms certificate.

"Cold enough for you?" the man commented dryly, his English good, but his accent thick and rhythmic Nordic.

King smiled. "No doubt you'll tell me it was colder in the winter…"

"You have been among Scandinavians before," he replied knowingly. "I myself am Norwegian, but it wasn't cold enough for me down there, so..."

"Only another eight hundred miles to go, then," King commented flatly.

"No bars at the North Pole. Not many customers, either."

"I need a rifle for my stay here," said King, looking at the row of rifles on the shelf behind the man. "I understand you only need to see a firearms certificate for me to rent one."

The man nodded as he scrutinised the pages. He folded it and handed it back to King. "We use point thirty-oh-six." He turned around and unhooked a well-used one from the chain. "I need a three-hundred-euro deposit and it's fifty euros a day for the gun. This is a Browning A-Bolt. Three shots, bolt action. Just a three-round magazine. But you cannot carry it around town with the magazine in the weapon, and you must carry it only with the bolt back and the breech open so people can see that it is not loaded."

King took the rifle from him and felt it, the weight, the balance and feel of it. The stock was what was referred to as synthetic, just a black plastic composite that required no maintenance, like modern military assault rifles. He could see from the bolt and magazine lips that the rifle had barely been fired, although it had been carried plenty of times, the stock and fore end were scratched, as was the barrel. "No telescopic sight?"

"You're not going hunting. This rifle is for protection only," the man said somewhat curtly. "The open sights are good for two-hundred metres, but if you need to use this, then you will have eight-hundred kilos of bear running you down at sixty kilometres an hour. In that scenario you do not want to be trying to shoot it looking through a magnified lens as you will struggle to keep up with the target. Scopes are no good for moving targets. If it is looking aggressive and coming straight at you, then wait until it is thirty metres away and fire. Miss and it will be twenty metres from you by the time you work the bolt. Miss again, and part of you will be in the beast's mouth and he'll already be eating you…"

King shrugged. He didn't exactly need a lesson on firearms, scopes or ballistics, but he'd never hired a gun for bear protection before, so he had listened and taken in what the man had said. "Can I have an assault rifle instead?" he joked.

"No," the man replied humourlessly. "Five-point-five-six millimetre will just piss the bear off anyway. We don't use anything that small up here."

King nodded. "Why this calibre in particular?" he asked purely out of interest.

Modern military weapons had bypassed .30-06 since the Second World War. He knew the legendary BAR troop support weapon chambered in .30-06 had been flawed by its heavy ammunition. Modern times called for a soldier to carry more ammunition and for the bullet to merely put an enemy soldier out of action, which in turn tied up more personnel in a support role, than simply killing just another soldier. That was why smaller, more specialised calibres were used on the battlefield. But a polar bear was an entirely different entity. A .30-06 was going to do more than sting a polar bear, but there were plenty more capable calibres out there.

"It packs a hell of a punch, without the huge recoil of the larger African game calibres. The government tested it against other calibres, and it ticked the most boxes for our unique purposes. Some of it had something to do with tighter necked bullet cases being affected by the extreme cold." He put a leaflet down on the counter. "That's the do's and don'ts. Remember, you're not here to bag a polar bear. The rifle is for your protection only. And don't relax just because you're in town. That's when we get the most attacks or encounters as people let their guard down and before they know it, they've wandered to the outskirts. That and down on the shoreline. And the police don't take kindly to not knowing if the rifle is unloaded or not. And they carry Glocks."

"And that's it?" King asked, mentally tucking away the fact the .30-06 performed well in cold weather, he'd be sure to discuss this with Simon Mereweather and see if he could take it to the MOD. Sometimes the simplest things could be overlooked.

The man shrugged. "You rent the ammunition, too." He put a box of twenty Hornaday red tips on the counter. "Soft-nosed, expanding ammunition. Fifty euros for the box, but it's returnable. However, I charge twenty euros per bullet used. Tends to keep down the number of people heading out of town to shoot beer bottles…" He said, then added. "But if you really must shoot something, there is a target range near Mine Two. It's easy to find."

King nodded as he strolled around the store and picked out an Arctic jacket, trouser and bib set and some more thermal socks. He also chose a pair of soft thermal boots and another pair of gloves. As he placed it all on the counter and the man started to tally it up, he added four chemical handwarmers and a Leatherman. The Leatherman was like a Swiss Army knife on steroids, with pliers, a sharp serrated blade and an array of other tools that could come in handy. He paid with the company card Ramsay had issued him with and shouldered the rifle on the leather strap. He tucked the bullets into his inside jacket pocket and slipped the overall trousers over his cargoes, swapped to the new boots, then loaded up with the bags. Outside, the air seared his throat and lungs, and he felt his nostrils stick together again as he breathed. King slipped on a pair of sunglasses he had bought back at Gatwick Airport. They were black Oakley wraparounds and as soon as he put them on, his eyes relaxed from the glare of sun on snow. He tossed everything but the rifle onto the rear seats, and rested the rifle on the passenger seat, with the stock in the footwell. He loaded three bullets into the magazine and tucked the magazine into his pocket. King wasn't overly concerned about polar bears. The only predator that concerned him was the man who had stared long and hard at him back at the airport terminal. He knew the look. And he knew that hostile forces would soon come into play. He felt happier with the rifle next to him.

Chapter Six

King checked his phone. The message just gave a time only. He had memorised the coordinates back in London, all that needed confirming was the time, and now he had that. He deleted the message and slipped the phone back into his pocket. Within less than a mile of driving, King knew he would have to abandon all thoughts of driving the pickup and find a snowmobile to complete his journey, so he turned around and headed back into town. The plan had been hastily put together, time being the overriding factor, and now he wondered what else he had overlooked, besides the near impossible task of boarding a submarine at a depth of over two thousand feet in Arctic waters and setting off charges before an international salvage team could attempt to bring it up to the surface. The more he thought about the mission, the more he felt he was doomed to fail. His motivation had been solely to discover what had happened after he had delivered a terrified woman to a submarine waiting for her underneath the ice of a fjord, and of course, keeping samples of the virus out of the hands of the Russians, and he had not given much thought to the environment he was operating in. The cold was savage, biting. Any exposed skin turned numb after less than a minute, and his clothing made movement both cumbersome and slow. He had bought the dry-suit and diving equipment he would need in case he could not get the submersible docked, but at that depth he would need trimix breathing gas of 10/70/20, that is 10% oxygen, 70% helium and 20% nitrogen. Naturally, the salvage divers would have the facility to mix their own gases dependent on the depth they were diving, but King was certainly no expert and deep diving required a team. The thought of piloting the mini sub was certainly more appealing, and in truth if he indeed had to dive, then he felt it was bordering on the very real prospect of becoming a suicide mission.

King pulled down his left glove at the wrist and checked his watch. The light was misleading. It was getting dark and still not yet three-thirty-pm. The locals had recently emerged from three months of darkness, so they would no doubt be in good spirits, but he had heard that the three months of daylight they would experience in the summer months was just as depressing as the months of darkness, with people working too many hours to get tasks done that would otherwise be difficult in darkness and colder temperatures and sleeping in perpetual light could take its toll as they suffered from insomnia. He pulled up at the hotel and saw the row of snowmobiles to the left beside a small convenience store. King parked up and got out, slinging the rifle over his shoulder on the leather sling strap. The cold air attacked his face and neck, and he pulled the collar up higher. He trudged up the steps, dusted with icy powder that looked like icing sugar. It was neither snow, nor ice and felt dry and grippy underfoot. It was like no snow he had seen before, and he realised why the Inuit people had a hundred different words for the various types of snow and ice.

There was a young woman of around twenty at the counter. King wondered what life held for a young person on the island. Whether they got out straight after university, of which he knew there to be a small campus, or if they remained and lived full and happy lives. Island living was one thing, but artic living was quite another. Put the two together with three months of daylight and three months of darkness, and an average summer temperature of just 5°C with winters down to as low as -40°C, then he saw it more as merely existing than living.

"Hi, do you rent out snowmobiles?" he asked.

The woman nodded, then replied in faultless English, but with a heavy Norwegian accent, "Yes. I need to see your passport and drivers' licence and take a five-hundred-euro deposit," she paused. "We don't actually take it from the card unless you damage the skidoo."

"Great." King walked cumbersomely over to her, propped the rifle against the counter and set about hunting for his wallet hidden somewhere within the many layers of thermal clothing.

"Are you from the research team?" she asked, seeming to study him intently.

King almost replied no but checked himself in time. "Yes. I'm a marine engineer," he said, finding the statement somewhat bizarre and alien to him.

"For the submarine?" she asked but didn't wait for his reply. "How exciting..."

"Yeah..."

She put a cross on a triplicate sheet and waited for him to hand her his card. When she took it, she slipped it into the PDQ terminal and tore off the permission slip when it printed out. She handed the copy to King, then placed the pen for him to sign where she had marked the crosses. "I hope you can return those poor sailors to their families," she said quietly. "Finally put them to rest…"

"Yeah," King replied hesitantly. Until the discovery of the vessel, the families had assumed they had still been on patrol, blissfully unaware of their demise. The submarine service was clandestine, with the crew not having contact with the outside world. Their only communication was a fortnightly one-hundred-and-twenty-word message, referred to as a FamGram, to which they could not reply. King felt treacherous somehow, guilt-ridden. The Royal Navy had played the long game, hedging their bets that there was a communication problem with the vessel, or at least hiding behind the fact until they traced their missing submarine. The story had gotten out and people empathised with the families, sympathised with the crew and their terrible fate. The top naval brass had known, of course, but nobody had reported the missing submarine as they continued to find the best way to announce it.

And now King was here to blow the vessel to the deepest part of the ocean and shroud the story in mystery forever. He realised he had shown no emotion at her comment, partly because he knew the outcome to be unlikely, but mainly because he felt responsible for the disappearance and the loss of lives onboard. He forced himself to say, "I hope they can finally rest in peace…"

Chapter Seven

The hotel foyer was basic but warm and King was shown to an equally basic and warm room. He wasn't a connoisseur of hotel rooms, settling for just either cool or warm – depending upon the local climate – and a comfy bed. Shower and toilet, naturally and tea and coffee making facilities were something he had come to expect in the Western world. But he had endured hardships in his career and had spent much of his life curled up and shivering at night in a freezing wadi or snatching sleep in the back of a vehicle when he could. If he was lucky, at the end of a mission there would be an airport hotel to revel in its comforts and order a good meal on room service while he awaited his return flight. During his time with the SIS and now with the Security Service, expense accounts didn't run to luxury suites and Michelin star restaurants.

King showered and enjoyed some time under the hot spray before towelling off and changing clothes for dinner. As was the way in Scandinavian countries, and in particular the Arctic, clothing was generally informal and outer layers would be required if going outside to nearby bars, so he was certain a pair of chinos and a shirt and sweater would allow him to blend right in.

King ordered a Borg pilsner beer at the bar and looked around the bar and restaurant. He perched on a barstool at the end of the counter, his back against the wall. To his left, waiting staff ferried out plates of reindeer meatballs, thick peppered reindeer steaks with fries, and slabs of Arctic cod with mashed potatoes and butter sauce. As he glanced at the menu, he could see it was both basic and small, but the food being whisked past him looked hearty and well-prepared. He watched as a pretty, young blonde entered and looked around. Disappointedly, she headed for the bar, then saw King and waved. King was trying to recall her name, got it by the time she reached him.

"Hello, Madeleine," he said. "Settling in?"

She frowned, mentally breaking down the language barrier, then replied, "Yes, the hotel is nice, thank you. How about you?"

"It's certainly warmer than outside…" He paused. "But I suppose you're used to this climate, being from Norway."

"Sweden," she corrected him. "Yes, sometimes we get cold winters, not as cold as here, but thankfully the summers can be warm."

King smiled. He hadn't made a mistake but was simply in the habit of testing the people he met. It was in his nature to spot anomalies in a person's story. You couldn't be too careful. "Sorry, my mistake," he said. "So, you were saying back at Oslo airport that you're a marine biologist?"

"Yes. I'm hoping to get work with Aurora, the organisation behind the green energy projects. I'm here for a two-month work placement."

"That sucks," he replied. "An organisation getting labour from the bright, keen and eternally hopeful."

She looked unsettled, innocent. "No, it will look great on my CV if I don't get the job," she said defensively, but shrugged. "But I live in hope…"

King nodded. This was why he didn't get invited to cocktail parties. He usually said what he was thinking and had never learned the art of subtlety. "Sorry," he replied. "I didn't mean to upset you. Here, let me get you a drink." He nodded to the barman and gestured to her. Madeleine asked for a peach schnapps with ice and the barman walked to the other end of the bar to use the optic.

"So, you're a marine engineer?" she asked.

King tensed. He'd read about what marine engineers did in his hotel room in Oslo and decided it would be better all-round if he skirted the subject. "Yes," he replied, then added, "Diving is my skillset." It was always better to use the truth in a cover story, and he had dived at many great locations around the world.

"Me too!" she said, the revelation meaning she had forgotten their previous conversation at Oslo airport. "Last year, I dived with Great Whites off Mexico in the Pacific, which was fantastic! We even got out of the dive cages, tentatively of course. Perhaps I will be lucky enough to see the elusive Greenland shark while I am here. It isn't just native to Greenland, but cold Northern waters like these. They live in Norwegian fjords as well, but it's not yet known if they migrate to Greenland. There is no funding for research in Greenland sharks, not at the moment at least."

"Right…" King remarked, his small talk not improving with practice. He didn't even know Greenland had a species of shark, and if it lived in Norway as well, then the name was probably somewhat redundant. He pushed himself out of his pedantic trait and said, "Well, I hope you get to dive before long."

"I have brought my equipment, but I suspect the chances of a dive will be slim. It's quite a specialist thing in these temperatures, and the former oil rigs that Aurora are using are anchored in deep water. Hey, I could always dive with you!" she said excitedly.

"Sure…" King paused as she was given her drink, then chinked her glass with his own. "Cheers," he said.

"What are we drinking to?"

"To thirst," King replied.

She smiled and took a sip. "Well, that's that taken care of!" She picked up a menu from the countertop and said, "Wanna get some dinner together?" she asked amiably.

"Sure."

"Great. I don't like eating in restaurants alone."

"Glad I could be of service."

She patted his knee and said, "Don't be silly! You're good company…"

King sipped some of his beer while he waited for her to remove her hand. She was an attractive woman, but he could honestly say that if he wasn't in a relationship with Caroline, then he would still not have been interested. She had a childlike quality and an enthusiasm in her eyes that would soon change if she got to know him. Caroline had seen tragedy and experienced personal loss, and together they made each other happy. Looking at Madeleine was like appreciating something pristine, something beautiful but wanting to protect it, rather than merely possess it. The feeling made him appreciate that if he wasn't exactly old, then he was certainly no longer young. He looked up as the young man whom she had been talking with at the airport entered the bar, scoured the residents, then confidently started to make his way over. No three's a crowd for this guy.

The man hesitated a moment behind her, then said, "Madeleine?"

Madeleine turned around, her satin blonde hair sweeping through the air like a shampoo advert. She beamed a smile and greeted him warmly. "Daniel! How wonderful, dinner with two handsome men!"

King shrugged, part of him pleased with the compliment, but he knew a gooseberry when he saw one, and knew that tonight it would be him. "Lovely as that sounds, I have some calls to make first, so you two go on without me," he replied, but he nodded at the man and said, "Can I get you a drink first?"

"Thank you," the man replied, but King sensed it was as much to do with making himself scarce as offering him a beverage. "A whisky, please. A Scotch."

King nodded at the hovering barman, then turned to Daniel. "Russian?" he asked.

"What?"

"Are you Russian?"

"No. Does it matter?"

"No."

"Well then, I'm Polish."

"I said, it doesn't matter…" King replied coldly. "But your accent sounds more Russian than Polish to me."

"Well, I know where I'm from." Daniel shrugged, took the whisky from the barman and looked directly at Madeleine as he toasted. "Cheers…" he said, raising his glass.

"Na Zdorovie!" King replied, holding up his glass and exhausting his knowledge of the Polish language. Then he realised that he'd mistakingly used Russian and Daniel hadn't corrected him. He should have said, Na Zdrowie. A subtle difference, but it was all in the pronunciation. Perhaps Daniel was being polite, but for some reason he doubted it. He didn't seem the type somehow. King turned to Madeleine and said, "I'm sorry, I don't know the Swedish phrase for cheers..." Again testing, as he knew it to be skol or skål.

Madeleine raised her schnapps. "We say cheers, too." She smiled and took a sip, the ice clinking against the glass.

King nodded and sunk half his beer. Most of the world said cheers, so he was no further ahead. He regarded Daniel for a moment, then turned his eyes to Madeleine. The two of them were closer in age. He put Daniel at thirty, but his eyes seemed older somehow. A maturity borne from professionalism. "What do you do, Daniel?" he asked.

Daniel took a moment to turn his eyes away from Madeleine, then looked back at King apparently with a degree of disinterest. King couldn't blame him. The last thing he would have wanted at that age was a cold individual a decade older being the third wheel. But it didn't make him like the younger man much more. "I'm a programmer and data analyst. I specialise in radar and sonar emissions and laser imaging."

"Sounds fun."

"It pays well. I get my fun elsewhere," he replied flippantly. "And what line of work are you in?"

"I'm a diver."

"At the coal face as it were," he smirked. "Bolting, drilling and laying equipment where people like me or my subordinates tell you to."

"Just a cog in the machine," King replied neutrally. He wasn't going to take offence at his cover story being looked down on. He had to focus on what was real. "Are you here to work on Aurora's hydroelectric project?"

"I am," he said smugly. "And to assist with raising the submarine, you British had so carelessly misplaced. Until now, that is. I was called in to survey the area in detail. Early reports are that it's on the edge of a precipice." He paused. "I'm sorry, you've bought me a drink and we are making small talk, but I didn't catch your name."

"I didn't throw it. But it's Alex."

Daniel stared at him for a moment, then said, "Nice to meet you…" He paused. "And are you working for Aurora?"

"Not directly. I'm just here to liaise on raising the sub."

"Liaise?"

King nodded. "Make sure Aurora don't get in the way. It's good of them to provide the rigs as a base for the project, but we don't want their interference to affect the process."

"It's in a UNESCO environmental zone. I don't see that it's any of your business."

"I don't make policy." King paused. "But Britain needs a non-military presence of private contractors here to champion its affairs."

"Clearly." He paused. "About the policy aspect, that is. You don't look like a man who makes important decisions."

"You'd be surprised. I've made a few life-or-death ones in my time…" King finished his beer and stood up. He noticed Daniel tense, then visibly relax as King stepped back a pace and put some distance between them as he picked up his jacket. "You two find a table together. I must make a few calls. I guess I'll see you both on the ship, tomorrow morning."

"We'll be there," Madeleine said breezily.

Daniel smirked. "Looking forward to it…"

"Well, until then," King smiled and walked out of the bar towards the foyer. He imagined that punching Daniel square in the face would have been most satisfying. There was an arrogance about the man that King did not like, or maybe it was just the man's competitiveness over Madeleine. Or it could have been his intention like King to spot foreign agents and elicit a response. King paused and checked his phone, glancing back at the two of them at the bar. Daniel's body language had changed, and he appeared to be more relaxed. King was sure he was pleased to be the only male on the scene, but Madeleine just looked sad. Could she have been interested in him? There was more than a decade and a half between them, so he doubted it really. He caught Daniel watching him and replaced his phone to his pocket as he headed back through the foyer and up to his room, the hairs on the back of his neck tingling and a shiver running down his spine.

Chapter Eight

King changed into his travelling clothes of jeans and several layers of T-shirts and sweatshirts and his leather bomber jacket with a wool lining, then made sure he did not forget to put on the pair of thermal socks. He covered up with the trouser bib set and threaded the ski jacket over his bomber jacket. He put spare gloves in his pockets along with two small plastic bottles of water and the chocolate from the minibar, then loaded the Browning rifle, but kept the bolt drawn back as he shouldered it on the strap. King tucked his gloves under his armpit and left them there as he put on his beanie and headed back downstairs.

Outside the digital thermometer in front of the hotel indicated that it was -25°c, the darkness shearing off another ten degrees or so from when he had landed and making it feel like another twenty. He walked across to the front of the convenience store and put the key in the ignition of a large Yamaha snowmobile. It was a 1049cc model and looked reasonably new in terms of aggressive design and wear and tear. King checked the gear selector was in neutral like he had been shown and used the electric ignition to start it seamlessly into life. He sat astride, buttoned up his jacket and took the rifle off his shoulder, drove the bolt forward and locked it down. He set the safety and slung the rifle over his head and shoulder to secure it firmly in place. He donned his gloves, his hands already burning from the cold. When he slipped the machine into gear it crept forwards ever so slightly, and when he touched the thumb throttle the snowmobile lunged forwards. The fastest accelerating vehicle he'd ever driven or ridden had been a snowmobile in Lapland, and he already knew this was on another level. He gripped the tank firmly with his knees and eased the machine forwards, then when he straightened the handlebars, he gave it plenty of throttle and took off down the street like a scalded cat. He couldn't help beaming the daftest smile he'd had in years, and the adrenaline surged through him, his heart pounding and his breathing becoming erratic. There was no gearing, simply a forward gear and a reverse like a boat's outboard engine and the noise sounded like a chainsaw at maximum revs. It felt two or three times as powerful as the fastest quadbike or wetbike he had experienced, and although he hadn't ridden many all-out sports motorbikes, he knew this was up there with them, or perhaps faster accelerating even still and he had to stop himself grinning like an idiot as he revelled in the rush the speed gave him. The belt-driven 'blades' underneath simply gripped harder the faster he went. A huge rooster tail of snow trailed behind him and the featureless terrain in the darkness made it difficult to navigate, but soon he was well outside the town limits and following the compass heading he had memorised earlier.

The instruments on the handlebars were shrouded in a sealed unit with a Perspex screen and indicated his speed in kilometres, fuel level, temperature – both ambient and engine temperature – all displayed digitally, as well as in the form of a coloured dial for the engine, compass, and oil level. He had not opted for the GPS option, as he did not want any evidence of his journey, especially of his destination, recorded. He had a GPS on his own phone and had started to use Google Maps in his room to plot his course, but it was a pointless exercise as the terrain was merely white and featureless. Instead, he had the coordinates and compass heading of both where he was aiming for, and of course, the town of Longyearbyen upon his return. All he had to do now was head North-West and follow the frozen shoreline for an hour. Which was easier said than done, because the cold was finding the stitching in his clothing, and what little exposed skin on his face remained, was burning with the cold. He had taken a pair of goggles with the snowmobile, and they were steaming up terribly, and that steam was now freezing – his own little snowstorm going on in his goggles. King released the throttle and the snowmobile stopped so suddenly that he almost went over the handlebars without any additional braking. He kept the engine running as he looked all around him to check for polar bears. Everything was monochrome, but despite the darkness and the sliver of moon in a cloudy night sky, there was enough ambient light to see for several hundred metres in every direction. He wondered how much better than his own a polar bear's vision would be in the darkness. He imagined they would have excellent night vision if they lived for three months of the year in complete darkness. He removed the goggles and wiped them out with his gloved fingers. The ice was already thick, and stubborn to remove. He got off the machine and stretched his legs, still cautious. And then he saw movement to his right. A lumbering mass of white. He only saw it because it had broken one of the rules of the six S's in camouflage and concealment. Shine, shadow, silhouette, sound, shape, and smell. This bear had broken the rule of silhouette, but King guessed it didn't know the rules and hadn't trained with the SAS, and that when an animal was hungry it needed to break cover at some point. It had the advantage of darkness and that would likely be enough of an advantage for it over a seal or a reindeer at night.

King wasted little time getting back on the snowmobile and checked the heading before easing off, mindful not to do anything rash that would spell disaster if he tipped the machine over. He checked over his shoulder, the polar bear now just fifty metres from him as he thumbed the throttle and lurched forward into the night. He risked another glance, surprised he had not put a great distance between them. He took the machine up to eighty-kilometres-per-hour and settled into his seat. Another glance and the bear was still scarily close. Trepidation setting in, King accelerated harder and it was an effort to keep his grip on the handlebars as the machine shot forwards like a bullet. He turned and looked again, but the tremendous beast had slowed to a lumber and broken off to King's right. The speed and agility of the animal had shocked him, and he wouldn't have to remind himself again of the danger they presented. He checked behind him regularly as he rode, and he kept well clear of ridges of ice the size of upturned vehicles, shaped by the savage and relentless north wind.

It was easy to lose track of time this deep inside in the Arctic Circle. The reflection of the snow and ice, even from just starlight and a sliver of moon, created a hue of white that was never truly extinguished by the darkness. An ambient glow. It hadn't changed since dusk at around three-thirty pm. After an hour of riding at half to three-quarters of throttle and keeping his distance from the large jutting forms of wind-blown ice on his right, and the icebergs peppering the shore to his left, he saw more polar bears ahead of him. King checked behind him, and sure enough a large bear was lumbering after him. A steep range of mountains rose a short distance inland and he got the sense he was entering a bottleneck where he would be forced to run the gauntlet against the bears.

Another glance behind him revealed another bear entering the chase, and the former bear slowing and turning back towards the shore. King checked the coordinates. He wasn't far away now, and the timing would be spot on, but he hadn't allowed for the bears. Even when he reached his destination, he would need time to get organised, and he wondered whether the animals would turn to cannibalisation if he was to put down one of the beasts with the rifle. He wasn't sure he even wanted to take the risk of adding an angry wounded bear into the mix. Perhaps a single gunshot nearby would simply scare them away. King increased the revs and veered inland, heading away from the shoreline. The bears ahead of him looked on, resolutely guarding the beach. Behind him, the pursuing bear had given up much like its predecessor and was heading for the icy grey sheet of ocean. Seals were more likely an easier prey than a man on a snowmobile.

King had just crested a hill, but the landing was hard and the scene ahead of him was difficult to take in. Dark and textured, the terrain giving way to shale, black sand, rock, and grass. The ice and snow had abruptly ended, and the snowmobile dug in hard, its steering next to useless and the skids catching. He tried in vain to regain control and the machine pitched and he was thrown clear, landing heavily on pebbles and sand. He rolled onto his back, winded from the fall and aware that he was wet and freezing cold. He had landed in a stream with ice on each bank and fast flowing water soaking into his clothes. Puzzled that it shouldn't be frozen, he assumed it was too fast flowing and had likely started to thaw in the daytime sunshine. He tried to sit up, but the layers of clothing restricted his movements. The snowmobile had spun and tumbled end over end and was resting the wrong side up, its engine stalled. King supposed there was an automatic safety cut-out, much like on a modern motorcycle. He had no idea where to start looking for the reset, but then again, he had more to worry about. A huge twelve-hundred-pound male polar bear was paused on top of the same hill, its head turning from side to side sniffing the air. King could hear a throaty gargling sound and rapid snorts. He hastily took the rifle off his shoulder, checked the muzzle to see if any debris had gotten into the end of the barrel. Firing it with a barrel blockage would be catastrophic and the entire barrel could split, and the breech could explode. He took out the magazine and worked the bolt to empty the chamber, then upended the weapon and blew down the barrel. The metal was cold and stuck to his lips, but his breath travelled freely down the barrel, steaming out of the breech. King looked back at the ridge where the polar bear was making its descent. He hastily slipped the bullet directly into the chamber and pushed the bolt forward, then he inserted the magazine. It was a backward load, but got the bullet where it was meant to be sooner. The Browning had a thumb safety behind the bolt, and he flicked it into the fire position. The bear was fifty metres from him when it hesitated, raised its head, and sniffed the air again. King watched the massive beast stare right at him, then lift his head and look past him. He was about to shoulder the rifle, when he glanced behind him and saw what the bear had been looking at. Less than a hundred metres behind him, two bears – one smaller than the other – were making their way towards him. The smaller bear, which King took to be a female, stopped walking while the large male continued, and King realised that he was in the centre of a triangle. He turned back to the bear on the slope, except it wasn't. In the time it had taken to spot the other two bears, it had traversed the gradient and was now standing thirty metres from him. King aimed at the beast's chest, then lowered his aim and fired between the animal's legs. The .30-06 sounded thunderous in the still, night air. Stones and sand sprayed into the bear's neck and face and it turned and bolted sideways a few paces, before looking back at King and raising itself to a full ten-feet tall as it half-roared, half-snorted. King worked the bolt and turned to face the other two bears. The female had closed the gap somewhat unnervingly, and King suddenly realised that it would possibly take more time than he had to get the box of ammunition out of his jacket and reload the magazine if the three animals charged at him. He was in it now, but he knew what standoffs could be like, and if he took another shot without killing one of the animals, then he was setting himself up for defeat. King visualised the box of bullets in his pocket. He would need to ditch his gloves, dig out the box, open it with already cold fingers and fish out another round. He decided he would be best off tipping the contents onto the ground and scooping up several of the bullets at once. He would need to eject the magazine with the push button. Would his hands be too cold already? Possibly. He'd have to take the chance. The snowmobile would act as cover between him and the bears, but not for long. He would have to be quick on the reloading.

King heard the other two bears join in on the aural display of prowess. Not a full roar, but the same snorting, moaning half-roar of the somewhat irked beast at the base of the slope. The humming seemed to grow loader and for a moment his heart sunk as he imagined more bears behind him. He turned and the noise grew louder, then reached a crescendo of pitch, but King now knew why and ducked his head instinctively as the shadow filled the sky.

The gatling guns opened fire and tracer rounds cut the ground just feet from the two polar bears. The Hercules C130 gunship banked hard to port, its wing precariously close to the jutting terrain below, then as it straightened and levelled, one of the gunners sent the burst of 7.62mm from its rear mini-gun close enough to the other bear for the tracer fire to light up its face in the darkness. King watched the three bears bounding off in all directions. The great aircraft was banking again and climbing, still way under the thousand feet hard deck it had been flying in on to keep below radar. King heard the engine pitch grow low and saw the airplane slow considerably in the sky. It must have been near to its stalling speed when the ramp lowered and one of the RAF "loadies" heaved out the crate and the parachute was instantly activated on its short tug line. It opened fully only fleetingly, then the crate hit the ground and the parachute billowed like a triumphant flag in the northerly wind.

King checked for bears again, but he doubted there would be one within a mile after the two bursts of machine gun fire. He looked back at the Hercules, but it had already settled to a height of five-hundred feet and was heading back out to sea. After a hundred miles or so it would climb back up to a cruising altitude of twenty-thousand feet and head back to RAF Lossiemouth in Scotland.

King wasted no time in righting the snowmobile back onto its skis. It was an effort, as he still felt the effects of the crash. He had landed heavily, but had assessed that nothing was broken, he was merely winded and bruised and he suspected he would feel it more acutely in the morning. He found the reset and started the machine, making slow and tentative progress on the rock and tundra, reflecting how bizarre it was that the ice and snow should randomly thaw. Although he soon got his answer as he passed several reindeer carcasses which had been mauled and torn apart by bears. There was little left but bone and hide and he imagined that the herd of reindeer had found the grass underneath the snow and ice and had dug and stamped at it as they had grazed. No wonder there were so many polar bears in the area.

The crate had snagged against two boulders and the parachute was wafting at the end of its lines like a kite. King gathered up the parachute and unclipped it from the webbing strapping on the crate. He used the Leatherman to cut the webbing, his hands already struggling with the cold, and after he had used the tool's handy pliers to prise open the crate, he put the Leatherman back in his pocket and put the gloves back on. King checked once again for bears, then loaded the cases onto the rear seat of the snowmobile and secured them in place with the set of bungees which had been strapped across the pillion seat. Next, he bundled the parachute underneath a reindeer carcass that had been picked clean, he supposed by Arctic foxes and seabirds. The bones had frozen against the ground, and he had to heave it free, before ensuring the parachute could not catch the wind. He kicked and stamped on the crate, then tossed the plywood lengths across the tundra so that it wouldn't be noticeable from a distance. It was the best he could do but reasoned it unlikely that people would venture this close to the remote coastline, the very essence of polar bear safety precautions.

King turned the snowmobile around in a gentle half-circle and started back up the slope. As he crested the hill, the skis met ice and snow and the belt-fed blades were once more at home. Sticking as closely as he could to his earlier tracks, he kept a vigilant eye on the coast to his right and the icy monoliths to his left in the shadows of the mountains. He was cold and hungry and wary of bears and looking forward to some hot food and the warmth of his hotel room as he unpacked and checked the equipment and explosives he would need for the mission. Anticipation and concerns about the objective had given way to excitement and adrenalin. He loved his work, enjoyed the challenges he faced and the feeling of worth he had adored since his recruitment all those clouded years ago when a tough Scotsman had handed him a lifeline in prison, and he had subsequently been recruited into MI6. He lived for the mission and never truly felt he was living unless he was operational. Caroline had seen it in him, knew what he was and what he needed to do. And, as he dodged a large male polar bear and checked over his shoulder as it chased him through the night, he knew it, too. He would no longer talk of retiring his skills, of settling down and starting a family. He wouldn't be the person he really was that way. He would merely be existing and living a lie. King enjoyed not looking past the mission, of taking each moment as his last and striving to win. He just hoped that the task ahead of him gave him at least a fighting chance of survival.

Chapter Nine

As was the case living in Arctic conditions, King found himself overheated once he was back inside the hotel. Living in these extremes was always a case of being too cold or too hot. The clothing which made living in such places possible, made inside habitation uncomfortable. King had dropped the two bags of equipment and shed the jacket and gloves, his leather bomber jacket, undone the bib of the trousers and untucked his sweatshirt on his way up to his room. He opened the door and dumped the bundle of clothing inside as he heaved the bags into the room and closed the door behind him. Once inside, he kicked off the boots and tore off the trouser and bib set and the rest of his clothing until he was in just his chinos and a thin T-shirt.

King looked around the room, then checked under the bed, in the wardrobe and the tiny bathroom. Nothing seemed out of place, but he stood on the bed and unscrewed the smoke alarm, took out the tiny wireless pinhole camera he had installed earlier and opened an app on his phone, then placed the phone beside the camera for them to sync. As they were working the magic of Bluetooth, he picked up the phone and ordered some room service. It was just after ten-pm and he was tired and hungry and needed a good night's sleep. A medium-rare reindeer steak and a basket of fries should settle his empty stomach and enable him to relax a little. The cold climate had sapped his energy, and he ordered a strong Norwegian beer and a slice of brownie to send him towards a good night's sleep. He picked up his phone and scrolled through the app's menu and headed to 'last action'. He watched himself clumsily enter the room bogged down with the cases and extra clothing, then headed back into the menu and searched 'previous action'. He watched the door open and smiled as he saw who entered and checked through what little belongings and luggage he had. He smiled again as he saw them rifle through his wallet and passport – both under the legend he was travelling under. He then watched them leave the room. King was not in the habit of leaving his wallet or passport behind when he operated overseas, but it had served its purpose. A breadcrumb of disinformation for his enemies.

"Interesting, but not unexpected..." he said quietly to himself. He closed the app and opened his newly set-up Facebook account. Ramsay had provided him with the login details and told him about the tracking pixel he had installed. King could see who had been looking at his account, that they had searched his photos and the limited number of posts and had flicked around what little they could see of his carefully displayed settings. It was enough to know that they were interested in him, but anything they had found tonight pointed to a divorced forty-something salvage diver who shared diving posts, pictures of reefs and sharks and oil rigs and displayed a potted history of college and university and work placements around the world. The friends displayed were all pictures of low-ranking MI5 admin staff who had volunteered a snapshot and the information was all fictional. Ramsay had been thorough and by using one of hundreds of existing accounts he had built King's 'legend' by simply changing the name and personal info displayed on one of these 'clone' accounts, which showed congruence and validity to the casual observer, and the tight security settings meant that they hadn't been able to dig any further. King smiled. It had been a good night. He had the equipment he needed, and he had weeded out the competition. And they had only learned enough to validate his cover and legend. They may not believe it, but they had showed their hand. The game had begun, and King was a little closer to knowing who all the players were.

Chapter Ten

MI5 wasn't getting its deposit back for the snowmobile anytime soon. King had apologised to the young woman behind the counter, but after several minutes of her admonishing him and declaring he'd been unduly reckless with one of her snowmobiles, he had simply shrugged his shoulders and left the store. He had taken out the insurance and if you were in the vehicle hire business, then those were the breaks.

After breakfast he drove the Toyota to the beach and watched polar bears lazily stalking seals on the shoreline, the cat and mouse game of bears pouncing and seals taking to the water played out in front of loaded tour buses with raised windows on gullwing latches for the tourists to photograph the animals in action. The seals were able to lurk in the water and the polar bears seemed so well fed as to appear lacklustre in their efforts, barely bothering once the seals came ashore fifty metres away. The bears certainly weren't hungry enough to bother with a small troop of enormous walruses at the far end of the beach. King wasn't interested in the local wildlife, and certainly not the polar bears. He'd seen enough of those last night for a lifetime. But he had heard Daniel suggest to Madeleine at breakfast that they go and watch the bears on the beach. The breakfast dining had taken the form of two large tables made from the smaller tables pushed together. It was an informal affair, and he hadn't eaten communally in such a manner since he and his wife Jane had once eaten at a restaurant frequented by locals near the Trevi Fountain in Rome. The thought had made him sad. And the realisation that he seldom thought about her now, nor felt the loss more regularly saddened him deeply. Time truly was a great healer, if only by erosion of the soul.

King had listened as Daniel had told some other people about the bears on the beach, but it wasn't why he wanted to go. He had seen another person's reaction and that had intrigued him.

King watched Daniel, Madeleine and two other people – a man and a woman from the breakfast table – standing beside a guide. The guide was a bearded man in his forties, and he carried a rifle over his shoulder on a leather sling, as well as a pump-action shotgun in his hands. The man looked to be a true Norseman and a round wooden shield and a Viking battle axe would not have looked out of place in his hands, although the modern orange ski jacket wasn't strictly historically accurate. King watched the man exude calmness as a bear meandered across the dark, grey sand towards them. He raised the muzzle of the weapon, and King suspected the weapon would be loaded with non-lethal bear rounds. A tightly packed beanbag filled with tiny plastic balls. Enough to put a person on their backside in a riot or sting an unsuspecting bear into backing away. King noted the short Winchester lever-action rifle on the Viking's shoulder, which would suggest that bears didn't always react well to being stung by a beanbag travelling at four-hundred-feet per second and may need a more permanent persuasion. After last night's demonstration by the RAF, King reckoned they did not like low-flying Hercules C130 airplanes and 7.62mm gatling guns, either.

King watched the man who was watching them. Even under the considerable bulk of his thermal snowsuit, he could see that he was both fit and relaxed in his movements. King estimated him to be a shade under six feet tall and had earlier noted that he was of slender, athletic build. A runner, perhaps. Not a weightlifter. King thought his mannerisms and demeanour at breakfast to be that of an American. He had a preppy look, loaded his plate with scrambled eggs, bacon and fruit and ate with only a fork in his right hand. Nobody from Britain put fruit with eggs and bacon, much less ate with just a fork in a restaurant and the European element were sticking to breads, pastries, and fruit, tearing the former into mouth sized pieces and dipping in their coffee, and eating the latter as a separate course. There was nothing else to distinguish the man as an American, but he had benefited from good orthodontist work a couple of decades before it had become the norm in Britain and Europe, and he looked as if he had a healthy country diet. Corn-fed, milk on tap and servings of beef several times a week. King imagined him playing quarterback in high school, perhaps even a college scholarship. He knew the type. Langley was full of them, and this man looked like he would have been poured into a suit and taken up office within the CIA. Young enough to be dangerous, old enough to have some standing, perhaps promoted above his peers in time to generate a clear career trajectory. King hated him already. A decade younger, on track for better things. All King had done was kill, steal, and deceive for his country. He had been ready, willing, and able. And that had bolstered his reputation, the belief that sometimes, he was the only man for the job. He could barely recount a mission that had gone to plan, or nor was he convinced even that the result had really made much difference in the grand scheme of things. He studied the man resting beside the Kia Sportage hire car, his attention on the small group on the beach, dangerously close to the bears and the frozen shoreline. What games had this young man been sent to play? King wondered whether he would have appreciated a man a decade older than himself advising him to give it all up and run for the hills. Not likely, he thought. He would have slotted the older man right there and then. He smiled at the thought. No, this young American was in play. The pieces were on the board. Britain had King, their American 'friends' had this young man, but what of the Russians? He would bet all he owned that the man staring back at him at the airport luggage belt had been Russian. He had the look, whatever the hell that was. But King was seldom wrong when it came to reading people. He knew the foibles that made every country unique. His life's work had been in reading both people and the situations he found himself in. But he'd read enough here. He could see that Daniel was a player, simply by the fact the American had taken an interest in him, and by that note, the American was a player, too.

The vehicle's heaters were on full and doing a fair job of clearing his rapidly freezing breath on the windscreen, but as King slipped the pickup into gear, he reached forward and cleared the edges of the windscreen with the back of his gloved hand. Both the rear, offside window and the driver's window shattered, the headrest erupting in a puff of fibre, sponge, and leather. King heard the gunshot a second later. He already had the engine running and the vehicle in gear, so he floored the accelerator and flung himself across the seat as the pickup slewed across the sand, heading for a polar bear that had been cautiously creeping forwards towards one of the tourist buses. King swung the wheel, missing the beast more by luck than judgement as he chanced a look and headed for the road. The Toyota's rear wheels sprayed two rooster tails of sand into the air, raining the tourists, buses and guides with stones and sand amid cries of protest and the growling of a fleeing polar bear. As the vehicle slewed onto the frozen dirt roadway, all four wheels gripped and the traction control managed the vehicle, guiding it back into a straight line. King sat up in his seat and focused on the road ahead. The bullet hole that had punched into the rear window was the size of an egg, but the driver's side window had blown out completely, the bullet having become greatly misshapen after passing through the headrest. So, he knew the direction of the gunman. But he still had no idea who had taken the shot. King glanced at the rifle beside him. Bolt drawn backwards, just three brass shells to call upon. With his thick gloves and zippered pockets, the box of bullets had just as well been back at the hotel.

Ahead of him, shipping containers met the dark, grey beach. King figured Spitsbergen's crime figures were low. No fence, no security. But the containers would have been the most likely place for a shot to have been taken. King checked the mirror, noted the distance to the buses and guides where he had been parked. It was a long shot for open sights. Nearing four-hundred metres. That was the sort of distance where the shooter would aim for the largest mass of the figure – the solid colour of the target – and not a precision shot, like the head or the heart. The shot had simply been too perfect, passing directly through the space occupied by King's head less than a second before. King would have estimated the bare minimum of a 3.9x40 scope and a competent marksman behind it. He slowed the pickup, glancing left and right for movement or colour that seemed out of place, and always using his peripheral vision to spot peculiarities and sudden movement.

The frozen dirt track wound past the stacks of shipping containers and skirted the beach once more. King eased the bonnet of the pickup past the outer edge of containers and killed the engine. He stripped off his gloves and tucked them into his jacket and took out the Beretta 92 Compact model that had formed part of his equipment drop the previous evening. It was a traditionally designed semi-automatic 9mm pistol with unmatched accuracy, reliability and durability, and a thirteen-round magazine. King had requested it because of the ergonomics of the controls and large trigger guard, making it a usable weapon in cold climates where fingers were either frozen or gloved.

He took the rifle and worked the bolt before slinging it over his shoulder. Polar bears were still the biggest threat, even with a sniper in the mix. King suspected the sniper would be long gone. No follow-up shot that he'd noticed as he had driven off the beach, and any sniper worth their salt would have either bugged out or taken up an alternative firing point by now. But King doubted self-preservation to be on this person's agenda. Spitsbergen was a remote and isolated island with only two ways off, both easily policed. The shooter had been willing to compromise their safety to attempt to kill King quite openly. And that meant commitment.

King edged down the side of a shipping container, the pistol in his right hand. His hands were cold, but there was enough adrenalin coursing through his veins to stave off the cold for a while longer. Above him, the perfect shooting platform remained unchecked and while he was moving, he knew there were simply too many tactically superior vantage points from which he could be viewed. He backtracked, broke left, and ran down the side of the area, pounding at a sprint until he worked his way around the unfenced compound. Around two-hundred metres later, his heart pounding and lungs heaving with the effort of breathing the cold air, King saw a rusted and broken tractor abandoned next to a single shipping container. He slowed to a walk, checking the open ground and when he reached the machine, he climbed up onto the fragile bonnet and precariously used it as a mounting block to pull himself up onto the top of the container. King rested on his stomach and surveyed the area. He saw the figure in an instant, lying prone and aiming the rifle in the direction of the Toyota, its bonnet only in view to them, the shooter waiting for some movement. A patient man, but ultimately too patient. And then, as if he read King's thoughts, he turned and stared right at King, uncomfortable that he had waited too long and that his quarry may try to flank him.

King fired the pistol. Not to realistically hit the man, but to put him under duress and stop him from getting the crosshairs of the rifle scope on him. He watched the bullets spark on top of the container, adjusted his aim, and sent another two bullets near enough to the man for him to flinch and recoil. King pocketed the pistol, reached for the rifle strapped on his shoulder, but realised that with the bulky clothing he was too slow and clumsy in his efforts, especially when up against a man whose kit was all laid out in front of him. He watched the man roll with well-practised grace, hugging the rifle close to his chest. When he had changed position, the rifle came out and up to the man's shoulder ready to aim and fire in an instant. King still did not have the rifle off his shoulder, so he dodged left and saw the muzzle flash of the rifle and the roar of the gunshot followed almost at once. He could see the man adjusting his aim, and he turned and leapt off the container, feeling the force of the bullet in his back and the sound of the gunshot reverberate through the containers as he fell. He landed heavily, his back on fire and curiously, a feeling of numbness filling him inside like icy water. He tried to move, but his head felt ready to explode, and his eyes started to close. He knew he was checking out, and his last thoughts were not of Caroline, nor of Jane, but that he was genuinely shocked that luck and fate had cashed in their chips. He had always won, always survived. But then he guessed that everybody else did, too.

Right up until they didn't.

Chapter Eleven

Dorset, England

She had moved the cross trainer into the lounge, butting it right up against the window so that she could look out towards the sea as she built on her physio routine. She missed their home in Cornwall, having taken a year's let on the cottage in Dorset while she rehabilitated, and they both re-evaluated. The Cornish property had been repaired and recently sold; too much had happened there to consider staying. They had made a little money on it and moved on. And now that she had time to reflect, she doubted their lives would ever reach a point where solid roots could grow. The risks were simply always going to be too great. The fact made her sad, but conversely it had made her realise that there was more to life, and that escaping the country with their yacht pipe-dream may be a step closer and not actually a pipe-dream at all.

She was up to fifteen-minutes, twice a day on a light setting with the cross trainer. The movement not only helped with her cardiovascular system, but with her back, legs, and arms, which had all suffered from fractures, breaks and contusions. Not only did she have to rebuild wasted muscle and increase flexibility, but she needed to mend mentally, and for that she needed to be able to control her body once more and get back to full strength.

Outside, walkers were heading for the steep, crumbling cliffs of the Jurassic Coast and the horseshoe bay below. Caroline had earlier attempted to walk the cliffs but had tried too soon. King had bought her the cross trainer and she now felt close to attempting another hike, but it was far too early to venture outside without the pair of crutches. She yearned to get outside and feel normal again, but now with King on assignment, everything felt far from normal.

Caroline watched the black Jaguar saloon pull into the side of the road and felt a pang of anxiety wash through her stomach, her heart beating faster in a few seconds than it had for ten-minutes on the cross trainer. She stopped pumping her arms and legs, stepped off the machine and felt her legs wobble, not through the exercise or pain, but because of what could now unfold. King had the luck of the devil, but she knew deep down that luck couldn't last forever. She wiped the perspiration from her face and watched as Ramsay stepped out of the passenger seat. Big Dave remained behind the wheel and she felt the anxiety grow further. She couldn't wait for Ramsay to make his way up the pathway and steps, and headed out to meet him halfway. Taking a deep breath and wiping a tear from her eye, she opened the door and looked at Ramsay expectantly. Holding herself against the wall and keeping the weight off her right leg.

"Caroline…" Ramsay said, surprised at the ambush.

"Is it Alex?" she managed to say, her lips quivering.

Ramsay looked at her awkwardly. "Can we talk inside?"

"Oh, my god…"

"King's okay," Big Dave said loudly, covering the ground in huge strides.

"Well, as far as we know. He's operational and beyond contact…" Ramsay protested.

"Shut up, Neil." Big Dave shook his head, then looked at Caroline and smiled warmly. "I knew he'd fuck it up…" He looked back at Ramsay and said, "What the hell's wrong with you man?" He paused. "It's about something else. Alright, well now I'm here, I'll get the kettle on so that you two can have that chat…"

"Thanks, Dave," she said quietly, the colour returning to her cheeks and the whirlpool inside her stomach starting to subside. "You'd best come in…" She paused, then added. "And for Christ's sake Neil, spit it out."

Ramsay shrugged and followed her up the steps. Big Dave closed the door after them and headed into the kitchen while Caroline showed Ramsay into the lounge and sat down, surprised how much the short workout had taken out of her, and how the sudden explosion of emotions had drained what little energy she had left.

"Interpol and the Italian police have uncovered an attempt to recruit an assassin to go after King," he said matter-of-factly.

Caroline stared at him, the colour draining from her cheeks for the second time in as many minutes. She shook her head, frowning at the thought, thoroughly perplexed. Her expression said it all: she'd thought it all behind them. "But…"

"When both you and King were attacked last year, we know that the Russian element was ultimately handled by Rashid and King, and a hostile takeover by a rival mafia brotherhood in Russia severed that link completely. Likewise, it looks like the Americans took care of their rogue agent. I have unconfirmed hearsay that it was the CIA director settling his account before an incurable illness forces his retirement. King and Rashid put down the Italian mafia hit team, but the family boss is still alive. Again, like the Romanovitch brotherhood, the Fortez family suffered a hostile takeover shortly afterwards. It's common for rival gangs to strike while the opposition is weakened. Giuseppe Fortez got out with some of his assets intact but left his operation and businesses to the rival mafia family. He now resides on Lake Como and will likely die a wealthy, but unremarkable man. Certainly, the likelihood of heading up a mafia family again are next to nil."

"I don't care about the man's career prospects," Caroline snapped. "What are we doing about it?"

"We?" Ramsay scoffed. "You're certainly not doing anything about it. You're on extended sick leave."

"Alright, then what are the service doing about it?"

"Firstly, I've come to warn you. To make certain that you are extra vigilant. Of course, we'll have to move you right away…"

"No."

"What do you mean, no?"

"No," Caroline repeated emphatically. "I'm done running." She paused. "We both are."

"Tea up," said Big Dave walking in with three mugs pinched between his giant hands, spread like they were throttling the life out of the three china mugs. "Popped some sugar in yours, luv, for the shock from the Samaritan here…"

"I think I need it," she replied, taking the mug, and cradling it between her hands while Dave Lomu sat down. "Thanks."

"Like I said, we will have to move you," Ramsay said. "Things caught up with you recently, this time you might not be so lucky."

"Lucky!" Caroline retorted. "You call what happened to me lucky?" She was about to add that she had lost her baby, but she still couldn't say it out loud and she was damned if she was going to say it to him.

"No, I just meant…"

"Forget it," she snapped, cutting him off. "What do you know about this attempt to hire an assassin?"

Ramsay shrugged. "Giuseppe Fortez has no pull and no men so even as a former boss of the Italian mob, he didn't have anybody to call on for the hit, so he hired a former associate to reach the dark web and trawl for somebody willing to take on the job."

"Any takers?"

"Not yet. But Interpol are involved because of the international nature. The Italian police…"

"Are as corrupt as Fortez is!" Caroline interrupted.

"… Are assisting Interpol with the investigation and because the associate he hired is based in Switzerland, the Swiss have handed over to Interpol as well. The thought is to create a sting."

"A sting? Big deal. He'll argue entrapment. At best he'll get five or six years, commuted to two or three with good behaviour."

"But he'll be out of your hair for a while," Ramsay replied tersely. "Both you and Alex can have some breathing space and re-evaluate your situation while Fortez rots in a prison cell."

"To make contact with any number of criminals who will take the job on! He'll be likely to dangle the job and money in front of inmates just to give himself some immunity with the criminal fraternity, the big hitters inside." She paused. "Screw entrapment. What else have you got?"

"It's not a task for the Security Service."

"Great," she said sardonically. "How's Simon Mereweather, the new boss? Just like the old boss, or so it seems."

"He's actually the acting director."

"And, by acting, then you clearly mean acting like a bureaucrat…"

Ramsay sighed. "We're here because he sent us. He understands the development and he wants you safe."

"For us to move, again." Caroline paused and sipped some more of her tea. "I have contacts in Interpol, from my sabbatical working with the people trafficking task force. I'll see what I can find out."

"No more than I have, I suspect."

Caroline glared at him. "I'm not moving," she said adamantly. "I'm staying put, getting back to health and then we're going travelling together."

"We'll call it a sabbatical. Keep the pensions running," replied Ramsay. "I know you two, you'll get bored. It looks like King has already…"

"Sod off, Neil," she said, standing up carefully. "I'll pack a bag and you can take me back to London with you."

"To what end?" he asked, exasperated.

"To answer the request for an assassin," she said.

"I didn't think you liked the idea of entrapment?"

"I don't. Not when it's the Italian police and their Ministry of Justice, no. But if we can get our hands on what Interpol have on Fortez so far, then we can control the parameters and see that he isn't handed a token sentence. That is, if any investigation even gets that far. This way, we're in control."

"I like the moxy," said Big Dave. "I've got nothing on, and Lake Como is nice this time of year."

"Technically, it would be a cyber operation. It could be done completely over the internet and the dark web." Ramsay said pointedly. "We only need an agreement, talk of a payoff and a trail."

Lomu smiled as he watched Caroline's face. "But the most thorough investigations with the greatest successes get out into the field," he interjected, winking at her. "Don't they, Caroline?"

Caroline smiled at him and said, "You're damned right they do..."

Chapter Twelve

Thames House
London

"This is Captain Gerrard Durand, formerly of the French counter-intelligence service and Interpol's senior investigator based here in London," Ramsay turned to the Frenchman and said, "And this is Caroline Darby, with the Security Service."

Caroline smiled pleasantly. Nobody was shaking hands these days, let alone cheek-kissing the French. Maybe the West would even start bowing soon like their Far Eastern counterparts. Anything was better than an elbow bump. "Pleased to meet you," she said.

Durand sat back down at his space at the table. Opposite him a woman in her late thirties with light brown hair and a weary expression sat awkwardly with an open file in front of her. Caroline knew who she was, although they'd never met. Ramsay did not pick up on the fact and sat down at the head of the table, while Dave Lomu poured himself a coffee at the counter. The room was a fifteen by twenty-foot windowless box room with an office conference table and utilitarian chairs. Coffee and hot water had been put out for them in large, pressurised thermos dispensers with a jug of milk and a selection of coffee, tea bags, sugar, and biscuits. Big Dave had loaded up with biscuits and taken the last remaining chair.

The woman realised she wasn't being introduced any time soon and caught Caroline's eye. "I'm Sally-Anne Thorpe," she said. "I came aboard last autumn. No doubt your other half will have told you all about me." Her tone was challenging and passive aggressive. Thrown out there to make of what she would. "He's a bit too old school, I fear. A blunt instrument when I see the future requires a little more precision. Especially as solid convictions will be what makes the intelligence services a viable entity in the future."

Caroline frowned and shook her head. "No, he didn't mention you," she lied. King had been adamant that having a former Metropolitan detective inspector in their ranks, tasked with keeping the team on the right side of the law and influence their approach, would in fact weaken their effect on fighting terrorism. She shrugged like it was of no consequence and smiled. "Have you ever operated in the shadows? Been to some of the worst places on earth and gone up against the worst people those places have to offer? It's not always so black and white. Sometimes people die and many people could be saved if swift action is taken."

Thorpe paused, regarding her sceptically. "No, I suppose I haven't. But ignoring the rule of law is the thin end of a moral wedge."

Caroline smirked. "And what is your particular role in all of this?"

Thorpe stared at her warily. In her mind, having been the brunt of King's feelings last autumn, she simply could not process the thought that King had not mentioned her or her remit. "I'm a former detective inspector with the Metropolitan Police Service."

"A thankless task, I should imagine. And hindered, I suspect, by your middling rank," Caroline interrupted her. "So, you've jumped ship while the going was good. What skillset do you bring to the role?"

"I might ask you the same..." Thorpe challenged her.

"I'm an ex-Army officer, formerly with army intelligence fighting the war on terror in Afghanistan and Syria. A few excursions into

Iraq as well. So, three warzones… officially, that is. Then I was recruited into the Security Service and have worked in the field ever since. Apart from regular liaisons with Special Branch and two sabbaticals with Interpol." She paused, feigning a look of bewilderment. "So, I suppose I've been fighting terrorism since university. Have you experience with terrorism, or is it just petty crime you were involved in as a policewoman?"

"I was a lead detective with MIT!" Thorpe snapped. "Murder was my speciality…"

"Mine, too. With the right weapon in my hand and a committed terrorist in my sights," she said, then looked at Big Dave. "Get us a cuppa, would you Dave? I've suddenly got a nasty taste in my mouth…"

Big Dave smiled and stood up, his imposing six-foot-four and eighteen stone frame towering over the table. "Anyone else?"

"Do you rank over Mister Lomu?" Thorpe asked. "For him to make you a cup of tea?"

"No, not really. But he is the nearest to the refreshments table, and makes a bloody good cuppa," she replied. "And we've got each other's back. He knows that and so do I."

"*Le combat de chat*," Durand mused quietly.

Caroline turned and faced him. "*À peine un ronronnement*," Caroline replied. "*Mes griffes ne sont pas encore sorties...*"

Durand laughed and sipped his coffee.

"What did you both say?" Thorpe asked somewhat aggressively.

"You didn't take French at school?" Caroline smiled, but did not wait for her to answer. "Well, there's no need for paranoia, my dear. I wasn't talking about you." She paused and shrugged like it was tedious and of no consequence. "Our colleague commented with the statement; the cat fight..."

Thorpe shrugged. "Well, maybe we got off to a bad start? I apologise for my part."

Caroline smiled like she was blissfully unaware of any animosity. "No need. My reply to him was that it was barely a purr..." She paused. "And that my claws haven't even come out yet..."

Thorpe regarded her closely but did not reply. Instead, she tried to save face by saying to Ramsay, "This problem in Italy, do you have any suggestions?"

Ramsay seemed bemused, having watched the passive-aggressive exchange. He'd known Caroline for long enough to know that Sally-Anne Thorpe's card had been marked from the moment she had criticised King. He had felt for some time that the team needed clearer remits and a code of conduct that could not simply be brushed aside when situations got tough, but he could already see that the former detective inspector's presence was going to be provocative at best.

"Giuseppe Fortez has used a former associate to make tentative enquiries regarding hiring an assassin. It is clear from this information that the man is no longer in a position of power and that he does not have men to call upon. Last autumn, five men were at his disposal to travel here and hunt for King. Now he has nobody. A rival mafia family moved in on his assets and his men were either recruited or killed." Ramsay paused. "His being able to settle in Lake Como is both a mark of professional courtesy, and one of humiliation. You can take it as either, but as a mafia head, he's done. He has nobody to perform this act of vendetta for him."

"Who is the associate with the computer skills?" Caroline asked.

"Milo Noventa," Thorpe replied. "By all accounts, a weasel of a man who is half Italian, half English. He lives in Switzerland on Lake Geneva." She paused. "Educated at a string of private schools, generally because of his father's work around Europe. He excelled in computers and communications, specialising in internet finance and security. Fortez used him to hide money, though not very well because he lost a great deal to the rival gang. Fortez transferred two-hundred-thousand euros to Noventa earlier this week."

"His fee, or for that of an assassin?" asked Big Dave.

"His own fee, or part of the fee for certain," Ramsay replied. "Noventa has set this up within the dark web, and he created a modular surface email account for the assassin to contact him directly, which would enable him to vet the applicants, leaving Fortez out of the mix, although Fortez does want final approval, so he's willing to give Noventa some free rein, which works for us. The surface email has software and malware written in and bounces itself between thousands of IP addresses bought from Russian black hatters in internet scams. There's no tracing Fortez from it alone, but we found out about this from Interpol from the other end. The Swiss police were monitoring Milo Noventa for money laundering through Bitcoin."

"And Interpol are running an entrapment with just the Italian police?" Caroline asked. "Surely the Swiss police should be involved as well?"

"That is where I come in," Durand said quietly. "The Swiss and Italians haven't had the best record of working well together in the past. There is still much government and police corruption in Italy, whereas the Swiss judicial machine moves as smoothly and reliably as one of their Rolex watch movements. The temperaments are different, too. No, Interpol have managed to wrangle this off the Italians and the Swiss and it will work better as a single entity, but with their input."

"But you are here, so it is now a partnership with MI5," Caroline said emphatically.

"No, Interpol will be calling the shots. The Security Service have been read in, but you are here for advisement and courtesy only."

"Bullshit!" Caroline snapped. "I was affected by the last attempt made on Alex's life. Believe me, I've spent months recovering. I've had to move home, and now I'm being told to move again!"

"Nevertheless, Interpol are best suited for this," said Thorpe. "For practical reasons, the Security Service being read into the investigation gives you a heads up, Caroline. You can stay in the loop and lay low if Fortez is successful securing an assassin."

Caroline stared at Thorpe and said, "I'm not prone to laying low when someone is out to kill my partner. I was drawn into this last year when someone used me to get to King. It won't happen again."

Chapter Thirteen

CWO (Clandestine Warfare Office)
CIA Headquarters, Langley
Virginia

"Are you saying we lost them?"

"It's a submarine, that's what they're designed to do."

"Don't get glib with me, Becker." Lefkowitz paused. "You're in that chair because I put you in it. I can take you out of it just as swiftly, though far more publicly."

Becker flushed red and nodded, looked back down at the file in front of him. "Yes, Sir, off the coast of Senegal, near the Cape Verde Islands…"

Director Lefkowitz looked at the man beside him. "And the intel fits?"

Admiral Casey nodded. The sight of the man beside him hooked up to a drip of amber liquid was somewhat intimidating. His nurse had been security cleared and signed up to accompany him throughout his treatment. She looked on unperturbed, caring only for her patient and not for the secrets inside the anteroom. "It does, Sir. As we know Iran has two branches of navy. The Islamic of Iran Navy and the Islamic Revolutionary Guards Corps Navy. They command a large submarine force, but no nuclear-powered subs, and none with nuclear strike weapons. As yet, Iran is not a nuclear power. The submarine we cannot account for is a Kilo-class, or what they call Tareq-class, one of seven attack submarines they purchased from Russia for the equivalent of a reputed six-hundred million US dollars each. It comes under the jurisdiction of the Islamic Revolutionary Guards Corps Navy."

"The Caspian Sea makes it easier to ascertain the strength and deployment of Iran's naval forces," Becker said. "Being a land-locked body of water, we know where they are pretty much all of the time from satellite footage and both thermal imaging and sonic pulse readings. Even the submarines are easy to track in the Caspian Sea and the Iranians have one Tareq-class hunter-killer operating there permanently, as well as four of their smaller SSM's, or mini-subs for special forces operations, oil field protection and surveillance on other nations."

Admiral Casey nodded. "The rest of the Iranian fleet are based in the Strait of Hormuz, but due to the savage currents, levels of salinity and depth, most patrol in the deeper water of the Gulf of Oman and the Arabian Sea. The Persian Gulf is extremely shallow, so Kilo-class boats, or in the Iranians' case the Tareq-class boats, can only access a third of the area. The waters are also crystal clear, which along with the limited submarine operation parameters, makes it great for tracking them with eyes in the sky."

Lefkowitz nodded. "And this submarine has been unaccounted for since…"

"Since the British Astute class sub was discovered in the Arctic by those climate change scientists and lobbyists, yes…" Becker realised he had interrupted and held up his hands. "Sorry, Director. But we really need to move on this." He glanced at Admiral Casey. "The US Navy needs to get a submarine up in those waters now."

Lefkowitz nodded. "Understood. But after being spotted refuelling off the coast of West Africa by an Iranian oil tanker, it could have headed in any number of directions…"

"Agreed," said Becker. "But essentially, it was heading northwards. If it changed course and headed west, then it may well be a threat to the United States. But it would need refuelling on this side of the Atlantic, and the Eastern Seaboard is well protected by our own hunter-killer subs and detector buoys, as well as a large naval surface presence. My gut is telling me that the Iranians are heading for that submarine on the seabed and Iran wants to get its hands on some serious military technology, either the Rolls Royce nuclear reactor or the Tomahawk cruise missiles on board. If they can board it by way of a docking port, then it's like leaving the shop door open."

"Bloody Brits. What the hell were they doing up there, anyway?" Lefkowitz mused.

"I imagine they…"

"It was a rhetorical question, Becker," the CIA director replied curtly. "He looked at Admiral Casey and said, "And this is your gut instinct, too?"

The Admiral nodded. "There are numerous Iranian tankers between Hormuz and Japan and at this time of year they use the Northern Sea Route over the top of Russia to head down into the Pacific and Asia. Hell, a ship did the route a few years back without the use of icebreakers. Global warming is making the route easier to navigate and there is now a constant stream of shipping vessels sailing the route in both directions. And with Iranian tankers to call upon along the way, the sub can refuel and keep its diesel-electric motors running and not only make it to the area off Spitsbergen but have a whole range of options getting back to Iran as well, either doubling back, or taking the Northern Sea Route across the roof of the world. These tankers could also resupply them with food and water for their journey through the Northern Sea Route, where they could refuel again off Korea or Japan. You see, unlike nuclear powered submarines, the diesel-electric models have to surface regularly and refuel, as well as clean their air circulators, scrubbers and pumps."

Lefkowitz nodded, his face pale and gaunt, his eyes deep in black sockets. The man's health was deteriorating and there was no hiding it now. But he was damned if he was going to leave the CIA in a worse condition than he had found it and that meant tying up a dozen loose ends before he went home and let nature take its course. "That Iranian sub must not get near the British submarine."

"Agreed," replied Admiral Casey. "We have a Nimitz class aircraft carrier steaming across the Atlantic as we speak. The premise is an Arctic warfare training exercise. It is equipped with MH-60 Seahawk ASW helicopters." He added. "That's the type used for anti-submarine warfare." He paused. "But that doesn't help us with the UNESCO green zone, which is after all, the size of France."

Lefkowitz nodded, but despite his pained expression, the other two men could tell he was unimpressed. "I already have an asset in the area," he said, holding up a hand to stop either of the men from commenting, pulling the drip enough for the nurse to readjust it behind his back. "I put them in place the moment news of the sunken submarine came to light. On the very next flight." He looked at the most senior ranking naval officer in the United States Navy and said, "Admiral, we need this to be a covert affair. We need a hunter-killer submarine to operate illegally in the UNESCO area, and it needs orders to sink that Iranian submarine the moment it detects it. A surface engagement just won't cut it. The President doesn't want an all-out offensive for the world to see and for Russia to fuel the flames. And we can't be heavy-handed and break the UNESCO embargo. We hit that Iranian submarine and then we deny the shit out of it."

Admiral Casey nodded. The submarine service was the most secretive wing of the United States Navy, and he could not comment on a vessel's location, but he knew the USS South Dakota - America's most advanced and deadly hunter-killer submarine - was en route from Alaska, travelling under the Polar Icecap to form an albeit covert 'presence' near the Svalbard archipelago. "Director Lefkowitz, rest assured, the United States Navy will have the means necessary."

Lefkowitz nodded. "Good. We can't be a day late and a dollar short on this one." He paused, rubbing the area around the cannula in the back of his hand. It was bruised and raw and the skin on the back of his hand was flaking from the itching to soothe the irritation. "Once it's signed off and we have the backing, the CIA will commit its asset in the region. Any intelligence cultivated will be shared with Naval Intelligence. I move to reconvene to Joint Intelligence Committee Clandestine Affairs tomorrow at zero nine hundred. By then, Admiral, you will have word on your submarine and Becker, you will have contacted our asset to give JICCA some meat on the bone."

Chapter Fourteen

Longyearbyen, Spitsbergen Island
Svalbard Archipelago

He opened his eyes, the bright light above him forcing him to blink defensively. His eyes were dry, although not as dry as his mouth, which felt somewhere in the region between flour, dust, and sand. There was a good reason for that, and he rubbed his mouth with the back of his right hand, noticing grains of the distinct looking black and grey sand glisten on his skin. He moved his left hand, but it stopped short, secured to the bed rail by a handcuff.

"What were you doing in the storage depot?" A woman's voice, out of King's view.

King strained his neck to see, winced as his shoulder seared with pain. His neck was stiff, too. "Show yourself," he said tiresomely. "I'm not talking to someone I can't see. Where am I?"

"Longyearbyen Hospital. The northernmost hospital in the world." A woman of around thirty-five stepped out from behind the separating curtain. She was blonde, a little weathered in the face from the climate and her activities but looked fit and athletic. Like a chalet girl who'd done too many ski seasons and not acquainted herself with sunscreen or moisturiser. "I am *Politiførsteinspectør* Karlsson," she said with authority. "Anna Karlsson. I am in charge here."

"Of the hospital?"

"Of the police."

"Like the sheriff," King mused.

"Like a sergeant in your own police service. It's a small and remote posting. No call for a more senior rank. Not much crime here. " She paused. "Until now…"

"I was shot at on the beach."

"I have witnesses who say you drove recklessly on the beach and narrowly missed hitting a polar bear." Karlsson paused. "Nobody said anything about hearing a gunshot."

King shrugged, but it hurt. "I want to see a doctor."

"You're fine."

"I've been shot."

"Not nearly enough."

"Why are you detaining me?"

"I'm not. Not yet at least."

King raised his left hand until the handcuffs chinked on the metal rail. "I beg to differ."

"Just a precaution."

"Then get it off me. Now!" He stared at her and she smiled, not in the least intimidated, but then again, he was cuffed, and she was the one with a Glock 17 pistol in the holster, next to her right hand which hung casually alongside it. "I want to see a doctor," he added, a little calmer after seeing her reaction. There was no sense sticking with the wrong approach when he was chained to a bed. He wasn't exactly holding any cards.

"You will," Karlsson smiled. She stepped out of his view and came back a moment later with the Browning rifle. The bolt had been removed, as had the magazine. She held up the stock for him to see. It had been struck by a bullet and as she spun it over, King could see a bulge in the synthetic material on the other side. "I'm surprised it stopped the bullet," she said. "It looks like a small round. I dug it out and have scanned it and emailed the images to the forensic laboratory in Bergen. I suspect they'll confirm it as point two-two-three, or five-point-five-six millimetre. Not a calibre we use up here, on account of the legal ballistic performance requirement for the threat from polar bears."

"Well, I'm sorry I got shot with the wrong gun…" He paused. "Now, unshackle me and fetch me the doctor."

"Ah, don't be such a wimp," she said quietly. "You have extensive bruising from the rifle stock, and bruises from falling off the container, but nothing else. No broken bones. It's a good job that rifle was hanging over your shoulder on the sling."

"Great, so unlock this and let me get out of here."

"All in good time." Karlsson paused. "Why would someone shoot at you?"

King shrugged. "No idea. I'm normally such an affable character."

"Who are you?"

"I'm a marine diver and salvage engineer."

She nodded. "So, you say. But tell me, why would someone who has been shot at go looking for the gunman?"

"I'm a vengeful son-of-a-bitch…"

"Most people would run away."

"I did. Or at least I drove. Ask the polar bear." King paused. "Apparently I got pretty close."

"Where's the gun, Mister King?"

"You're holding it."

"There were shell casings found on top of the container. Nine-millimetre. Where is the gun you used against the other gunman?"

"So, you now admit there was a gunman to start with, although the bullet in my gunstock already told you that."

"A gunman at the yard, but there's no proof you were fired at on the beach. I should write you up for dangerous driving."

"Take a look at my truck and you'll see it was shot up. Someone was shooting at me." King frowned. "And you say there were casings from the most popular calibre handgun in the world, but no gun found at the scene, where I must have been discovered in a state of unconsciousness…" He looked at her and said, "Well, it wasn't me. I was looking for the person who shot at me. I found him, and he shot at me again. It was foolish to go after him, and I have learned my lesson. Now, about the handcuff and my arrest…"

"I haven't arrested you."

"Then you'd better get this thing off me before it's too late. You're imprisoning me without due process." King stared at her, but not as cold as he could have. His grey-blue eyes were cold enough to start with, like glacier water. There was no malice in his expression, but she could be under no illusion as to the seriousness of his mood. "And your techniques are disingenuous. You start off by denying I was shot at, but clearly the truck I hired was at the scene and it doesn't take a CSI level of forensics investigation to see the windows are broken and my headrest has been shot out."

"There was no vehicle at the scene," she replied. "But you were seen driving a silver Toyota Hi-lux and you couldn't very well hide it at the yard before we found you…" She stepped forwards and walked around the bottom of the bed, reached down, and unlocked the cuffs with a stubby-looking silver key. "I'll be in touch," she said, as she headed for the door.

"You'll leave the rifle, bolt, magazine and bullets," said King. "It's illegal for me to leave town without them."

"You're planning on leaving town, Mister King?"

"I haven't decided yet," he replied, rubbing the feeling back into his left wrist. "But I don't see that you can do anything about it, as I'm not under arrest…"

"Be careful, Mister King," she said. "There are many new faces around here because of the green energy project, and many more since your country's submarine was discovered. I think you have already met someone with an agenda that does not align with your own. You should take care." She rested the rifle against the wall and nodded to where he could find the rest of his things on the other side of the room. "Stay out of trouble."

King watched her leave, then swung his legs over the edge of the bed, grimacing as he felt a twinge in his back and his head started to spin.

"You can't leave yet."

King looked up at the doorway where a tall, balding man with thick spectacles stood wearing a white medical coat with a stethoscope hanging loosely around his neck. He didn't look happy with his patient.

"No harm done, I hear," King replied.

"You've had a serious concussion. You should rest and remain under our observation."

King nodded. "I've had a few concussions in my time, I know the score."

"I can see you've suffered a few traumas. You are a former soldier, yes?"

King shrugged. His employment had never looked good on a form. He found silence was sometimes the best answer he could give, or the people asking the questions could hope for.

"You have bullet wounds, the scars from knife wounds and your body has suffered many blunt force traumas." The doctor stared at him. "Whatever you do, you should perhaps stop doing it…"

"Do you need my medical insurance details?" King asked, changing the subject.

"You will see the reception desk on your way out," the doctor replied. "You know, it's illegal to die in Svalbard." He mused. "If a citizen has a terminal disease, then they must return to Norway. The permafrost prevents the digging of graves."

"I'll be careful not to die, then."

"I'm thinking of the people who get in your way." The doctor turned and hesitated in the doorway. "Don't fall asleep until tonight, and if you suffer a headache take a couple of paracetamols and call the hospital if it persists. Likewise, you should contact us if you suffer from double vision or dizziness. But I'm guessing you know the score…"

King watched the man leave and got off the bed, the hospital gown was gapping open at the rear and catching a draft as he gathered his clothes and the rifle and pulled the cubicle curtain around him.

Chapter Fifteen

King had never experienced a fog like it. He had filled in the forms on the desk and left the hospital, unable to see more than twenty feet in front of him. He had supposed the Toyota was still at the cargo storage compound, but from what Karlsson had said he could only assume the gunman had stolen it. There couldn't be many places to hide it and making it roll into deep water would be about the only way of disposing of it, but a can of petrol and a match would be more effective and a lot less discreet. He could not see to what ends it served the gunman to steal the pick-up, other than to escape in and now there would be their DNA inside.

He had asked someone for directions, a spectre appearing before him out of the gloom, but the man had not spoken English and King's Norwegian was about on the same par, so the two had parted ways and disappeared from each other after a few paces. Thankfully, the hotel was on the main street and once he worked out that he was at least on the right street and the correct side of the road, he was able to make his way there, slipping under foot as the ice had started to melt on the surface, making progress treacherous.

As he entered the lobby King was met by Madeleine who looked pleased to see him. "Oh, thank goodness you're okay!" she exclaimed and hugged him closely. "There was a shooting near the beach! Somebody said it was a handgun, but apparently the police could not find the shooter." She realised King had winced when she hugged him and she pushed him away at arms-length and looked at him full of concern, still holding him by the arms. "What happened to you, are you injured?"

"I fell, it's nothing," he said defensively. She hugged him close again, then released her grip a little awkwardly.

"I thought I might have heard a rifle shot," Daniel said, walking over to him. "But it may have been a vehicle backfiring because some idiot raced across the beach in a pickup and nearly hit a female polar bear. Maybe it was an accidental gunshot, and the idiot made his escape before anybody could question him. They hire out firearms to people with no experience, just so long as they can get the forms filled in on time." He paused, looking at the rifle on King's shoulder. "Anyway, it's been quite a morning…"

"Sounds like it has," King replied, ignoring Daniel's comment. Had he seen King driving and entered into a passive-aggressive rhetoric? King suspected so but decided to let it go.

"That doesn't explain the other gunshots," Madeleine protested.

"I didn't hear them," said Daniel. He looked at King and asked, "Did you?"

"No," King lied.

She shrugged. "I didn't either, but somebody said that was what the police were questioning people about. Anyway, the sailing has been cancelled because of the fog. Not because of the ship and navigation, but because of the issue of loading it with the cargo and passengers. They're all used to it up here, the fog can be some of the worst on the planet caused by the warm Gulfstream and cold Arctic currents meeting head on."

"Is there fog forecast for tomorrow?"

"Not as thick," Madeleine replied. "We're having some lunch, care to join us?"

King looked at Daniel, whose expression was somewhere between disinterest and ambivalence. King could think of nothing he'd rather do less, but he agreed. Something wasn't quite right with these two, and he figured he could find out what that was over a plate of something hot. He looked around for somewhere to put the rifle, then ended up handing it over the desk to the receptionist, who received it like it was an everyday occurrence, which he supposed it was. She put a tag on it and asked his name, writing it on the tag along with his room number. King had drawn out the bolt and kept the magazine.

The restaurant was busy with people who should have been making their way to the port but had been left with a last-minute change in plans and from the way the front of house staff bustled about the place, King got the impression that this was an impromptu lunch service. After they had been seated on a table laid for four diners, they ordered drinks and food from a special's menu of three choices. King chose the reindeer stew with potatoes and Madeleine ordered king crab claws with dill butter. King wasn't necessarily interested in what Daniel chose but when the food came, it was the thickest slab of cod he'd ever seen. The fillet had been cut a mere inch wide and still filled a third of the plate. He started to regret his choice of reindeer, which he could see was the Svalbard or Norwegian equivalent of a shepherd's pie. Madeleine was handed a plate containing a small faux bucket of cracked crab claws, a pot of the melted dill butter and a finger bowl with a slice of lemon.

"The food here really is excellent," she commented. "Simple, but brilliant."

"Agreed," said Daniel, but King suspected it was merely to agree with her and not that he was a fan of the menu.

"Have you heard about the seed vault?" Madeleine asked, looking at them both.

"No," Daniel replied.

"I have," replied King. He glanced at Daniel, and the man seemed visibly irked that he had answered honestly.

"Isn't it simply the most wonderful idea?" She exclaimed. She turned to Daniel and said, "It is an underground vault located here on Spitsbergen. Naturally being the most northerly town on the planet, and with a year-round permafrost, the place is a natural freezer. Well, every country on the planet stores its most staple crop seeds in the vault in case of disaster or famine. That way, they can withdraw seeds and grow them in times of crisis. It's incredible because the United States keeps its seeds right next to those of North Korea! It's a neutral facility and kind of ground zero for feeding the planet if we ever suffer a disaster like an ELE."

"ELE?" Daniel asked.

"An extinction level event," King replied casually. "Yes, it's a marvellous facility, or the concept is at least. Four and a half million varieties of seeds are held in what is referred to as the Doomsday Vault. Even cannabis is stored there."

"Cannabis!" Madeleine exclaimed.

"Yes," replied King with a wry smile. "That was what the Dutch chose to store…"

Madeleine laughed. "You are terrible!"

"Do countries ever withdraw their seeds?" Daniel asked, not looking in King's direction.

Madeleine shrugged and King said, "Syria is the only country ever to have made a withdrawal. Which gives you an idea of the situation out there…"

"Oh my god…" Madeleine said quietly.

Everybody was quiet for a few minutes as

they ate. King paused to sip his beer and said, "It's a shame this fog is so thick, we should have been able to see the Northern Lights tonight."

"Yes!" exclaimed Madeleine. "I have seen them before, when I was a child we stayed at a cottage in the north of Sweden, and we watched them every night."

"What about you, Daniel, have you seen them before?" King asked.

Daniel nodded through a mouthful of cod. He finished chewing and said as he swallowed, "Yes. Like Madeleine, I saw them as a child growing up."

King nodded. "Nothing new for you, then."

"They're pretty, but you get used to them."

"In Poland?" King sipped his beer and stared at Daniel. "I didn't think you could see them that far south."

"Well, you can."

"Surely not?"

"It's about light pollution, not strictly northern geography."

"But still…" King stared at him. "It's not a common occurrence."

"I grew up in a rural location, in one of the largest forests in Europe. The nights were dark, the stars were clear, and the sky was big. We saw the northern lights on many occasions..." He looked at Madeleine. "How is your crab? I was tempted to try it myself."

Madeleine dipped a fleshy piece of claw meat into the butter and passed it over to him. King watched as he ate and agreed how wonderful it was. If he cared he would have felt awkward, but he wasn't interested in Madeleine, Daniel could have her. But he did care why there was the pretence of including him. King had only spoken with her briefly in Oslo and she appeared to have met Daniel on the flight to Svalbard, and yet there was an easiness between them. They may well have slept together since arriving, and that was their business. Until he had met his wife Jane, King had always made it his business never to turn down sex when it was even a remote possibility, so he wasn't one to judge what people got up to. However, sharing food was a long way down the dating line for him, and if two people were getting along so famously, so comfortably, then why include a rugged-looking man in his forties? There were plenty of people sitting alone in the restaurant, it was that sort of place. King could only come back to the thought that they wanted to keep him close. But why?

The conversation soon drifted to King and his line of work, and he soon realised that it was always Daniel, in his passive aggressive manner, that steered the conversation. The sort of questioning that would ordinarily lead the person being questioned to justify their position. King couldn't be sure if Madeleine followed on through politeness or was part of the act.

"So, where did you train?" Daniel asked, taking a mouthful of cod.

King was aware of the technique – ask a question, then make it difficult to ask another, forcing the other person to fill the void. There was a reason why CEOs preferred to interview their executives over lunch. Anybody pleased with a lunchtime meeting in business and thinking they'd arrived was kidding themselves. King took a sip from his beer, recounting the legend Neil Ramsay had made for him, the faked, but designed to look little used social media account, the potted history. "I did an engineering degree at Brunel, then worked in the field for a number of years before deciding to specialise in marine engineering because of my love of diving."

"Then you will have needed to retrain," Daniel commented, suddenly having finished his mouthful.

"Indeed," King replied, taking a sip of beer. He knew the technique well and decided to offer nothing else as he took another mouthful of the strange reindeer and potato stew. He'd lucked out, the dish didn't work for him.

"Well?" Daniel prompted.

"Sorry," said King, apparently done with the conversation. "Southampton University." King had helped Ramsay keep the legend close to real events. King had in fact been working and living on the south coast at the same time, although he had been labouring and taking part in prize fights while on the run from several London gangs who were intent on getting their stake money back for a boxing match that he won but should have hit the canvas. Something had sparked in King that day, and he realised that he couldn't lose or step away from a fight. The same trait had seen him in prison on a double manslaughter conviction. That all seemed so long ago now. Despite being a trained killer, he was a far better man now. "I didn't realise I was attending an interview. Would you like to hear about my grades next?" King stared at him coldly, enjoying the effect it had on the younger man. He smiled, softening his eyes to let the man know he had been joking, but Daniel didn't seem too convinced. King turned to Madeleine and asked, "What will you be doing with Aurora?"

She smiled and said, "I'm hoping to study cetaceans."

"Right... That's seals, isn't it?" King asked, rolling the dice.

"No, they're chordata, which break down into three families of odobenidae, otariidae, and phocidae. For example, walrus, sealions and fur seals, and true seals." She paused. "No, cetaceans are whales and dolphins."

"I see," said King. "And if Aurora don't have an opening in ocean mammals?"

"Sharks," she replied emphatically. "I'm interested in cetaceans because of the numerous pods of orcas to be found there, where it was previously thought all orca pods were known. There are the orcas in Northern California and Oregon that hunt great white sharks solely for their liver, the orcas of Patagonia that have developed a beaching method for hunting seals and in Norway there are the super fishers, the orcas that have developed herding and stunning to hunt herring. Yes, there are many more pods around the world, but orcas are great travellers and migrate to different locations, scientists think, to communicate with other orca and learn their techniques." She sipped some of her beer and smiled. "Sorry, I get passionate thinking about it. But if not, then I would be interested in sharks and in particular the Greenland Shark, which has recently been found in the cold climates of Iceland and Norwegian Fjords."

"You must have dived with sharks," Daniel said, looking at King.

"Both a pleasure and a natural risk in my working environment."

"Not as much of a risk as people would assume."

"It depends," he replied, thinking of Cuba and an experience he had there not so long ago. It hadn't worked out too well for somebody else. "Some species are simply curious, while others are downright dangerous. I don't like getting in the water with bulls and tigers, but we dive in buddies and avoid dawn and dusk as much as possible. That's the common feeding times."

"I doubt sharks are even in the water half the time," Daniel commented dubiously.

"I have a test that always works. If you do it, then you will never fail to know if there is a shark nearby," replied. "It works in every ocean."

"Really?" Daniel frowned. He looked at Madeleine. "Do you know about this?"

"No, I can't say I do." She frowned, looking somewhat bewildered yet interested, nonetheless.

King smiled. "It's easy, really. What you do is when you arrive somewhere, make your way down to the shore and dip your finger in the ocean." He paused, looking at them both in turn. "Now, take your finger and place it in your mouth…"

"Your mouth?" Daniel asked incredulously.

King nodded. "Now, here's the thing. If it tastes salty, then there's a decent chance that a species of shark is nearby…" The other two looked at each other, then Madeleine started to laugh. Daniel didn't quite see the joke, nor the truth in King's statement. Regardless, King had had enough of the food and the company and had plenty to go and check on. He drained his beer and stood up. "Lunch was on me," he said. "I'll let them know at the desk to charge it to my room. Please, enjoy some dessert. But I'm afraid I have some calls to make, but imagine I will see you both later…"

Chapter Sixteen

Back inside his room, King inspected the bullet damage to the rifle. Karlsson had cut some of the synthetic material away in her effort to extract the bullet. He could see from the bulge on the other side, and the way the colour had drained from the black composite that the bullet had been close to penetrating and passing through. Another calibre up the ballistic chart, or ten metres closer for that matter and the outcome would have been entirely different. He loaded the rifle, applied the safety, and propped the weapon beside the bed. He wasn't a fan of unloaded weapons. Next, King checked the pinhole camera again, but he hadn't received any unwanted visitors. The room should have been made up, but as the occupants of the hotel had nowhere else to go, and the flights from the mainland had been cancelled, his room was available until the fog cleared and the boat from the port of Longyearbyen could set sail. King checked under his bed and pulled out the two samsonite cases containing the explosives and detonators. The cases were secured by double four-digit combination locks. King had been told the codes before leaving for Norway and steadily turned the dials, the lids snapping open when he had completed the combinations. He slid his index finger inside the lip of the lid, ran it across until he found the secret internal catch, then unhooked it and cautiously opened the lid. The catch was attached to a grenade and although it wouldn't have detonated the packages of plastic explosives, it would have killed, or maimed anyone inside the room. King repeated the process with the second case, then breathed a deep sigh of relief. He hated grenades and he despised boobytraps. One had to remain so alert in their presence.

King studied the explosives, the RDX detonators and the detonation cord. There was also Velcro, glue, and duct tape – all the things needed to hold things in place. Because of the nature of the detonation there were electronic timers, spare batteries, and a roll of tools he would need including screwdrivers, pliers, snips, a boxcutter and spare blade and a wire stripper. King weighed up the necessity for the grenade boobytraps and decided to remove them. The samsonite cases were difficult enough to damage, and the combination locks provided tens of thousands of possibilities, but a probability of zero in solving. The grenades were not only unnecessary, but simply too random for King's liking. When he was called upon to kill, he did so with a heavy heart, and in most cases through the sights of a gun or with his hands or a knife. When these methods were not possible or appropriate, he targeted with an explosive device or chemical agent, but only when he could be sure that there would be no collateral damage. King checked the split pins holding the spring-loaded levers down on the grenade bodies, and opened the pins up making it difficult to remove them by accident. He then tore off a strip of duct tape, tore the tape in half lengthways and fastened it around the grenades, which would hold the levers in place even with the pins removed. Then he stored them in his leather bag. He cursed himself for losing the Beretta but was more puzzled why it had not turned up in Karlsson's search at the scene.

King sat down on the bed, his back screaming as a jolt of pain shot through him. He was still aching from the fall from the snowmobile, let alone the terrific impact from the bullet into the rifle stock and the fall from the top of the shipping container. He thought about the size of the rifle stock and how far through the bullet had penetrated. The hard synthetic composite material had stopped the bullet and he knew that a wooden stock would have told a different story. One he probably wouldn't have been around to hear. The choice of calibre had surprised Karlsson, but King already knew the rifle would have been an assault type. The calibre just didn't fit for the island and the reasons for owning one. He had seen a large scope attached but had not been able to identify the weapon at such a distance, but the rapid follow-up shots had meant that it was a semi-automatic, and in that calibre, that meant assault rifle. He had felt the impact of the bullet against the rifle stock but had lost consciousness when he had landed so heavily and did not hear any rapid follow-up shots. Although that would mark the gunman as a pro. No target, no shot. Karlsson had not elaborated further on the gunman or the incident, which told King that she either had her suspicions, or didn't have a single lead. More likely it was the latter and she probably hoped the incident would go away as soon as King boarded the ship to the Aurora platforms a hundred miles to the south. No harm, no foul.

King took out his smartphone and opened a browser. He first searched for the Northern

Lights, or *Aurora Borealis*. The effect of disturbances in the magnetosphere caused by solar wind. The disturbances caused by the sun are sometimes strong enough to alter the trajectory of charged particles of electrons and protons in the upper atmosphere where they collected hydrogen particles. The resulting ionisation emitted light of varying colour and complexity, seen best the nearer you are to either poles – the South Pole's equivalent being Aurora Australis, visible from Southern Australia. To see the Northern Lights, it was generally agreed that you needed to be far to the north and away from light pollution. King knew that the further north you went, the less light pollution was an issue, but as he searched where the lights could be seen he saw that it was in fact possible to view them from Scotland and the north of England, particularly in Northumberland. It was what enthusiasts considered to be a partial observation, at around forty percent of what you would see in Canada, Alaska, Russia, and Scandinavia. King continued to search and discovered it was in fact possible to occasionally see the sight in Poland. Not regular, and certainly not the full show, but possible. He cursed, hoping that he had found a lie in

Daniel's story. Next, he searched for seals and whales and Greenland sharks. He recalled most of what Madeleine had said, and he figured that she was either legitimate in her claims to be a marine biologist, or she had a well-rehearsed back story. King decided he would delve deeper when he saw her next.

Since landing on Spitsbergen and checking into the hotel King had had his suspicions. Aurora was hosting the international delegation of salvage workers that would make up the team to raise the submarine and tow it to the Faroe Islands, where the Royal Navy would assume command and receive their vessel. Hostile forces would be among the salvage crew with their own agendas, just as King was there to defend his country's interests. He had earmarked Daniel and the American, but both had been on the beach at the time he had been shot at. But he still had reason enough to suspect the young American. The man he assumed to be Russian, staring at him across the luggage carousel had disappeared. King couldn't identify the shooter, so was nowhere nearer to hunting him down, or remaining out of harm's way. He stood up slowly. There was pain in his right knee now; his landing had been heavy, and the ground had been frozen solid. King walked over to the window and stared outside. The room was on the second floor and he could not see the ground below, such was the thickness of the bank of fog. Outside, vehicle headlights made slow progress, like eerie spectres in the ether. He doubted the crane operators could even see the ship, let alone load the supplies and equipment safely on board. He looked back at the two samsonite cases and again felt uncomfortable without the pistol, but more so at its disappearance. With the fog outside there was little more he could do today, and it felt as if his enemies were circling, and he had no move to play.

Chapter Seventeen

50° 00' 08.99'' N 6° 38' 24.38'' W
Atlantic Ocean
30 miles off the Cornish Coast

Keshmiri Pezhman studied the ship in the periscope. It was a Panamanian registered tanker and sailed under the name Golden Star. The ship was in fact Iranian owned and loaded with unrefined oil on her way past the Scilly Isles off the coast of Cornwall having made an unsanctioned delivery to a West African nation suffering from trade embargoes, on her way to the Northern Sea Route across the north coast of Russia, where it would arrive for processing in what the world knew as North Korea, officially and somewhat ironically called the Democratic People's Republic of Korea. As two countries both the subject of world sanctions, Iran had kept the oil fires burning in North Korea for more than twenty years, while its neighbour China traded in food and coal. The submarine would follow the tanker for another one-hundred miles and then refuel from the vessel's vast diesel tanks midway between the Scilly Isles and the southern Ireland coast. When there was no other shipping for miles the submarine would surface and the tanker's crew would secure them while the fuel was pumped and the submarine's engine crew would clean the scrubbers and recirculate the air, while fresh water was pumped in and waste swapped for supplies. The entire process would take no more than thirty minutes with the Golden Star's radio operator studying the radar and sonar array for approaching vessels.

Keshmiri Pezhman was the rank of *Nakhoda Dovom* - or Commander – in the Islamic Revolutionary Guards Corps Navy. The elite corps of submarines trained in covert surveillance and the hunting of enemy ships and submarines. The hunter-killers. The young Iranian was proud to hold such an esteemed position, and although the West spoke of their superior technology and advancement in submarine design, Pezhman knew that both he and his peers across the corps had one thing their Western counterparts did not have and that was faith in the Almighty, the one true God and it was Him who would see them prevail, because they were willing to give their lives if required and that gave them the biggest edge of all.

Chapter Eighteen

Geneva, Switzerland

There were many exclusive restaurants along the Quai du Mont Blanc. It was the same in most cities along a waterfront where bars, cafes, hotels, and restaurants could charge at least half as much again as their in-town rivals just for the view and the sound of sailboats bobbing up and down on the water, empty rigging blocks tapping away on masts. With views of the snow-capped alps, the Mont Blanc ridge and Geneva's historic architecture – and not least the monied clientele this part of Switzerland appealed to – the eateries along the Quai du Mont Blanc could command a higher tariff than most places on earth.

Milo Noventa sipped his second espresso and read from a copy of the Financial Times. He had the look of a carefree man easing into another day, in no particular rush and not quite sure where it would take him. His black, slicked-back hair went well with the grey Armani suit and the gold chain he wore over his red T-shirt underneath. There was money there, a certain sense of style, but little class.

"He'll have a ponytail for sure," said Big Dave.

"Why so sure?" Sally-Anne Thorpe asked.

"He looks the type."

"And that is?"

"Apart from slippery and slick, he looks like an arsehole. And if you lift the tail of a pony, or a man's ponytail, you'll always find an arsehole underneath…"

"Cute…" Thorpe smiled, keeping her eyes on the screen in front of her. The camera was rigged in the wing mirror of the van, enabling her to watch and control focus from where she sat with the laptop on her lap in the rear of the vehicle. Another camera was fixed between the two kayaks strapped to the roof racks to provide them with some cover. Big Dave controlled this one, and it took in the wide-angle view.

"He looks like a double-glazing salesman from the nineties," Big Dave commented, adjusting the focus slightly.

"He's pushing Bitcoin. How else was he going to look?" She watched as Noventa turned and watched a woman in tight leather trousers walk past. "Yep, you were right. A thin ponytail down his collar."

"I think most Bitcoin dealers are arseholes, too."

"That's because you don't understand it."

Big Dave nodded. "And you do? I didn't realise until this operation that Bitcoin was even a thing. I thought it was just a con."

"I don't have a PHD in computer software and mathematics, so no matter how many times I read about it, I'm still lost…" Thorpe agreed.

"It's a decentralised digital currency without a central bank or single administrative body that can be sent from user to user on the peer-to-peer Bitcoin network without the need for intermediaries. Transactions are verified by network nodes through cryptography and recorded in a public distributed ledger called a blockchain. Bitcoins are created as a reward for a process known as mining. They can be exchanged for other currencies, products, and services." Neil Ramsay paused. "What's not to understand? Network nodes can validate transactions, add them to their copy of the ledger, and then broadcast these ledger additions to other nodes. To achieve independent verification of the chain of ownership each network node stores its own copy of the blockchain. At varying intervals of time averaging to every ten minutes, a new group of accepted transactions, called a block, is created, added to the blockchain, and quickly published to all nodes, without requiring central oversight. This allows Bitcoin software to determine when a particular Bitcoin has been spent, which is needed to prevent double spending. A conventional ledger records the transfers of actual bills or promissory notes that exist apart from it, but the blockchain is the only place that bitcoins can be said to exist in the form of unspent outputs of transactions."

Big Dave glanced at Thorpe and smiled. "Thanks, Neil. Glad you could clear that up for me."

"So, Neil, have you invested in Bitcoin?"

"Not likely," Ramsay said mockingly. "I have a mortgage, teenage girls and a senior-leader salary. What little I have sits in a well-known bank. I don't like any risk in my portfolio." He paused, glancing over Thorpe's shoulder at the screen. "My, he is a thoroughly unlikeable looking character, isn't he?"

"He's fishing for an assassin in the dark

web, he was never going to be saint-like," Thorpe replied.

Ramsay didn't respond. Looking at Big Dave he said, "It looks as though he's ordered another coffee. He's not going anywhere soon, and there's a seat free at the nearest table. Dave, go and have an espresso. Hide your earpiece and make sure your mic can pick up everything. He's most likely waiting to meet somebody." He paused. "And don't blow it…"

***

"Big Dave is up," Caroline said quietly inside the Mercedes hire car. She watched the man-mountain slide into the empty seat and sit with his back to Noventa. Although Dave Lomu was six-four and eighteen stone, he moved with a cat-like grace, agile on his toes and with good spatial awareness. Wearing cargoes and a body-hugging woollen sweater with a zipped neck, he looked fit and comfortable, and did not look like a typical tourist. Caroline watched as the man ordered, then sat back to watch the lake on his right, and the rest of the street straight ahead of him.

"He is a good man, no?" Gerrard Durand asked.

"Big Dave? The best," she said. "Cool in a crisis, a good sense of humour and as tough as nails." She glanced at the French counter-terrorist captain and saw him nodding approvingly.

"You have, what is the term, friction with Sally-Anne Thorpe?"

Caroline shook her head. "I don't like to be policed. What we do is by its very nature, a bit of a grey area in a world of black and white." She paused, looking back at Noventa. "Ramsay brought her in for her investigation skills. She was a top murder detective, apparently. While I appreciate her expertise, our remit differs from what the Security Service is both widely seen and believed to do."

"A hammer to crack a walnut..." Durand interrupted. "I get it. I deal with ISIS and other Islamic extremists, endemic to France." He shrugged. "My heavy-handed techniques got results, but put it this way, I did not volunteer for this posting. In France, too, there is seen by politicians the need to finesse when really, as I say, a hammer gets the job done."

Caroline smiled. She thought Durand had much in common with her, and she thought King might agree as well. The thought of his absence saddened her, and she turned her attention back to Noventa and Big Dave at the Café du Lac. She hated not knowing where King was or if he was even safe. He was on his own and there was nobody to have his back.

"Are you carrying?" she asked, not taking her eyes off the subject.

Durand hesitated, then shrugged and said, "Yes."

"What?"

"A Glock Nineteen."

"Where did you get that?"

"I have contacts. Getting a pistol in Europe is easy."

"Give it to me," she said uncompromisingly.

"And if I say no?"

"Then I'll take it from you."

"I'd like to see you try."

"Then just try saying, no…"

Durand shook his head in exasperation and pulled the weapon from his jacket pocket and handed it to her. "It's loaded…"

"Not much good to anyone empty," she said, but taking nothing on face value she pressed the release button and ejected the magazine. She pulled back the slide, caught the ejected bullet and pressed the lever to hold the slide backwards while she inspected the breech and set about reloading the magazine with the loose round. "I'll look after it," she assured him, as she inserted the magazine and dropped the slide forward. The weapon was ready, and she tucked it into her shoulder bag and opened the door.

"What the hell?" Durand glared at her. "You are only here because you wore me down! I agreed to the Security Service taking part in the surveillance and moved the goal posts for you, and now you are moving them again! We are only meant to observe!"

"So, observe…" she replied, getting out stiffly. She had brought along just one crutch and had been pushing herself at that, but she looked at it on the back seat and decided to leave it. She shouldered the leather bag, checked the catch was open and there was easy access to the pistol, then bent down, looking back inside the vehicle as she said, "I'm not playing Neil Ramsay's games and making this a tech-based, internet-heavy investigation. By the time we get to play this idiot, he could already have a contract in place."

"He will have worked out a code word, something to alert Fortez. You could blow this completely…" Durand said earnestly, but his protests were drowned out when she slammed the door behind her.

Caroline limped across the road, wishing she had used the crutch by the time she was halfway across. When she reached the pavement, just a few steps from the café, she paused to regain her composure and take a breath. The pain in her right leg was excruciating, and ever since she had left her home in Dorset, she had been taking painkillers as if they were sweets. She had three pins in her leg and all of them told her she was pushing herself beyond her limits.

***

"What the hell is she doing!" Thorpe exclaimed as she saw Caroline come into her field of view on the laptop screen.

"Her job," Ramsay replied.

"Her job was to observe!"

"Then I suppose she changed the parameters…"

"For god's sake…" Thorpe shook her head and said in dismay, "She's a loose cannon, just like that King character. No wonder you're getting flack for this team…"

"You're a damned good investigator, Sally-Anne. You got us here. You found out more about Milo Noventa and his whereabouts than anybody I know could have. And you did it in record time." He paused, but kept his eyes firmly on the laptop screen. "But Caroline Darby is good at this sort of thing. Yes, she's a giant pain in the arse sometimes, but she can adapt and improvise like nobody else can. So, let's just sit back and see where it takes us…"

***

Caroline caught the waiter's eye as she approached, rather unsteadily, and asked for a double espresso, and another for her friend, pointing at Milo Noventa who was thoroughly immersed in an article in his paper.

She walked around the table and sat down opposite him, catching Big Dave's look of surprise as the big man glanced her way. "I'd like to say you're a difficult man to find, but I'd be lying," she said.

"Who the hell are you?" Noventa asked bemused. He then looked at the waiter who placed two espressos on the linen tablecloth, along with more sugar and two cat's tongue biscuits. "No, I…"

"Relax," Caroline interrupted. "I ordered this." She dropped a brown sugar cube into her double espresso and stirred deliberately with a tiny silver spoon. "I use the dark web a great deal and I peel the layers from the onion," she said. "Just like you. But I also employ a technical genius who not only found this job for me but found the gatekeeper as well."

"I don't know what you mean," Noventa replied belligerently. He pushed out his chair. "I'll be going now," he said tersely.

"Dave…" Caroline said quietly.

Big Dave turned around and with a swift motion, pushed the chair back under the table with his size thirteen boot. Noventa was about to protest, but as if Dave Lomu's size wasn't enough, he caught sight of the pistol in Caroline's hand. She had placed her bag on the table and tilted it for Noventa to see, and now she slipped the bag back into her lap. "If my colleague doesn't grab you and force your chin backwards until your vertebrae pops, then I'll just put three nine-millimetre bullets into your spine."

"People will hear…"

"I'll refer you to the first scenario. The two hundred and fifty pounds of muscle seated right behind you." She paused. "Anyway, the gun is loaded with Russian-made cartridges from their PSS project. The cartridge contains a propelling charge which drives an internal piston in contact with the base of the bullet. Upon firing, the piston propels the bullet out of the barrel with enough energy to achieve an effective range of twenty-five metres. Hell, that's about it for a pistol, in a firefight, anyway. At the end of its travel the piston seals the cartridge neck, preventing noise, smoke, or any blast from escaping. These cartridges are over a thousand euros a pop and quite silent, but I dare say I can part with three or four of them without worrying too much about the cost."

"What is this?"

Caroline smiled. "Just a quiet drink between the middleman and a prospective client who is telling you to go to your paymaster and tell him you have a suitable person for the hit, and unbeknown to your client, you close the contract down."

"And if I don't?"

"I gave you two scenarios, I have a third, but didn't want to have reason to give it to you. Two scenarios should have been enough." She paused. "Oh, okay, I can see you're the kind of guy who needs to see all of his options spread out in front of him. So, I'll give you another. Let's say, we take you someplace quiet where I'll get my colleague here to hold you down while I flail the skin slowly from your back... Is that good enough for you? Or how about, I remove your testicles using two bricks and a whole lot of clapping...?" She sneered and said, "I promise if you test me, the worst scenario will be the one we use."

"Okay, I get it!" Noventa shuddered. "Look, it's not as easy as that. My client will want a résumé of previous... er, assignments..."

"Hits. You mean, hits."

"Whatever."

"Well, let's just say this. The advertisement is pulled. I've shut you down. You will only get your finder's fee once a person is hired for the contract. And that person, under whatever guise you chose, will be me. That's it, job done. So, you bloody well sell me to your client, or you don't get your fee, get your balls removed between two bricks, get your neck snapped, do not pass Go and do not collect two-hundred pounds. Got it?"

Noventa nodded pathetically. "Okay, I've got it…"

"Now, the job was a million euros. That's not going to work for me. But two million? I can live with that," she said. She reached into her bag and took out a small sheet of paper. "That's my account number, forward it to your client when you inform them that you've found someone, but only when they agree. Not before," she said curtly, putting it down between them. "Standard operating procedure is half before the contract commences and half when the contract is completed. Those will be the terms I work under."

"My client requires a face-to-face meet."

"Then they'll have to pay half before we meet."

"That's not going to work."

"Then, see that it does. I'll kill whoever he wants for two million euros, but I'll happily kill you for free."

Noventa slipped the piece of paper into his pocket and took a sip of his espresso. "How can I contact you?"

Caroline smiled. "I'll contact you. Be under no illusion, you won't give me the slip, you won't get out of this, and if you try to run, I'll kill you. Or my friend here will. But look on the bright side, your finder's fee has just gone up. Don't sell yourself short, Noventa. This isn't selling Bitcoin to people with more money than sense. This is dark stuff, and it commands a high price."

Noventa nodded. "Am I free to go?"

Caroline shook her head. "No, but I am. I suggest you give it fifteen minutes. I have another friend with a sight on your back. We don't want to let off a six-point-five Creedmoor in the city, but needs must…"

"What the hell is that?"

"It's a rifle calibre. A relatively new one. Damned effective and with a wonderfully straight trajectory." She paused. "It's another scenario that I didn't want to mention. A fail safe if you will."

"Who the hell are you?" he asked belligerently.

Caroline smiled thinly. She wore a pair of large Gucci sunglasses and the lenses were dark brown, hiding her eyes. Even with her striking looks and her mousey hair cascading around her shoulders, she would be difficult to recognise. The sunglasses and her lack of expression were all the disguise she needed. "We are just a few people with specialist skills and the will to exploit them effectively."

Noventa nodded. "How did you trace the dark webwork back to me?"

"As I said, specialist skills. And my man hacked you. Don't worry, it happens." She paused. "But be under no illusion, we can get to you whenever we want and wherever you are."

"I get it," he replied tersely.

"When you leave here you will start the ball rolling and contact your client. Whatever they want, whatever you have to do, you make sure I get hired."

"I'll need a résumé."

"You'll get some details. I'll email them to you. Yes, I have your email address. Nobody admits to what they have done in this game, so there will have to an element of trust, as someone like myself has in getting the second payment. Your client wants anonymity, and that leaves me not knowing who they are, or where they are. Like I said, trust."

"But you already know who my client is…" Noventa commented wryly. "Otherwise, why else do you want this?"

"You are a clever enough man to realise that some questions do not get answered without consequences. No, right now you are a middleman. Only, you now work for me…" She stood up, her leg giving her some pain, but she tried her best not to show it. "I'll be in touch."

Milo Noventa turned to watch her leave and Big Dave said, "Eyes front, greasy." He paused. "See what she doesn't want you to see, and you won't live to regret it."

Noventa picked up his espresso, his hand shaking. It was his third, but it wasn't the overload in caffeine that made him unsteady. The man was shaken to the core, and his options did not look good. After a few minutes he sighed and said, "How long do I have to stay here?" There was no reply, and he risked a glance, but Big Dave's seat was empty, and the man hadn't heard or sensed anything as the man-mountain had left.

Chapter Nineteen

"Jesus Christ! What the hell was that?"

"Improvisation," Caroline replied tiresomely.

Sally-Anne Thorpe shook her head, glancing at Ramsay for support. "We were mounting a surveillance operation. You and Durand had barely got eyes and ears on at Noventa's property. What did you think? You'd roll up at the stake-out and just wing it?" She watched Caroline move around the table and drop heavily into the chair. "You're not even fit. You could have got into trouble facing off with the target like that."

"I had Big Dave looking out for me."

"Dave was caught unaware and had to improvise." Thorpe paused. "And improvisation breeds mistakes."

"I thought I was okay," Big Dave chipped in. He had made a foot-long sub, and it was busting open with smoked meats, but he squeezed it closed and took an almighty bite. "Went well enough," he added, speaking through a mouthful of coleslaw, salami, and salted roast beef.

Thorpe shook her head. "And where the hell did you get the gun?"

"That was me," Durand interjected. "I have it back in my possession now…"

"We aren't allowed to be armed," she replied.

Durand shrugged. "I am an officer with my country's counter-intelligence service, on secondment with Interpol. We are routinely armed and I can travel with my weapon under the Schengen Agreement."

"And that's your official weapon, is it? You wouldn't have carried one in London and I seem to remember flying here with you direct from Gatwick Airport…"

Durand shrugged, took a sip of his coffee, and returned his attention to the laptop in front of him. Milo Noventa's property had been put under electronic surveillance using pinhole cameras with audio throughout. Durand had intercepted the telephone line and an encrypted scanner would take care of the man's mobile phone. The Active Financial Crime Unit of the Swiss police had handed over the IP address details and email trail logs to Interpol as part of their investigation, which Durand had used to great effect, and he was now logged into

Noventa's computer and capable of searching documents and emails without the man knowing.

"Let's get some perspective," said Ramsay. "I see what Caroline has done. Either Noventa works for us, or he works against us. If a genuine assassin gets wind of who is hiring, then we could have a situation where an assassin is in place and the contract is activated without us being in the loop. With Caroline posing as an assassin, and with Noventa coerced into presenting her to Fortez, we can now control the situation."

"It's called entrapment!" Thorpe paused. "It's what we wanted to avoid, not least because it will never stand up in court."

"Excuse me…" Caroline stood up, shuffled a step then used her crutch to walk towards the balcony door. She had overdone it earlier, exerted herself too much. She would have to take it easier, but she wasn't the best patient for that. "I need some fresh air." She opened the glass door and stepped outside, the hubbub of the city below, the tranquil waters of the lake in the distance above the rooftops in front of her. She took out her mobile phone and scrolled to the number King had given her before their last operation. She would need it now and she looked at the number, working out the simple code in which she had entered it into her phonebook. She had left the zeros and sevens in place, but every number was altered either one up, or one down numerically. There was no sense in altering zeros and sevens because they appeared in all UK mobile numbers, but by altering the subsequent numbers so simply it was easy for her to remember, and almost impossible for someone else to recognise. She looked up as Captain Durand stepped outside and lit a cigarette. He offered one to Caroline, but she politely shook her head and continued to text. She sent the opening text and waited.

"She is not used to operating in such a manner," Durand ventured.

"No, she is not."

"And I think both you and she have not taken to each other."

"I'm a pro, Durand. I don't partake in idle office gossip. Thorpe has her remit and I have mine, but I'll be damned if I let someone stand in my way when I see an opening." She paused. "I'm a big girl and I've been doing this long enough to know when to hold and when to fold."

"Or when to walk away?"

"Meaning?"

Durand looked at her leg, the crutch, and the way she was holding herself up against the balcony. "She is right about one thing... You are not fit for active service."

"Bullshit. I can still hold my own."

"You must appear credible to Fortez. He won't buy it if he thinks you cannot complete the contract."

"I'm not taking a real contract. I need to get past the man's security and speak to him face to face."

"You need evidence of a crime for an effective and successful arrest to be made." He paused. "Far enough along the process that Fortez makes a payment."

Caroline nodded. She read the reply to her text, then typed out one word: Reaper. The text was replied to almost at once and she typed out what she required in just two short lines. She glanced up at Captain Durand before sending it. "I know what needs to be done," she said, sending the text and smiling as she thought about her request. "Like I said, I've been doing this long enough…"

Chapter Twenty

Fifty miles south of Spitsbergen Island
Svalbard Archipelago

King looked at the pistol in the man's hand. He'd been there before, and he'd never got used to it. The impotence of being unarmed and staring down the wrong end of a gun. The man wore thick thermal gloves against the cold and his trigger finger was still nestled against the frame. The sign of a pro. Little chance of a negligent discharge, but given the cold, the thick gloves and the immediate proximity, King would have had his finger on the trigger. But then again, King did not have the gun and the man in front of him did.

The ship trundled onwards, its diesel engines thumping and droning lazily in the background, the steel hull striking occasional slabs of sea ice the size of a single bed. King could see the man's breath in front of him, almost frozen by the time it reached his own face. The breath crystalising slowly and falling to the deck like a snow globe that had been given only a lacklustre shake.

"They warned me about you in Moscow…"

King shrugged. "Whereas I don't even know who you are."

"That makes for the better operative, don't you think?"

King looked at the man's gloves. They seemed thick and cumbersome and half an inch in diameter too big for the trigger guard of the Makarov pistol. But then again, the man was a Russian and they tended to be at home in the cold. Although as he felt the sharp, icy chill on his face, he seriously doubted anyone could get used to this. But King knew that if the tables had been turned, he would have taken off the gloves before he had reached for the gun. Experience counted for so much in this game, and the thought that his opponent hadn't thought this through as thoroughly as he would have, gave him some hope at the very least.

"What do you want?" asked King.

"The same thing as you do."

"I seriously doubt that."

"Well, I suppose I want what's ours, and you want to make sure the world never finds it." He paused, his breath all around him and falling steadily to the frozen deck. "But essentially, we're after the same thing. We both want something and are prepared to kill to stop the enemy getting their hands on it."

King glanced at the ice under the man's feet. Behind him, the rail was heavy with a build-up of icicles, large stalactites hanging down several inches. Eight inches or more in the darker recesses behind the lifeboats. King had the advantage of standing on galvanised steel grating, his footing feeling both firm and secure under him. He realised he was still holding the mug of tea. He looked around for somewhere to put it, then simply dropped it on the deck between them, the tea flooding around the man's feet, the tin mug clattering across the deck towards the lifeboats. "There's a manifest," he said. "If you kill me, they'll know in no time." He nodded at the gun in the man's hand. "And you certainly can't kill me with that, or they'll be looking for a murderer."

The man shrugged like it was nothing. "People have accidents all the time. They slip on ice, fall overboard. It happens."

"Not with nine-millimetre holes in them."

The man waved the pistol to the port side. "Step this way…"

King smiled and shook his head belligerently. "Not in a thousand lifetimes, sunshine," he said. He watched the hesitation in the younger man's eyes. "You shoot me, and there'll be an investigation. People will recall conversations, they'll have alibis. But where were you? As soon as we dock, you'll be the number one suspect."

"I'll be gone way before then," he said, looking at the inflatable tender with its forty-horsepower engine.

"There will be a reception committee at the rigs. You're going nowhere before the ship gets there." He paused, glancing down, and watching the spilt tea freezing around the man's feet. "You made your move too soon, son. Inexperience, that's all."

"Don't you dare patronise me!" He stepped closer. King noticed the finger was inside the trigger guard now, the material of the glove had bunched up. He could see that the Makarov's hammer was not cocked. The trigger could still be pulled, but the weight of the pull on the double-action Makarov was up there with gym equipment. Twice that of a Glock, at around fourteen pounds.

"That RIB won't do you any good out here."

"Let me worry about that. You should worry about yourself. The water will be cold, but it will make your death swift. Give into it, you'll know next to nothing about it…"

King moved quickly, grabbing the pistol, and pushing it back towards the man as he kicked him in the shin with all the force he could muster. Not to cause pain – which it invariably did – but to shove him backwards in the ice formed from the tea he had intentionally spilt. The man had pulled the trigger, but King's grip had eased the slide of the weapon back just enough to disengage the striker and as long as he kept up the pressure, the weapon was useless. The man slipped and tried to regain his balance, but King kicked out again, and followed up with a headbutt onto the bridge of the man's nose. The younger man recoiled, his eyes closed, the pain excruciating, but King gripped him by the windpipe, adding a further dimension for the man's instincts to wrestle with – three different areas for the pain receptors to signal the brain and for the brain to become confused how to deal with each - and pushed him back against the railing. King had the weight and strength advantage, and the man was struggling for traction on the ship's slippery deck. Then King changed tactics and instead of kicking the man's shin again, he hooked his foot behind the man's heel and pulled his leg towards him as he pushed hard on his throat, forcing him backwards against the railing. Momentum, inertia, and gravity came together like the independent notes of a symphony and the man pirouetted over the railing and fell silently twenty feet or so into the icy water. Not even a grunt, let alone a scream, as the man's instincts were to take a deep breath in mid-air, nothing more.

King did not hear the splash above the monotonous thump of the engines. He had the Makarov in his hand, and he tucked it into his pocket as he walked the length of the railing and searched for him in the water. There was plenty of ice, but no yellow and red flashes of colour of the man's ski jacket. King realised he had underestimated the ship's speed, and he looked further out to the stern and saw the man floundering in the water. He turned around and watched the bridge. Above him he thought he saw movement on the upper deck, somebody stepping into a doorway. The light was dim and grey, and it was difficult to judge both distance and movement. But no alarm sounded and nobody else appeared. King turned and looked back at the water for his would-be killer, but the man had gone. Succumbed to the cold and the inevitability of death in such a hostile, merciless environment. Perhaps he had remembered his own hollow words and simply given up the struggle in favour of a swift end. A lungful of water and short struggle under the surface to end the searing pain of the cold. Whatever the scenario, the wake of the ship rolled on, there was no colour in the grey water and King's mission was unimpeded.

For now.

King turned around and watched the bridge once more. Daniel was gone. Sinking to the depths. He had mentioned Moscow, and King's suspicions had been confirmed. The man had tried to pass himself off as Polish, but there was something about him that had seemed so familiar, his mannerisms. The way they had toasted with drinks, King's attempts to trip the man up. So, he had been proven wrong about the Northern Lights, the fact that they could occasionally be seen from the wilderness in Poland, but he'd been right about toasting that first drink. He'd used Russian, a subtle difference, but from Daniel's later prickly attitude and the jibe about King being merely a diver, diving where people like Daniel told him too, he knew that he'd slipped up. Daniel would have corrected him, had the toast not been natural. From that moment on, King knew Daniel hadn't been who he said he was.

King slipped the Makarov into his pocket, then bent down and picked up the tin mug, which was rolling lazily on the deck. He was cold and he needed to get back inside the hubbub of the rec-room and prepare for the inevitable charade when Daniel was eventually noticed to be missing. But he wanted to make sure he was near Madeleine when it happened.

Chapter Twenty-One

King entered the recreation room as subtly as he could, but he was an imposing man at a shade under six-foot and weighing in at just over fourteen stone, but most of that weight was in his muscular shoulders, chest, and arms and as he discarded his jacket and hung it on the only spare hook, he could see people looking at him. Although he was oblivious to the fact, he was viewed by many women with interest, while most men saw him as a threat. There was an animalistic quality to him that gave off warning signs, backed up by the coldness of his glacier-cold, blue-grey eyes.

The room was hot, the windows steamed up completely and after the stillness of the icy, clean air outside, the room had become a miasma of heat, voices, the smell of strong percolated coffee, and body odours. King eased his way through the crowd of people and reached the coffee station, where he found teabags, a flask of hot water and some milk. He made a strong mug of tea and spooned in some dark sugar, which was all he could find. He took a sip, then looked around the room at the groups of people. The conversation hadn't changed much. He guessed he was used to a profession where one never really spoke about their work, and that even in the company of other intelligence agents, nobody talked about the job at hand. It was different within the team, and of course between himself and Caroline, although neither spoke about an operation the other was not involved in. His thoughts ran to Caroline and her recovery. She was such an athletic soul, so tenacious, too. She had been through the wringer and now carried the mental, physical, and emotional scars. King knew many of these scars would heal over time, but even time gave no succour to the deepest of wounds, the mental traumas that could not be seen, but always so painfully felt.

"I was wondering where you had gotten to."

King turned around and Madeleine was right in front of him. She was a good deal shorter than himself, and he looked down at her and smiled. "I needed some fresh air," he replied. He held up his cup. "Would you like a tea?" he asked.

"No, thanks. But I'll get a coffee and perhaps we can find somewhere to sit?"

"Of course." He watched her pour a cup of black coffee and she turned around, catching him looking at her. She smiled coyly and he could have sworn she pushed her bottom out a little. She certainly touched a lock of her glossy blonde hair. There wasn't much more she could do than come right out and say she was interested in him. King could read most people like a book, but he had never been adept at reading whether a woman was interested in him or not. In his late teens he'd been invited in for coffee plenty of times, but he despised coffee and only drank tea and had made his excuses and left, only to realise later in life what the phrase had meant. To his consternation, now that he was in his forties and had found the woman that he wanted to spend the rest of his life with, he could now read the signs perfectly well and noticed that he was never short of female attention for long.

Madeleine led the way through the crowd and to a row of seats near the starboard window. Outside the sky and sea were grey, but the windows were so steamed up it almost looked dark. She gave the window a wipe with her sleeve and said, "It looks monochrome out there. Like a black and white film. Like the fog as the

boat approaches Skull Island in King Kong..."
She sat down, the seats all facing forwards for
riding out rough seas. "Have you seen Daniel?"

"Not recently."

"Strange, he said he was going outside as
well..."

King shrugged, sipped some of his tea.
"There are two sides to a boat."

"Ship," she corrected him, then smiled.

"What's the difference?"

"Well, I thought a marine salvage diver
would know."

King nodded. "I'm not entirely sure
where the cut-off point is. I suppose it's like
when a pony becomes a horse. A definitive
measurement. I don't have a tape measure
handy..."

She laughed. "In sailing, a ship has to
have square rigged masts and must have at least
three masts. Anything else is a boat."

"Do you sail?"

"Not so much lately," she replied. "But at
university I joined a project to recreate a tall
ship, and that was the definition. I was invited
back, along with other alumni over the ten years
it took to build and finally sail her, but I was on
a research vessel off the Great Barrier Reef

involved in climate change research into the sun bleaching coral. It was that research that opened the door for the placement with Aurora."

"And you just met Daniel on the flight?" he asked. "It's just that you two seem rather close. Are you two an item?"

"No!" she protested a little indignantly. "What makes you ask that?"

King shrugged. "You were always together. He couldn't wait to get one over on me. I think he resented my presence, saw me as competition."

"He is on the ship, you know. You're using the past tense like he didn't make the journey," she chuckled. "Anyway, no, I'm not into him." She paused. "But because you've noticed all these things, might I take it that you could be interested in me… even if just a little?"

"You can," he lied. He smiled as Madeleine glanced around and reached out to touch his fingers delicately. He gave her hand a little squeeze in return. "And it feels good…"

"Yes, it does," she said.

King was quickly working through some boundaries. Attractive though she was, she was twenty years younger, more girl than woman, and as flattering as he found her attention, the fact she was declaring her attraction towards him made him dubious. And then there was Caroline. King had never cheated on his wife, Jane. And he had never cheated on Caroline. He took a serious relationship with all the name implied. But what if getting close to Madeleine aided his operation? He had taken an oath for Queen and Country when he was recruited into MI6. He hadn't exactly been sworn into MI5, more swept along with events, but it amounted to the same thing. He worked, put his life on the line, for his country. Not for the government – governments and Prime Ministers came and went, made the same mistakes, and never learned from their time in power - but the citizens who relied upon him, and people like him, to do unspeakable things in the shadows, so they may live in the light. He looked down at her and smiled. Her lips were moist and plump, and she had a habit of nibbling at her bottom lip. It looked seductive and inviting. He could feel a surge within him and knew if he didn't check himself in time, he'd be getting in too deep.

King unwound his fingers and released her grip. He looked past her and wiped the window clear. "We're here!" he said, a little too excitedly. His reaction sparked the interest of his fellow passengers, as he knew it would, and everyone started to shuffle closer to the windows, some picking up their coats and heading for the starboard deck.

Madeleine looked out of the window and said, "It really is a marvel." She paused. "A wonder of engineering and resourcefulness..."

King nodded. "Come on, let's get up on deck and take a closer look." He did not give her any choice, heading for where he had hung his jacket. As he unhooked it, he knew the weight was off. He swung the jacket on like he was unaware and glanced around for a watching pair of eyes. The heavy little Makarov pistol was no longer there.

Chapter Twenty-Two

The sheer size of the first oil rig was remarkable. Four hundred feet high by some two-hundred and fifty feet wide and capable of withstanding one-hundred-foot waves as well as a twenty-knot collision from a five-thousand tonne vessel. There was a helicopter landing pad on the top deck and the drilling equipment had been removed and replaced by an experimental wind turbine which added another hundred and fifty feet in height. This turbine used a series of magnets to double the torque effect and generate four times the electricity as a standard wind turbine. As well as this, solar panel platforms had been attached around the second deck, jutting out a full hundred feet from the structure. The temperature may not have been warm, but clear skies generated enough power to work in tandem with the wind turbine and give the platform all the energy it would require, while a desalination plant provided an unlimited supply of fresh water. King had heard about the sustainability of the project, greenhouses and polytunnels made use of treated human excrement to fertilise the soil, and plants were heated and watered by an offshoot from the central heating system, providing sub-tropical growing conditions for tomatoes, herbs, salad leaves, strawberries, legumes, and potatoes. These plants were considered the easiest to grow in hothouse conditions, requiring just a few weeks from gestation to harvest. To compliment this self-sufficiency, weighted hook lines were lowered for a few hours a day using the waste remains of the previous day's prepared catch and yielded daily hauls of cod, haddock and pollack to name but a few species of fish in plentiful supply, which were drawn to the molluscs and small fish that made the legs of the rig their home, which in essence was an artificial reef. Scraps of fish were also placed in crab pots and dropped to the seabed, where they would be hauled up every few days with a sizeable catch of crabs and lobsters.

"It's enormous…" Madeleine said quietly. "You see there…" She pointed at a large boom jutting out several hundred metres. "That's the hydroelectricity boom Aurora are testing. It remains deployed in the roughest weather, generating electricity twenty-four hours a day."

King studied it, noticing the red flashing lights fitted along the top at intervals to warn shipping of its presence. The ship had slowed, the captain wary of the obstruction. Another boom connected with the neighbouring rig and in the lee of the rig, an identical boom jutted out several hundred metres. "Booms connect all the rigs as well in calm weather," he replied. "And there's seven of them in all..." He marvelled at the scale of the project. Seven out-dated oil rigs now used for the experimentation of hydroelectricity and regenerative power. King could see the nearest two rigs, both one-thousand metres equidistant, but the grey hue of the sky and matching greyness of the sea meant he could not see the other four rigs in the chain.

"These platforms could generate enough electricity to power London. That is, if it wasn't being grounded on the buoy a mile south of here," a voice behind King said. "Amazing, isn't it?" King turned around and looked into the eyes of the man who had been on the beach watching Madeleine and Daniel. The man he'd had down as American, and CIA. "They just need governments to take on the technology, invest in similar projects."

"But other companies need the technology, otherwise Aurora is a monopoly and that wouldn't be fair on people. Sooner or later the tariff would go up and the supply chain could be affected." King paused. "Who are you?" he asked, deciding not to beat around the bush and be direct.

"David Newman," the man replied.

King stared at the man, a nagging feeling that he'd seen him before he had arrived in Svalbard. "What do you do?"

"I'm a salvage diver."

"Small world." King paused. "And what are America's interests here?"

"Green energy," Newman replied sardonically.

"From the country that pulled out of the Paris Accord, yet are the second largest polluter on the planet."

"Another President's policy. No, we're all about the green these days."

"In America's case, the green usually means all about the dollar," replied King. "Which is about right."

Newman shrugged. "And you're here because?"

"I'm helping Aurora salvage the submarine."

Newman nodded. "Our paths may cross again, then."

King looked at him, unsure whether their paths had already crossed. There was something vaguely familiar about the man, but he could not for the life of him remember where he had seen him before. He turned his back on him, confident that the man would not try anything here, and continued to look at the rigs, impressed not only by the size of a drilling platform up close, but the ambition of the project and the scale of the investment and organisation needed to bring it to fruition. He had read the articles in Forbes, National Geographic and USA Today about how Aurora had heard about Shell and BP's issue of how to dispose of old drilling platforms in an environmentally friendly manner, and how the CEO of the new clean energy start-up had thought the opportunity too good to miss. Taking the rigs from them, the petroleum conglomerates had paid Aurora half what they would have spent scrapping them, and the irony that Aurora used these funds to further their clean energy ethos was not lost on the company's investors.

King turned around and Newman was no longer behind him. Madeleine had pretended not to notice the curt exchange between the two men. King also thought it strange that she had not queried Daniel's absence more. The ship had a manifest of passengers, but King suspected it would operate like a buddy system. They were grown adults and it wouldn't be like a teacher holding a role call on the steps of the bus on a school outing. Daniel had only been in the company of Madeleine on Spitsbergen, so it would be likely only she would draw attention to his whereabouts.

The ship had moored alongside a large floating pontoon that jutted out some fifty metres and was tethered in place at the base of the platform. The pontoon looked to be constructed from a series of thick, hollow plastic containers chained together. Each section was around the size of the rear section of a small van, and the top surface had non-slip sheeting adhered in place.

"All constructed out of recycled plastic bottles with added natural colouring. The small sections make it more buoyant, but are also a safety feature, if one is damaged, the others remain afloat." Madeleine said as they got in the orderly queue. She smiled up at him and added, "I did some reading up on it while I was on the plane. Speaking of which, where is Daniel? I still haven't seen him."

King pointed to the cage lift that was making its way up to the former drilling platform, the first passengers on their way to the top level, where the offices, accommodation and admin were located. He studied the lift and the queue and estimated that there would be another four or five trips before they got their turn. "I saw him get on board," he lied. "I expect he'll be putting first dibs on the best room."

"Dibs?" She looked at him quizzically.

"Yeah, like calling shotgun." He paused. "It's a British thing."

"Oh…" She watched the lift come back down and said, "I was told everybody gets off here then boats ferry them to the other platforms."

"That's right," King agreed. The formalities were a fog, the operation so rushed that it was all he could do to concentrate on what needed to be done next. He still needed to meet his contact. "So, Daniel may well be remaining on this platform. We'll have to see how it works out, it could be us who get ferried away."

"Oh well." Madeleine bumped her hip against King's and said quietly, "Three's a crowd…"

King smiled down at her. His old mentor Peter Stewart, the man who had recruited and trained him what seemed like a lifetime ago, would always say, "You're always in the shit, Son. It's only the depth that varies..." King had begun to realise what the man had meant. There was no good outcome from allowing the flirtation and acknowledgement of the attraction between them. The shit level was about up to his bottom lip at this stage. He would have to be careful.

Chapter Twenty-Three

Lake Como, Italy

Located in a large basin within mountains giving way to numerous steep valleys through which funnelled wind met the water, Lake Como was renowned for its complex weather system. Often the lake could be seen dotted with masts and spray from sailing boats crashing through troughs, sails full and tacking dramatically tight courses, only for those same boats to be stranded in the middle of calm water, held hostage to still air and a mirrored surface from which there was often no escape for hours on end. There were few places on earth with such complex and fickle sailing conditions, and the locals even had names for the winds. There was the *Breva* - the prevailing wind, with its anticyclonic rotation it blew frequently. In the Alto Lago di Como, compared to the rest of the lake, the Breva wind was strengthened by an intensity that easily exceeded twenty-knots, accompanied often by significant wave motion. The *Tivano* was the morning thermal wind, with lower intensity. And the *Ventone* or *Vento* was the northerly wind that blows in strong gusts during the afternoons, often reaching forty knots. The *Fohn* was a wind that was accompanied by a rise in temperature, and the *Garzeno* or *Garzenasco* wind descended from the valleys of Garzeno and was usually associated with thunderstorms concentrated on the high ground above the town of Dongo.

Giuseppe Fortez did not tire of watching the lake and its turbulent waters. Since arriving here, he had noticed how the wind whipped up the lake, but how the conditions never lasted long, and as the days had warmed to spring, he could now set his watch by the change in wind and the daily temperature. There was little else for him to do here. Of course, he had been lucky to live through the takeover. What his grandfather had built up, the empire born from unions and workers' rights had swelled to organised crime, wartime profiteering, switching of wartime allegiances and heavy-handed domination of the backstreets of towns and cities, and then entire regions of his beloved Italy. His father before him had commanded the regions of Tuscany and Umbria with the same ruthlessness as the Dons of Sicily but had remained out of the witch-hunts that had followed, paying off the right people and the wrong people with a little bit more. After he had succeeded his father Giuseppe Fortez had ruled with an iron fist, and had built a fortune, but in handing over the reins to his two sons, that fortune had been slowly eroded. Poor investments, battles with rival gangs and families, encroaching foreign organised crime and the reliance upon drugs and weapons as their stock-in-trade had weakened the family. The focus had changed, and his sons had forgotten the old ways. To intimidate and harm one's enemies, rather than merely kill them meant that there was the chance for further extortion. Yes, the previous generations of Fortez men had killed, but to kill too soon was to close an account, a line of opportunity. His sons had also failed to invest in gold. The precious metal was the true measure of one's wealth and governments the world over used it to value their currency. Instead, his sons had used Bitcoin and invested in dot com companies that had subsequently folded. They saw their father's reluctance to change his ways as a failing, but in truth, he had remained with the tried and tested methods. Giuseppe Fortez had resisted investments in stocks and settled only on gold, because everything else in life was a risk that was only profitable for as long as the smart money remained invested. But gold was gold and since the ancient civilisations had dug up the first nuggets, the value and desire has never satiated. But of all things it was their involvement in drugs that had been the beginning of the end. Drugs created stiff and ruthless competition, holes in the supply chain, informers and undercover police, junkies who would sell out their own mother for a fix.

Giuseppe watched the boats tacking back and forth across the water. His villa was located on top of a fifty-foot cliff and surrounded by three acres of gardens. He had more bedrooms than he needed and had managed to negotiate his classic Alfa Romeo Spyder and Mercedes S-class, but his son Gennaro's vehicles had been shared among the Marino family, as had every remaining asset. Giuseppe had the money he had kept away from his sons in Switzerland, as well as some physical gold bullion in Liechtenstein, classed as offshore investment. The fact that the head of the Marino family allowed Fortez to live and relocate to Lake Como was not lost on him every day. The act may have been seen as weak by some, but Marino used it as testament to his victory. Fortez was a prisoner, a reminder that Marino could have killed him, but had allowed him to run away like a coward instead. The Fortez family dynasty had been ended, and the figurehead now rested in abject poverty, his business and assets carved up and his son's wives and children cast to the streets with nothing. And there was nothing Giuseppe Fortez could do about it. A stipulation. The price for his life. And to his consternation, he had accepted those terms. However, what he hated most, more than the sad reflection of his wrinkled face as he shaved in the mirror each morning, more than the loss of his family home and the sight and sound his grandchildren running around the terraces, was the Englishman Alex King. The bastard from MI5 who had used his son Luca merely to get to their Russian mafia rivals and had left his son to his fate. The man who had killed his younger son Gennaro in Britain last year. Shot him as he had fled in a light aircraft. He knew that his son had disregarded his own orders, gone to search for the man who had killed his brother, but he could not sit back and leave his sons unavenged. It was not the Italian way, and it was not the Fortez way. He may have lost everything including his dignity, but he was damned if he was going to lose both of his sons and leave their killer walking the earth.

Giuseppe Fortez moved his chair a few inches and felt the sun on his face once again. Like a cat tracking the sun across the floor, ever escaping the shadows. The light across the lake had cast a golden hue on the surface, and a sailing boat had a full sail and was sailing the length of reflective gold, its stern glistening in the sunlight. Fortez reached for his espresso and tested the liquid. It had cooled slightly, and he drank it down, savouring the caffeine hit and with it the thought of having the English assassin killed, but not before his killer delivered him a message, leaving him in no uncertain terms who was behind his execution.

Chapter Twenty-Four

North Atlantic

Keshmiri Pezhman kept his eyes to the periscope and watched the frigate two-thousand metres to the east. It was an Irish Naval Service vessel running close to Scottish waters, two hundred miles north of Ireland, and as he watched, it turned hard to port and headed towards them. Pezhman gave the order to dive as he dropped periscope. The frigate could have detected their presence, or it could have been a chance manoeuvre, but his objective was to avoid contact at all costs and complete his mission.

The helmsman controlled the plane, while the ballast tanks filled with water and the boat propelled steadily downwards. The crew leaned back in unison as the vessel tilted forwards and headed for a depth of three-hundred feet. They had been making twenty knots, or twenty-three mph. But the Iranian Commander gave the order to slow until the Irish Navy frigate was clear of them. The submarine couldn't run silently at speed. They had enough fuel and supplies to run for thirty-five days, but it would take just two more to reach their objective. The air scrubbers had been cleaned and vented at the last refuel stop and they could carry out their mission and escape through the Northern Sea Route and the Bering Strait, where an Indian registered tanker now under North Korean ownership and crew, and skirting the trade sanctions, would meet to resupply them and exchange cargoes south of the Andreanof Islands. Their journey should take no more than twenty days. Another twenty and they would return to Iran as heroes. And Iran would have no reason to fear its enemies again, and its enemies would quake in its shadow. A new world order was possible. With riots on American streets, democracy proven to be a myth as half the US felt cheated and disillusioned in recent years, Iran and its allies would grow stronger, while the great Satan that was America grew weaker and frequently less vigilant. The submarine commander smiled at the thought. The scales would soon balance in Iran's, and the Great Ayatollah's favour.

Chapter Twenty-Five

500 miles north of Svalbard Archipelago
Beneath the Polar Icecap

Commander JT McClure gave the order for silent running. No crew member other than the two helmsmen and the sonar operator, along with his second in command (XO) and the Weapons Division Officer (WEPS) could speak. And even then, anything but a low tone a quiet voice was a court-martial offence. All crew members were frozen in their spots. Above them, just eighty-feet of water between the conning tower and the first of the dramatic polar stalactites and a steady eight-foot thickness of solid polar icecap. Just one-hundred feet below their hull, the Russian submarine was suspended in eleven-thousand feet of water, at a steady eight-knots.

The Virginia class Submarine was America's deadliest and newest hunter-killer in the US Navy's arsenal. The sonar warning system had identified the propeller as a Yasen-class Russian submarine, and both the sonar operator and the Commander had confirmed the pulse. A team of US Navy SEALS had rigged recording buoys under the surface of the water outside Murmansk in the extreme north-west of Russia, home to their nuclear submarine base, with the sole intention of recording the pulse and pitch of the new Yasen-class submarines. Months of classroom-based scenarios had taught US submarine officers and sonar operators what to look for, but this was the first time Commander McClure had been so close to a Yasen-class submarine, and the feeling was unnerving to say the least, although he did not show his concern to his crew. The Yasen was Russia's newest, fourth generation nuclear powered attack submarine. A hunter-killer.

The vessel's distinctive design with such a forward placed and low conning tower, was state-of-the-art. The Yasen-class nuclear submarines were presumed to be armed with land-attack cruise missiles, anti-ship missiles and anti-submarine missiles, as well as anti-ship and anti-submarine torpedoes. The Yasen could also detach mines and retaliate with countermeasures to missile and torpedo attack. It was also the first Russian submarine to be equipped with a spherical sonar. CIA intelligence reports had shown that the Yasen was crewed by just sixty-four, while the US Virginia class submarines were typically crewed by one-hundred and twenty-eight – indicating that the Russian's had a great deal more sophisticated computerised systems and technology than previously thought.

"Hard to port, maintain speed." Commander McClure ordered quietly. "WEPS, Harpoon Torpedoes in tubes one and three," he said quietly, then added. "Maintain silent running."

The Weapons Division Officer passed on the order, nodding that he'd heard. Normally he would have repeated the order loudly to confirm but with a hunter-killer submarine directly below them, he did not dare risk it.

"Do you think they know we're here, Commander?" His second in command asked quietly.

McClure shook his head. "They've stumbled into us, I think they're oblivious. They're not taking any defensive action…"

"And we should continue to stalk them?"

"Lieutenant-Commander Jacobs, it's always better to keep your eyes on a predator rather than to turn your back…"

"Yes, Commander…"

Commander McClure looked at the digital map above him. They were heading on a south-westerly course. He could see the marker indicated by Svalbard and the Aurora Project rigs. He could draw an imaginary line directly on their present course. All the way to the sunken British Astute class submarine, some fifty miles south of the Aurora rigs. "Okay," he said quietly to himself. "Let's see how this plays out..."

Chapter Twenty-Six

The Aurora Project

"I'm Thomas Grainger," the man said. Nobody shook hands anymore, so King gave an extra meaningful nod. "Call me Tom," he added.

"King."

"Simon said you were a man of few words. He also said that you tend to make up for that with your actions."

"Mereweather wants you to keep an eye on me?"

"Not in the slightest. Not sure I could, anyway." He paused. "I'm here to lend a hand, help you navigate Aurora, the protocols etcetera."

King nodded as Grainger turned and led the way down the painted metal corridor and up a flight of galvanised mesh steps. "You and Mereweather were at university together?"

"Indeed. The good old days."

"Post or pre-Segwarides?"

"Oh, post! I can't believe he told you that!" Grainger laughed. "No, I'm in the Simon camp, always known him as that."

"He didn't tell me his real name," King replied. "That was his old man."

"Sir Galahad!" Grainger paused at the top of the steps. "Wonderful man. Helped get me some useful contacts. A true Royal Navy man, then went into the secret squirrels, rather like yourself."

King started to climb, not enjoying the vulnerability of talking to a stranger while still on the stairs. Surviving in his profession was all about the advantages of position and holding ground. "It's moved on, by the sounds of it."

"I imagine so," replied Grainger as King passed him and paused in a recess in the corridor. He eyed King with a tentative respect. It was clear to him that King wasn't walking in Simon Mereweather's shoes. The two representatives of MI5 could not have been more different. "He's a real Sir, as well. So, a real-life Sir Galahad!"

King nodded. He wasn't knowledgeable about the court of King Arthur, but he understood it was far more mythical than historical. Although the Mereweather family had seemed to have taken it all quite seriously. "What has Simon told you?" he asked, as Grainger continued down the corridor. Either side of the corridor there were health and safety posters for everything from gas leaks, power cuts and water ingress to full scale evacuation procedures. The metal walls were painted in cream enamel and reminded King of the bowels of a ship.

"He's requested I assist you, as has Sir Galahad. Naturally, I didn't need persuading, I've been a surrogate family member for years! I first went down to the estate to have a sort of assignation with Simon's sister. She was horse crazy and mother Mereweather thought I could get her out of the saddle. We ended up riding horses of course. She was practically born in the saddle."

"A spot of fox hunting, what?" King replied sarcastically, trying his best at an impression of the landed gentry.

"No. But we did draw some pegs and join the pheasant shoot for a few birds," Grainger smiled wryly. "To be honest, it's a different world and Horsey Harriet wasn't really my type..." He paused. "Simon is solid, though. And the thing about Simon being in his line of work, well I imagine one could always trust him."

"How so?"

"Well, the family is richer than Croesus."

"Who?"

"Ancient Greece, around six-hundred BC. He was the King of Lydia who, according to Herodotus, reigned for fourteen years until his defeat by the Persian king Cyrus the Great."

"Why do I always get a bloody history lesson?" King muttered.

"Well, he was colossally wealthy, hence the expression."

"Was he as rich as Bill Gates?"

"I doubt it."

"Well, that would still have been a better analogy, then."

"School of hard knocks, university of life?" Grainger grinned.

King smiled. "Got expelled from the school of hard knocks, still at the Open University version of life, as a mature student. In a crap subject. Probably won't graduate."

Grainger chuckled. "I expect there are more than a few things you could teach me."

"Don't be so sure." King paused. "We are what we are…"

"Never a truer word spoken," Grainger said with a smile.

"So, what has Mereweather being wealthy got to do with anything?"

"Why, don't you see? The man is completely incorruptible. I mean, his family have a net worth more than some countries. Nobody could ever hope to bribe the man…"

King thought of Mereweather's position, how he occupied the chair of a man who had been bribed. Not everything came down to money. King had been put in a similar position, too. In this business your loved ones would always be the most effective leverage, but he got Grainger's point. Grainger caught hold of the door handle on his right and said, "My office…" He paused. "Now, your extra bags have been taken to my dive unit. They will be quite safe. I will see that they're padlocked anyway." He sat down behind a small wooden desk and gestured for King to take a seat opposite.

King closed the door behind him and pulled out the chair. The office was cramped, with a few photographs of various marine expeditions on the wall, the obligatory health and safety posters and curiously, a golf bag and clubs.

Grainger saw King looking and said, "The

helicopter landing pad is a great place to drive a few balls."

"Not very environmentally friendly." Grainger smiled. "I suppose not…"

King stared at him for a moment, watching the discomfort in the man's eyes before saying, "You're here for something else, aren't you? No self-respecting eco-warrior would drive golf balls into the sea. What's the depth here, three-hundred metres?"

Grainger smiled. "More than ten times that in places. That sub is lying on a ledge that drops off to over twelve-thousand feet."

"So, you're here for reasons other than the submarine, but you're not a committed member of Aurora?" King said quietly. "And you've obviously been here for a while."

Grainger nodded. "I check for listening devices twice a day, but I've never found anything, we should be fine." He paused, resting his elbows on the desk and steepling his fingers. "I took the marine engineer job with Aurora because Aurora subcontracted the company I work for, but Simon asked me to look into the operation. He's not satisfied that Aurora is on the level. Well, not him per se, but the British government."

King nodded. "Too good to be true?"

"Exactly." Grainger paused. "But while I'm here, I am uniquely placed to give you the assistance required."

"You know what he has planned?"

"Yes. I can get you down in our submersible, and I can get you onboard through our dry-docking system. It's quite simple, really. You see, the water pressure would mean that the hatch could never be opened. Either from the inside or outside of the submarine. Our system uses a gaiter which surrounds the hatch, the pressure is equalised to that inside the submarine and the pressure holds the gaiter in place. We open our hatch, then we open the submarine's hatch, and you slip inside. I'll be at the controls of the submersible. You do all your secret squirrel daring-do heroics, get back on the submersible, hatches replaced, pressure restored, gaiter removed and back to the surface for tea and medals…"

King smiled and nodded. He just couldn't help thinking that it wouldn't be that simple.

Chapter Twenty-Seven

Geneva, Switzerland

Captain Gerrard Durand waved them over, his eyes on the screen of the laptop. He stared transfixed, as if taking his eyes off the screen even for a moment would have a detrimental impact on events.

"Noventa has sent his first message to Fortez through the dark web. It is an integrated messenger service bypassing traditional surface internet mailing hosts."

Ramsay and Thorpe gathered round, but Caroline was slow to move. She winced as she straightened up, seeing that Thorpe had noticed. She did her best to walk over unaided, but in doing so earlier at the café on Quai du Mont Blanc, she had aggravated the injury. She continued, ignoring her crutch but she knew that if Thorpe hadn't seen, then she would have willingly used it to take the weight off her leg. Both legs had been broken in the incident, but there had been extensive surgery to her right leg with multiple plates and pins and her recovery had been slow.

"You really should use that stick of yours…" Thorpe said somewhat unsympathetically without looking up from the screen.

"Yeah, I might well do that…" she replied, imagining her smashing it against the woman's windpipe.

Durand read out the message, despite the three of them already reading it over his hunched shoulders. "Contact made…"

"He's sent it," Thorpe said, eyes transfixed on the screen.

"That's it?" Durand asked quietly.

Ramsay took out his phone and dialled. He watched the screen as it rang, then switched the phone onto speaker. "Dave, it's Neil. Where is Milo Noventa?"

"Right in front of me, not going anywhere."

"You're with him? You were meant to keep him under surveillance."

"What's the point? The man has been given an ultimatum. I'm just making sure he does what he's told. Besides, it was hot in the car and the man makes a damned fine cup of coffee, too. He's got one of those steam machines baristas use…"

Ramsay scowled and shook his head

despairingly. "So, we're seeing he's sent the email."

"That's right."

"Look, it makes sense not to divulge too much," said Caroline.

"Why?" Thorpe asked briskly.

Caroline shrugged. "Fortez has to think he's in control. If Noventa throws a recommendation at him too hard, then he may get spooked. Noventa is on a commission, but if he seems biased, then Fortez may think there's more to it. He'll assume that Noventa is on the take. Sharing the contract with the assassin."

"That's what I said," Big Dave's voice echoed out of the phone in Ramsay's hand. *"Slowly, slowly, catchy monkey…"*

"Okay, it makes sense." Ramsay paused. "Are we sure Noventa isn't under surveillance from Fortez? As an insurance policy?" He looked at Thorpe and said, "Sally-Anne, get round there immediately and keep watch. Dave, when you leave, be friendly with Noventa. Make it look like two friends having a catch-up."

Caroline beamed a grin. "The file shows that Noventa is actually a practising bisexual and not currently in a relationship," she mused. "Give the guy a kiss when you leave, Dave. Make it look like you were there for a reason…"

"Fuck off…" Big Dave jeered.

"No, it's a good idea," said Durand. "It will look convincing if Fortez has surveillance on him."

"And you can get fucked as well. You Frenchmen may go in for all that kissing each other, and you can keep it…"

"It's called taking one for the team," Caroline chided.

"Well, make sure he's not under surveillance first," replied Big Dave. *"Sally-Anne, get around here quick smart!"*

"No, good surveillance can always be missed," Ramsay said firmly. "That will teach you to go off-piste."

"You're bloody enjoying this…"

Tell me more… The words appeared in the text box and everybody simmered down, except for Sally-Anne Thorpe, who was getting the car keys and checking her phone battery as she readied to leave.

"I'll get round there now," she said, but only Ramsay nodded.

Noventa: A man and a woman. The woman seems to be in charge. The man is huge. They said there was a sniper covering them.

Fortez: You have met them?

Noventa: They found me and used that skill as part of their interview. Impressive.

Fortez: Or a trap…

Noventa: No, I doubt that. If they were law enforcement, then they would have enough on both of us by now. They are far from the type, anyway.

Fortez: What do you mean by both of us?

Noventa: If they could find me, then they can certainly discover who you are and find you.

CONNECTION BROKEN

"Merde!" Durand cursed. "He's scared him off!"

Ramsay held up a hand. "Dave, the connection has been lost. Watch Noventa and make sure he doesn't leave."

"On it."

"Sally-Anne is on her way to check on the area around Noventa's place for any physical surveillance."

"I'm not kissing this dickhead…"

"Well, you shouldn't have gone beyond your remit."

"Bugger off…"

"He's back." Durand paused. "User Man Child, that's Noventa, and user Orcus, that's Fortez."

"What the hell is Orcus?" Ramsay frowned.

"Roman god of the underworld. The Greeks had Hades, the Roman's had Orcus," Caroline said matter-of-factly.

"Oh," Ramsay said tersely.

"Delusions of grandeur, I think," Durand commented. "Considering he was spared and has been exiled. Consequently, he cannot see his grandchildren or either of his daughter-in-laws. Hardly a god of anything, let alone the underworld…"

"I imagine it could be taken a number of ways. You may see the underworld as meaning he is a god of organised crime, deviousness and anything that pushes against the system." Caroline paused. "Or, he could be living in purgatorial Hell, so much so that he is god of the place. The ultimate person living such an existence."

"Oh." Durand shrugged. "Okay, I like your one better…"

Fortez: What guarantees can you make that this is not a trap?

There was a minute before the response, with all three staring at the screen, waiting impatiently. Caroline realised she was gripping Durand's shoulder, but he hadn't seemed to notice. She released her grip, embarrassed that she didn't really know him that well. Ramsay's phone rang and he ignored it. It must have gone to answerphone but rang again instantly. Ramsay sighed, fumbled for the phone, and stared at the screen.

"It's Dave," he said, but nobody was taking any notice. "Hello, Dave… what the hell's going on with Noventa's response?"

"Thank god! I was shouting down the phone, but you can't have heard me. I rang a couple of times, too. Look, I've got a bit of a situation here…"

"What?" Ramsay switched to speaker for everyone's benefit. "Tell Noventa to get his response sent. And tell him he's in it up to his bloody neck, so he'd better make it good!"

Eventually, the response appeared on the screen.

Noventa: They were convincing. The woman was injured quite badly. Law enforcement wouldn't allow an agent to work in that condition.

"Fuck it, I can't multitask," said Big Dave. *"I'm typing here and talking to you!"*

"Why, what's happened? Why the hell are you typing?"

"Noventa pulled a knife on me. It's my own fault, I should have checked. I checked his drawer for a gun, but didn't think he looked the type to carry a flick knife, much less have the bottle to use it..."

Fortez: What kind of injury?

Noventa/Big Dave: Recovering from a broken leg. Don't let that put you off, as I said earlier, she is part of a team. My guess is disgruntled law enforcement and ex-soldiers.

"Shit, I don't know how to play this," said Big Dave.

"Can Noventa type? What's wrong with him?"

"No, we had a struggle for possession of the blade, he lost. He's not going anywhere anytime soon."

"Soon?" Ramsay asked tersely.

"Ever. I punched him in the face and his neck didn't agree with it."

"Bloody hell..."

"Dave, listen," Caroline said clearly into the phone. "Thorpe's on the way over to check for watchers. You don't want to let her know what's happened…"

"Caroline!" Ramsay snapped. "We're a bloody team!"

Caroline shrugged, glaring back at him. "Then tell me she'll be okay with Dave killing our lead asset…"

Fortez: It seems curious they would seek you out.

Noventa/Big Dave: Nah, I think it shows they know their shit.

Fortez: Shit?

Noventa/Big Dave: Stuff. Know their stuff.

"Christ, he's only typed three lines and it even sounds like him," Ramsay commented and then said into his phone, "Tone it down, you don't sound anything like Noventa."

"Sound? I'm fucking typing here!" Big Dave snapped back at him.

"It's your digital signature, it reads like you, and not him…"

"Bollocks…"

Fortez: I think I'll pass.

"No…" Durand said quietly.

Noventa/Big Dave: That's a mistake.

Fortez: It is mine to make.

Noventa/Big Dave: Consider me out. I'm closing down the site and wiping the emails. You're on your own, old man. They'll likely come for you in your sleep. They aren't the type of people to mess with, and I had to agree to them taking the contract to leave the meeting alive. They'll think you stiffed them, and that's what I'll say when they come for me. You're on your own.

"Bloody hell!" Ramsay screamed. "Dave, what the hell are you doing?" he shouted into his phone but was met with the sound of the calling ending abruptly.

"Wait," Caroline said. "He's gone all in. Cards on the table…"

Fortez: You dare to threaten me?

Ramsay and Durand stared at the screen, but Caroline walked back to her chair, her leg aching terribly. She sat down carefully, dropping the last few inches, and breathing out heavily. She started to count quietly. "One… two… three… four…"

Fortez: Noventa?

"Five… six… seven… eight…"

Fortez: Noventa, are you there?

"Nine… ten…"

Noventa/Big Dave: I'm here.

Fortez: OK. Do it. I'll send the details through. But if there's a problem I'll hold you responsible…

Chapter Twenty-Eight

The Aurora Project Rigs
100 miles south of Svalbard Archipelago

King left Grainger in his office and made his way down to the dive centre to check on his kit. He felt aggrieved at having Daniel's pistol taken from his own pocket on the ship. He hadn't noticed anything obvious, anybody to stand out amongst the crowd. Newman, the man he had down as CIA, hadn't been in the rec-room at the time, or at least King had not spotted him, and the man who had attempted to stare him down at the airport hadn't been seen since. Although he was sure he had been the gunman at the storage site, for the simple reason that Newman and Daniel had been on the beach. But ultimately King felt no further ahead, and somewhere out there someone had been armed at his expense. Twice.

The dive centre was located on the lower deck, but still a hundred feet above the ocean. The entire floors, or more accurately the open decks of the platform were constructed from galvanised steel grating to allow for the huge waves and to make scrubbing down easier. Dive tanks were chained up inside a cage and both dry-suits and wetsuits hung from solid-looking racks in an open-fronted metal shipping container. A door led off to a briefing room and shower room, and there were clipboards hanging on hooks, which King supposed were dive logs, as well as bunches of keys with floats on them which King presumed were for the stack of RIBs, or Rigid-hull Inflatable Boats on the lift platform below. Above him, the ceiling was the same heavy-duty grating that he stood on. He was aware of somebody's presence above but could not make out whether they were male or female. He was sure they were watching him but doubted they would have any better view of him than he did of them. There was at least forty feet between them. Turning his attention back to his two cases that had been stacked alongside others, he ignored whoever was above him and crouched down beside the cases and checked on the locks.

The sound of the silenced gunshot was unmistakable. The clang of a bullet striking the grating, the 'phut' of the moderated gunshot and the clatter of the ejected shell casing on the metal floor came all at once, and King heard the ricochet of the bullet as it zinged out to sea. He dived to his right, but the shooter anticipated this, and the second gunshot came instantly, but the bullet was thrown off its well-aimed course by the metal grating. King darted left, then right and threw himself into the briefing room. Behind him, another 'phut', another clatter, and another ricochet. King searched for a weapon, but only found three sheathed diving knives hanging up from their rubber leg straps. He snatched one out of its sheath and held it by its hilt, the blade facing downwards in a classic stabbing grip. This way he could still punch, parry and stab, as well as hook at his opponent. He edged back outside and could hear hurried footsteps on the steel grating of the staircase. King readied himself and walked collectedly to the edge of the platform, his legs gently lowering and shifting into a fighting stance from years of practice and instinct. Thirty percent of his weight on his front foot – ready to kick or avoid being swept – with seventy percent of his weight on his back foot – to drive the power of the kick home. He moved, shuffling left foot forward, so that he could have all his power behind the knife when he twisted his hips into it – like a reverse punch in karate – the move that the martial art was renowned for. Finally, his left hand led the way, ready to block or jab or grab, so he could follow up with the diving knife and its eight-inch surgical steel blade.

King estimated the running footsteps were merely a pace or two away, so he made his move, edging out from the corner to greet his attacker head-on. The man rushed on and King caught his arm and scythed the blade towards him but registering the panic upon the man's face just in time to pull his arm back.

"Rashid!" he snapped. "What the hell?"

"King!" Rashid replied breathlessly, his face pained. "You're okay?"

King looked at his friend and colleague, pulled him around the corner to stop them both being exposed to the gunman. Above them, the grate flooring had given way to solid sheet steel – the floor of part of the solid super-structure. "Yes, I'm fine. Did you see the shooter?" King was glad to see his friend. The fact Rashid was here lifted his spirits immensely. Rashid was ex-SAS and the youngest solider of Pakistani descent to become an officer in the British Army promoted from an NCO. Prior to his passing SAS selection and officer training Rashid had been a sniper and had proven himself to be a world-class shot. He had certainly been there for

King in the past, covering him on several missions.

"See him? I wrestled the gun off him…" He held up a silenced Makarov pistol. King could not be sure if it was the same weapon he took from Daniel, but it looked identical. King noticed Rashid's other left hand was nursing his groin. "But he kicked me in the balls and ran. It was lucky I kept hold of the gun when I fell and it put some distance between us, I think he realised his options were better to get the hell out of there," he explained.

"Who was it?" King paused. "A neat little guy, preppy, American?"

"No, but I noticed him, too. Back on Spitsbergen and on the boat."

"You were on the boat?"

"I've been in your shadow ever since you landed. Simon Mereweather sent me out two days before you, to back you up."

"So, it was you who took my gun at the storage yard," King mused, finally making some sense of it. Rashid obviously couldn't get King out of there before the police arrived, so he did the next best thing and cleaned the scene. "Thanks."

"No, that wasn't me. I don't know anything about that. I saw you nearly run over a polar bear on the beach, saw your smashed window and figured you'd been shot at." He paused. "I had to take off, the police were on the scene within minutes."

King frowned, the disappearance of his Beretta still not making any sense. He shrugged it off and grinned at his friend. "And you call that backing me up?" He shook his head. "You didn't even bring me grapes at the hospital."

"You weren't really shot, were you?" Rashid paused. "I was trying to make enquiries and saw you walk back into the hotel in that fog white-out."

King shook his head. "No. I was lucky, the bullet hit the gunstock and I took a bit of a spill off a shipping container."

Rashid laughed. "I remember you pushing me off the top of one around the back of a mosque a few years back. I'd only just had surgery and you split my bloody stitches open. Finally, some bloody karma catching up with you…"

"Dickhead…"

"Anyway, it looks like you were a lot luckier than the man who pulled the gun on you on deck, at least."

"You saw that?"

"I was working my way around from the other side of the boat. By the time I got around the bridge, you'd sent the bloke off for a swim."

King nodded. "So, one out of three. I get shot at on Svalbard and a gun is pulled on me on the boat and you were too late both times? Do the world a favour, when the Security Service eventually fire you, don't become a bodyguard and head out onto the circuit…"

"Well, that's gratitude for you…" Rashid shook his head. "I save you from an Iranian agent and that's all the thanks I get?"

"Iranian?"

"Yeah, you had a little staring contest with the bloke at the airport. I photographed him and had Ramsay run his face on the system."

"Shit, I thought he was Russian."

"Does it make a difference? The last time I checked, they were all still the bad guys."

King frowned. "It makes all the difference. The Russians could be here simply because it's just what they do. I don't have a problem with the Russian people, just the old guard who have remained in government and in the intelligence services. And organised crime, of course. The Russian mafia are a plague on the West. The Russian people are fine, but the bastards at the heart of governance haven't changed in sixty years. No, if Russia were here, it would be to play silly but dangerous games. The Iranians on the other hand, well they don't have nuclear weapons. For an Iranian agent to be involved makes me feel uneasy. They have a lot to gain, and nothing to lose."

"But there's no nukes on that sub," Rashid replied. "Cruise missiles, various torpedoes, and of course, the nuclear reactor, but no nukes. The Astute-class submarines don't carry nukes. Those are Trident nuclear missiles, and they are on the Vanguard-class boats…"

King walked back into the dive briefing room. He snatched the empty sheath off the wall and replaced the knife but tucked it down the waistband of his trousers underneath the cumbersome pair of outer ski pants. "Well, that's what the world is meant to think. Mounting tension with Russia at the time the submarine went missing caused the government, or at least the PM and the defence minister to give the

Royal Navy a secret directive. The Astute boats were all armed with the W80 low to intermediate yield two-stage thermonuclear warhead. This is what the US Navy use and commonly called dial-a-yield. Meaning you can dial in five to one-hundred and fifty kilotons of yield. The latter flattens entire military installations, towns and small cities, even." He paused. "Which means we have nuclear capabilities off all of Russia's coasts including the Black Sea, as well as the Mediterranean, the Gulf and China. North Korea, too."

"I'm guessing this decision wasn't ever going to be discussed in the House of Commons…" Rashid mused, taking up position in the doorway, the weapon held down beside his leg should an unsuspecting innocent round the corner.

"I'm sure no more than the PM and one or two cabinet members know." King paused. "But the whole bloody world will know if Iran gets its hands on our weaponry."

"Not likely, though. Is it?"

"The plan is for me to get on board using a submersible."

"What?" Rashid asked incredulously.

"You don't know?"

He shook his head. "I was tasked to watch your back and assist if required. Mereweather's words, to the letter."

King considered this then said, "If it's possible for me to get on board using a small submersible, then what if the Iranians have a submarine in the vicinity? They could dock and offload the cruise missiles."

Rashid shook his head. "I'm not so sure they could offload entire missiles, but they could certainly remove the warheads. The Iranians would know that no international military presence is permitted within the UNESCO green zone, so they would be clear to interfere."

"The nuclear reactor is a Rolls Royce unit. I imagine they could get hold of the plans if they wanted it badly enough. But the uranium is another matter entirely," said King. "So, we need to get our hands on this Iranian agent and get him to have a little chat with us."

"By chat, you mean interrogation, don't you?"

"Whatever works."

"Yeah, I just want to make sure I'm on the same page."

King smiled wryly. "Don't worry, you'll catch up…"

Chapter Twenty-Nine

"Show him your phone," King said to Rashid, adding, "You sent Neil Ramsay a picture of this Iranian guy to identify, let Grainger see it."

Rashid unlocked his phone with his thumbprint and scrolled. "Hormuzd Shirazi, although presumably he'll be travelling under another name." He showed Grainger the man's photograph and waited while the man scrolled on his laptop.

"Nothing by that name on Aurora's manifest." He continued to scroll, glancing at the image on Rashid's phone. "Ah, here. This is him. He's down as Ali Vakilov, from Azerbaijan." He turned the laptop around for them to see. "A marine biologist wanting to introduce environmentally sound techniques for the farming of Caspian Sea sturgeon fish. Caviar is big business, and the world is cleaning up its act. Even in that part of the world. It's a good cover story, especially as China are now producing seventy percent of the world's caviar through mass fish farming. There are plenty of countries trying to get a stronger hold on the market."

"And a nice cover profile as well," said King. "He doesn't look traditionally Iranian. I suppose he's of Azerbaijani descent. There's a large Azerbaijani population in Iran. They look similar to the Russians, which was why I assumed he was a Russian at the airport."

"Well, the Soviet Union ruled there for years," Grainger commented helpfully. "One of its many satellite countries."

"Where can we find him?" asked King.

Grainger sighed. "There are boats and ships all over the green zone and the projects that Aurora are running are both complex and extensive. He's not here to aid with the salvage of the submarine, so that goes above my remit, and if we bring this to Aurora's attention, then your cover will be blown." He paused, fingering the stubble on his chin. He reminded King of a naval or commando officer who would normally have been well-groomed and smartly turned out but had allowed himself a rustic look while deployed. "The weather and sea conditions are calm, and will be for the next two days, so the inflatable booms are out and connecting the rigs."

"I didn't notice that," said Rashid.

"Me neither," King added. "So, can we assume that with all the rigs connected, people tend to meet up?"

"Meet up, socialise, get laid…" Grainger shrugged.

"What are these booms?" Rashid asked.

"Inflatable walkways that are tethered together and to the neighbouring rigs. They form a ring. Most people do a circuit for fitness and a change of scene. They have wire handrails and flashing beacons to alert boats. Sometimes they are down for a week, in most cases they are not out for weeks at a time."

"So, our man could be anywhere," King commented flatly.

"This rig and the next two in the chain are connected, the others are still working on it, but the maintenance crew won't close the circle until all the boats are outside the ring and moored seaward side."

"Okay," said King. One of us will have to wait and start the circuit anti-clockwise while the other two start out clockwise."

"Two?" Grainger asked curiously.

"Yes," replied King. "You'll be coming along for the ride…"

Chapter Thirty

King and Grainger took clockwise, while Rashid waited for the last of the boats and ships to get clear from the centre of the ring and the boom to be fixed to the rig before heading in a counterclockwise direction. King had the diving knife and Rashid had kept the silenced Makarov, which had four bullets remaining. It was getting dark and the lights along the boom lit their path perfectly.

"It's pretty sturdy," commented King. "You could run along it." As if to confirm it, two women appeared out of the gloom, chatting to one another, and maintaining a decent pace. Even this far north, they wore running attire, although they wore leggings and jackets. As they drew closer, King could see their breath on the air.

"These rigs are huge," said Grainger. "The fact we're doing this won't help much. This Shirazi fellow could be anywhere. He could double back while we search the next rig."

"Well, it's all we've got," King replied. He stepped aside for the two women and they smiled at him as they passed by. "We'll have to cover the recreation rooms, refectory and communal places, there's not a lot more we can do. As you say, if we request more information or assistance from Aurora, then our cover will be compromised." He paused and watched as a man headed towards them. King slipped his hand underneath his jacket and gripped the handle of the diving knife. When he was close enough to make out the man's features, he relaxed and released his grip on the knife. "There's more people ahead," he told Grainger quietly as the man passed.

"There'll be loads more before long. Some of the rigs offer better food, simply by having better chefs. Everybody has a card with credit on it, or spare cash for when the credit isn't applied for something like chocolate or sweets. Most of the rigs cater well, but the last one in the ring has an American chef and he does great burger nights and makes a mean stacked pizza. Chicago style. You know, like a pie with the cheese on the bottom, then the toppings and the tomato sauce on top. He does proper Mac and cheese as well. When the conditions allow and the boats can go out or the booms are tethered, his refectory will be heaving." He paused. "The Aurora corporation tends to practice what they preach, so a lot of the food is normally plant-based, and of course, each rig has fishing lines out. Fish features high on the menus out here."

King nodded. "It's like a town on the sea."

"It can be, but don't let this fool you. I've seen fifty-foot waves for a month and a real shortage of supplies. When the rigs get together it gets a bit hectic, especially if people are seeing someone on another rig. Aurora only allow people to purchase alcohol on a Saturday night, so if the stars align…"

"Are you married?"

Grainger nodded. "Five years now."

"Is she understanding?"

"He is, and I can control myself…"

"Oh."

"Does that bother you."

"No. Why should it?"

"You just assumed."

"No, but I guess I can see how the Mereweathers trying to set you up with Horsey Harriet was always going to be a non-starter…" King smiled wryly. "Actually, because it sounds like this place has a bit of a party vibe, I assumed your other half would have to be understanding. That was wrong of me. I'm sorry. And being gay has nothing to do with me, nor does it bother me." He paused. "Besides, I'm one to talk about understanding partners. I met a girl out here who clearly likes me, and I've been leading her on because it may aid my mission. I'm engaged and my fiancée is at home recuperating after a terrible accident. I've actually been working out how far is too far in this sort of scenario."

"Oh, what like a kiss?" Grainger laughed. "Trust me, if you're contemplating what is too far, then it's already too far."

"I suppose."

Grainger shrugged. "Why don't you just reverse it."

"What?"

"What's your partner called?"

"Caroline."

"And what does she do?"

King shrugged. He thought Grainger was on the level, and he liked him, too. "The same line of work as myself."

"Ah, well that's easy! Just suppose that Caroline has to find out something and going down on a man is…"

"No!"

Grainger laughed. "Okay, she lets the man go down on…"

"Still a big fucking no!" King paused. "Okay, I get it."

"Maybe a mutual fondle, a passionate, kiss with lots of tongue…"

"You'll be swimming in a minute sunshine…"

"Hah! You're welcome!"

"For what?"

"For working out the boundary thing for you. In a mutually exclusive relationship, if that is indeed what both you and Caroline have, your boundaries should be identical. I'm guessing you got your answer."

King nodded, but he would have to mull over on Grainger's words later, as they had reached the end of the last segment of boom and were at the neighbouring rig. He checked his mobile phone, but there was only a weak signal.

"The signal varies, but it's an at sea network, like the operating system used on cruise ships. They changed it because it was costing people a fortune to call home." Grainger paused and said, "Anyway, there was nothing wrong per se with Horsey Harriet, she just wasn't my type. I didn't truly find out that I was attracted to another man until I met my partner. I never considered myself to be gay, or in the closet when I dated women at university."

King didn't answer. He wasn't adept at personal conversations. He was watching the signal bars on his phone. He knew the display was wildly inaccurate. You either had a signal or you didn't. Phone networks and phone handset manufacturers added the five-bar system to give people hope and to hedge their bets that the user would soon reach a signal. That was why that one or two-bar signal lurking on the screen disappeared to zero when you tried dialling. There was no point in calling Rashid for an update, but he typed a quick text to say they had arrived at the first rig in the chain and slipped the phone back into his pocket. It would send if or when the signal increased.

"What's the plan?" Grainger asked, steering the conversation back to business.

"Just look for Shirazi." King paused. "But don't confront him. He'll be dangerous." King knew the agents of the Iranian Ministry of Intelligence to be well-trained and ruthless. He had heard that during the war with Iraq they trained their assassins on Iraqi prisoners of war, and each agent honed their skills in every conceivable method from simply using their bare hands to knives and small arms and even sniper rifles. Chemical and biological agents were also tested on the prisoners. King had no idea whether the Iranians employed similar training today, but he knew of the human rights violations and the lack of judicial rights. With many people still 'disappeared' in the system in Iran, it wasn't a stretch of the imagination by any means.

"Don't worry, I won't," Grainger replied nervously. "I haven't had a fight since I was twelve, I don't want to start now. Christ, what the hell has Simon got me into?"

King patted him on the back as he took the steel grate staircase. "Just look out for him. I'll find you and we'll move onto the next rig."

King took the stairs two at a time, veered off at the first deck, which mirrored the dive centre on the other rig. There were two men filling tanks and another working his way down a checklist on a clipboard. Neither man looked up and after a glance inside, King took the other staircase up to the next deck, where the walls and floor were enclosed, powerful heaters circulated warm air from knee level and the suites of offices, recreation rooms and kitchen were situated. People were heading out in tracksuits and running gear, others were reading magazines and sipping coffee. King glanced at his watch – a vintage Rolex Submariner he had bought with his first three month's salary all those years ago with MI6. Only, it hadn't been a vintage model then, but it had barely left his wrist since and never let him down over the years. He'd lost track of time, the dark hue from early afternoon onwards had confused him. It was still only four-pm, and some people were jostling between offices or working at computer terminals. He wondered whether typical office hours even applied out here. Just a month or so ago, the rigs would have been in three months of perpetual darkness, and in a couple of months the summer would give them three months of constant light. He supposed a different work ethic would be required, making use of the warmer water and constant daylight.

As King rounded the corner outside one of the recreation-rooms he saw Madeleine ahead of him in the corridor walking towards him.

"Alex!" She beamed, hastening her step before flinging herself at him. "You'll never guess what?" she asked but gave him no time to answer. "I got orcas!"

"Sound's painful…"

She punched his arm playfully and said, "Silly… No, there is room for me to study the pod of orcas, you know… killer whales… they patrol between here, Bear Island and Svalbard. They almost stick entirely to the green zone. It's uncanny. We, or rather the other marine biologists think they dive deeper here than anywhere else on the planet. They feed on king crabs that have spread from when Joseph Stalin did a deal with America and introduced them to the northern Russian waters to help feed the nation. The species were hugely invasive and have spread prolifically to Norway and beyond. The team have recorded an orca diving to three-hundred and fifty metres. Normally they do not dive deeper than a hundred metres, although the previous recorded deepest dive was just over two-hundred and fifty metres." She paused for breath, excitedly recounting what she knew, then shrugged when she saw King's expression did not match her own enthusiasm. "But I'll get to fit trackers to them and use the data for my thesis in my master's degree," she added excitedly.

King smiled. "That's amazing," he replied. He could see that she was genuinely fired-up about it, and she had a new project. He was no longer the source of her affection, and somewhat bizarrely, he felt rejected. "We'll have to meet up, so you can tell me more…"

"Yeah, sure… I have so much work to do first, though. So much reading to get up to speed, to see what the other scientists have observed and noted. Behavioural, anecdotal, and then of course there's the work. After tomorrow I'll be on the Amity, the ship used for the project. She's berthing tomorrow evening, and then we're off in the morning." She paused. "I don't think I'll see you after that, what with your work raising the submarine, I mean…"

King was a good judge of character. He recognised a young woman, scared of the choices she'd made. To go and work for a company based in the middle of the ocean, a thousand miles from the mainland. Not knowing a soul. That was why she had interacted with him when he helped her with her equipment back in Oslo. And that was why she had bonded with Daniel on the flight, and with them both at the hotel. She wasn't a naturally confident person and needed company and reassurance. King was in no doubt that he could have slept with her if he'd wanted to. Her confidence would have been bolstered by the bond between them. People like her craved company. And if it hadn't been him, then it would have been someone else. Perhaps even Daniel. He could see now that the man had pulled her in, used her as a stalking horse to get closer to him.

"No problem," King replied. He held her gently by the shoulders and kissed her on the forehead. More out of relief than anything else. He had suspected her to be working with Daniel, and he could well have killed her by association. "Go study your orcas and nail that thesis. Good luck!"

"Thank you," she replied, her eyes still sparkling with excitement.

King released her and carried on down the corridor. He saw Grainger heading down the stairs and the man shrugged. "Anything?"

"Nothing."

"Right, let's try the next rig…"

Chapter Thirty-One

Geneva, Switzerland

"Admit it, you'd have done anything not to have kissed him," Caroline teased.

"Yeah, probably," Big Dave replied. "I've buggered things up good and proper, though."

"So, what do we do?" asked Durand. He had lit a Gauloises Blondes cigarette and was sucking on the thing so hard that the tip glowed like the bright embers of a fire in a draught. Ramsay, normally an anti-smoking authoritarian hadn't seemed to notice the smoke wafting around them.

"We call the police," Thorpe said emphatically. "A man has been killed…"

"What, and hand ourselves in?" Caroline shook her head. "The Swiss take an extremely dim view of foreign intelligence agents operating on their soil without their express permission. They handed over to Interpol, not MI5."

Thorpe frowned. "No more than a ticking off, surely? Dave on the other hand, will have to answer for what he did and if it was as he says it was, then he should be in the clear. It was self-defence."

"No," Ramsay replied quietly. "We'd all remain in custody either until they gathered enough evidence for a trial, or they came to an agreement with the British government. There'd likely be a few years of diplomatic wrangling, and we wouldn't get bail while that was going on."

"Indeed," Durand agreed. "We've seen this with French agents. And we're their neighbours. Nobody likes the British," he added with a wry smile, trying to ease the tension.

"Want to quit?" Caroline asked, staring at her. "I wasn't exactly sure what you were bringing to the party, anyway."

"Now, now…" Ramsay said sharply. "We need to think what can be done to rectify the situation."

"I could get a shovel?" Big Dave suggested. "Noventa ain't that big, it won't take me long to did a hole."

"For crying out loud…" Thorpe shook her head in frustration and walked to the window. She stared out onto the quiet, tree-lined street below. She hadn't spotted any surveillance on Noventa's property earlier, and Durand had watched the area for twenty-minutes before circling the property. After a further twenty-minutes he had announced that he concurred with the former Metropolitan Police detective. Noventa was not being watched, and the all-clear was given for Caroline and Ramsay to proceed inside.

"Right, let's keep it simple," said Caroline, moving on. "We've got a single blow to the face, a broken neck and fractured skull would be my bet. So, there's Dave's DNA on Noventa from the punch." She looked at Big Dave and asked, "Did you rough him up, hold him in any way?"

"No, the guy was compliant, right up until he wasn't." He stepped around Noventa's twisted body on the parquet floor and held up his hands, re-enacting what had transpired. "He came at me with the knife, so I blocked..." Big Dave stepped forwards, swung his left arm out to the side, then twisted his hips and dropped his left knee a few inches as he drove through a straight punch from his hip, almost all the way out with his massively long and well-muscled arm until it was a few inches from fully extended, when he brought the punch upwards and rose to his full height. "Like that," he said.

"Like a steam hammer, by the looks of it," Durand commented flatly. "Noventa must have lifted into the air. I'm surprised you didn't knock his head off…"

"Well, I imagine inside the skin, he did," Ramsay said quietly.

"It'll have to be made to look like a robbery gone wrong," Thorpe said with her back to them. "Get some gloves on and take what valuables you can. Don't ransack the place, just pull out some drawers. It needs to look like they'd just got started and Noventa disturbed them. The guy's wearing a Breitling watch. Probably worth ten-thousand euros, maybe more. Take it off his wrist. Someone will have to throw it into the lake later." She turned around and nodded to Durand. "We'll need a household spray cleaner. The type with a trigger pump. Empty it and fill it with one third bleach, and two thirds water. Spray over everything that has been touched. In fact, get a light spray on everything in the room, then spray all over Noventa's body. That will corrupt Dave's DNA, and any trace elements from ourselves." She paused. "Neil and Caroline, go wait in the car. I'll supervise… and Dave, you need to get some gloves on. The spray bottle comes with us, and we need to cover our tracks with it all the way to the pavement outside."

Chapter Thirty-Two

Beneath the Polar Icecap
500 miles North of Svalbard Archipelago

"Slow ahead, reduce speed to four knots and dive to six-hundred feet."

"Aye, aye, captain."

They were still silent running, so the orders were distinctly murmured. Not a whisper – that made the sound more distinguishable under water – more a gentle hum of the throat.

"Dive to six-hundred feet, check," replied the lead helmsman.

Commander JT McClure turned to the WEPS and said, "WEPS load tubes two and four, countermeasures at the ready…"

"They're increasing speed, now at twenty-two knots."

"Slow to twelve." McClure turned to his second in command and said, "Some distance and increase in their speed will allow our torpedo tubes to be loaded without detection." He paused. "XO, do you concur?"

"I concur, Commander," the Lieutenant-Commander replied.

McClure listened intently, the Russian submarine's increase in wake and propulsion emitted a more distinct tone. The Russian vessel had dived as they left the icecap behind them and the only way to remain undetected was to travel directly in its wake. Six-hundred feet above them, floating sea ice played havoc with the boat's sonar, but it also gave them the advantage of irregular sonar pulses, which could be easily ignored by the Russian submarine's sonar operator.

"They're changing course, Commander. Contact bearing one-twenty, south and east." The lead communications officer paused. "Now at twelve-hundred metres."

"Helmsman, contact bearing one-twenty…"

"Aye, aye, skipper."

Commander McClure looked up at the Perspex map. The heading would take them directly to the sunken British submarine. He was surprised, knowing he would have taken a different, and somewhat more devious route. Perhaps zig-zagged nearer, then made his course more deliberate with the last leg. He wondered what the Russian commander's orders were. His own crew knew nothing of the task ahead of them, only that they were to patrol an area with the high likelihood of enemy activity. As standard operating procedure dictated, Lieutenant-Commander Jacobs knew the orders and the remit they sailed under. Should anything happen to Commander McClure, then as XO, Jacobs would be in charge.

"Torpedo! Torpedo! Torpedo!" the sonar operator shouted, there was no point now in obeying the silent running protocol. "Port side, five-hundred metres and closing at twenty-five knots!"

"Hard to starboard, bearing one-twenty! Depth two-hundred," he ordered, the submarine already in a dive. "Maximum propulsion!" Everybody had their own job, and the three commands could hardly be missed. "WEPS countermeasures, now!"

"Four-hundred metres, Commander!"

McClure did not answer as he waited for the explosions from the countermeasures. Four charges shot vertically and slowly sank in their wake. When they levelled out to the same depth as when they were launched, they exploded and super-heated phosphorus burned at 2000°c and white-hot metal ball bearings were shot out twenty-feet in every direction.

"No change, torpedo still on course!"

"Vent chambers! Helmsman, hard to surface!" McClure gripped the rail beside the watch desk and nodded to his XO who instinctively picked up the PA and ordered the crew to brace. The crew would now be hastily finding something to hang on to, or wrap themselves around, or strap themselves to. "WEPS! Countermeasures!"

Again, the counter measure charges shot out vertically, but were left in their wake as they started to climb. The flotation tanks were flushed with compressed air and the vessel lurched upwards, its prow leading with such angle that all crew remaining on the control deck leaned heavily forwards to counter the effect.

The explosion rocked them, blowing the submarine wildly to port and seats were emptied of their occupants. Commander McClure stuck out his right floor and pinned the primary weapons officer to the deck as he slid past him. "WEPS, back to your station, if you will…" He nodded to Lieutenant-Commander Jacobs. "Prepare for breach," he said calmly. "Helmsman, breach the surface then dive hard immediately. Ballast tanks to reverse, prepare for hard descent. WEPS, two Barracuda torpedoes away as you locate target…" He paused. "Let's put this bastard on the bottom of the ocean…"

There were gasps from the crew as they waited for the submarine to surface. Nobody aboard had ever issued or heard the order for live torpedoes to be fired upon a real target. The Weapons Division Officer relayed to the torpedo room, the helmsman and his co-controller readied for the hard breach and the divemaster relayed that the now empty ballast tanks should be immediately pumped with water to allow a hard dive upon his order.

"Two hundred feet… one-seventy… one forty…"

"Twenty-two knots, Sir…"

"One hundred feet…"

McClure took in his crew's feedback, then said, "Brace! Brace! Brace!"

The ordered was repeated on the PA system.

"Torpedo! Torpedo! Torpedo!" the PWO screamed. "Directly on our stern, three hundred metres!"

"Shit!" Commander McClure responded. "Countermeasures! Immediately!"

The WEPS gave the command to the torpedo room, but there was no time. The weapons crew would be holding on for dear life between checking the locks, straps and clips on the torpedoes and ground attack missiles.

The Submarine broke through the surface, two-thirds of the vessel breaching the water like a humpback whale. The belly of the vessel slapped down hard on the surface smashing onto blocks of floating sea ice, each block the size of a family car. A mighty bow wave broke ahead of them, capsizing the bergs of sea ice and driving them fifty metres away from them. Inside the submarine, there were screams and shouts as crew members were sent in all directions, injuries sustained and alarms sounding. In the galley a fire alarm was sounding, and the crew were starting to respond, the years of training becoming second nature. Already, the submarine was into its dive. Behind them, the wire-guided torpedo was still gaining on them. The countermeasure charges scattered and sank behind them, but the Russian torpedo operator had not yet armed the device, and if it could pass through the web of falling charges, then the torpedo would be unaffected.

"Enemy sub located! Two torpedoes away!" the WEPS shouted triumphantly. Unlike the wire-guided Russian torpedo which was fed out on a large spool of command wire, the Virginia class was armed with the Barracuda Mk IV and once fired at the enemy, used powerful electro-magnets to remain on target, as well as a conventional noise source detector, like that of heat-seeker missiles fired from fighter jets, but sensing the pulse of the submarine's propeller instead of heat.

Commander McClure leaned back against the heavy angle from their descent and said quietly to his second in command, "Let's just hope ours can get to them before theirs gets to us..."

"Amen..." Jacobs replied, watching the sonar screen beside them.

The two Mk IV Barracuda torpedoes were equidistant from the Russian submarine and the wire-guided torpedo to their stern.

An explosion rumbled and the Virginia Class submarine tremored and vibrated. The WEPS announced, "Their countermeasures have destroyed one of the Barracuda..."

"Add a real prayer to that Amen, would you...?" McClure said quietly, but Lieutenant-Commander Jacobs just stared at the sonar and said nothing.

Behind them, the countermeasures were sinking and exploding with white-hot phosphorus balls which glistened like deep-sea phosphorescent plankton. The Submarine was diving hard and the torpedo, which had been steered a devious and circuitous route, was getting ever nearer. The barrage of countermeasures was scattering around the nose cone of the torpedo, and finally one exploded dead-on. The burning, 2000°c chemical fire of the phosphorous melting the hull and letting in enough water for the torpedo to be put off balance and lurch to starboard, exposing its command cable to the starburst of super-heated chemicals. The wire was severed by a clump of burning, sticky phosphorous and the torpedo continued, but deviated steadily off its course with the American submarine.

Another explosion rumbled and shook the submarine and crew. The Weapons Division Officer looked at his commanding officer and said, "The second Barracuda has been destroyed, Sir..."

"The enemy torpedo is off course and heading directly for the Russian sub!" the sonar operator shouted. "The Kilo-class is turning broadside into it!"

"Helmsman hard to surface! Vent ballast tanks, hard ascent!" McClure turned to the sonar operator and said, "Get us back under the ice…"

"Yes, Sir. Head twenty-five degrees north…"

The helmsman acknowledged and steered to port, whilst the ballast tanks vented.

"Reduce speed, fifteen knots. Slow ascent." Commander McClure paused, turning to his second in command. "Damage report?"

"Nothing serious reported. Small oil fire in the galley, but it's out now. Expect sandwiches for dinner…"

McClure nodded then gave the order, "Silent running…" He turned to the sonar operator but said nothing yet. The sonar display showed the Russian torpedo close to the Russian submarine. There was a sudden explosion and a tremor vibrated through the hull. "Impact?"

"Negative, Sir. Self-destruct. Russian sub is veering to the east, full engines."

Commander McClure nodded. "Maybe that's the last we'll see of her, then..." But he didn't think so for a moment.

Chapter Thirty-Three

The Aurora Project Rigs

Hormuzd Shirazi had seen King and another man leave one way, and after the last pontoon had been attached, the Asian man who he had fought with for possession of the gun had left in the other direction. Shirazi had been using a pair of powerful Zeiss binoculars with light enhancement, although it was now too dark to use them. He had sprinted to the third rig in the chain, but his accommodation – a bunk in a shared room - was in the second rig and he was now in a position where he could be shepherded into containment. He figured the Englishman would want to maintain his cover, so they would not have announced the fact they were searching for someone, much less the reason. And they would be unable to search the individual accommodation rooms and sleeping quarters. He glanced at his watch. He had missed his first scheduled communication and had only three minutes until the next. His lips and nose were sore, his ribs too. The Asian guy had put up a tremendous fight for possession of the pistol, and he had lashed out in return with an almighty kick to the man's balls, flooring him. Unfortunately, the man had fallen backwards and kept hold of the pistol and by kicking him to the floor, Shirazi had put too much distance between them. He had darted for the stairwell, hearing the gun fire its muted silenced shot after him, the bullet ricocheting around the metal staircase. It had been close, but he had lost the weapon he had stolen from the English agent, and he had shown his hand. He knew he would be hunted and there was nowhere to go, nowhere for him in which to flee. Seven former oil rigs in a ring covering five kilometres did not offer much in the way of escape. His options were limited. He had already seen where the inflatable boats were stowed, and the larger ships were anchored a mile away on the outside of the ring. They would remain while the Aurora scientists got organised, and while the weather conditions remained calm. The crew raising the submarine were still arriving and getting organised over the next two days, and then they would leave and not return until the submarine was floated on the inflatable bags similar in design to the large booms forming the pontoons between the rigs. That gave him a night at least. Enough time to make contact, confirm the coordinates and kill the Englishman. After he had completed his mission, he would steal an inflatable and rendezvous with the Tareq-class submarine commanded by Keshmiri Pezhman of the Islamic Revolutionary Guards Corps Navy and continue his journey.

Shirazi checked his watch. Just a minute to spare. From his position on the top deck, he could no longer see the Englishman or his kafir subordinate approaching in their pincer movement. The rigs were now shrouded in complete darkness and he was also aware of a dense fog looming in from the east. The fog could help him, but it could also hinder him. He took the Iridium satellite phone out from his jacket pocket and dialled 8816 followed by the eight-digit number from memory. The signal was achievable, but when the phone line opened, the sound was both tinny and echoey.

He spoke the Takbeer nonetheless. "Allahu Akbar, my brother." He awaited the reply and nodded in respect of His name. "My brother, our time frame is short. The salvage crews are massing, there will be a consultation period while they analyse the data, then work will commence in three days. You will need to complete your task before then. I will be at the

prearranged coordinates at the agreed time..."
He stopped talking, hearing a movement behind
him. Shirazi broke the connection and locked the
phone using the six-digit pin code. He backed
away into the shadows and watched as the
Englishman appeared at the top step. There was
something about him. Something predatory,
animalistic. He had been lucky before. Lucky at
the storage depot on Spitsbergen and lucky on
the other rig when he had shot at him but been
thwarted by the kafir. When the time came, or
when opportunity presented itself, he would
enjoy killing the Englishman, but he would
enjoy killing the kafir even more. He loathed his
kind – a Muslim doing the bidding of a capitalist
nation of non-believers. Fooled into believing the
myth of multiculturalism in the West. A man
who Shirazi imagined prayed little, no longer
practised a halal diet, and dated non-Muslim
women while listening to lurid lyrics in music
and drinking alcohol before engaging in casual
sex. No, he would enjoy killing him, and he
would do it the Islamic way, by cutting the
man's throat.

Chapter Thirty-Five

Tremezzo
Lake Como, Italy

They had always planned on staying in the small Italian town of Tremezzo for its location, but not as soon as they had been forced to. With Milo Noventa dead and with contact made to Giuseppe Fortez it was time to get out of Geneva. The villa they had rented before leaving England was a six-bedroomed stone-built farmhouse, although any farmland once surrounding it had long been built on. Shrouded in gardens with off-road parking and even a small swimming pool, the quiet property acted as a welcome sanctuary to them after recent events. The chance to reset and reflect on what had gone wrong, and how they could put things right now that they had put Switzerland behind them.

Captain Durand had set up the laptop with its added external processor and routed it back through Noventa's IP address in Switzerland. No further contact had been made, but the ball was in their court. Fortez wanted a meeting to discuss his stipulations in the contract, and driven by vengeance he had allowed them in. Noventa had been the middleman, the expert needed to negotiate the dark web, but Fortez was still just an old-fashioned crook, blinded by revenge. He could have allowed Noventa to act as go-between, never dirtied his hands or put himself at risk, but King's death meant something to him. Which was what worried Caroline the most. The man would stop at nothing to carry out his revenge, near Shakespearian in its magnitude and audacity – a true bloodlust that would never see him rest until it had been achieved.

They had eaten a basic meal of takeaway pizzas and calzone in near silence and each member of the team had found their own space afterwards. Durand was now checking the laptop and surveillance equipment, while Neil Ramsay worked at his own laptop and was busy filing reports and firing off emails to London. Big Dave had gone outside to check the vehicles. Tyre pressures, oil, water, and fuel meant everything when your life depended on them. Once they arrested Fortez they had decided it would be beneficial for all concerned to whisk him away to Switzerland. The Swiss police had cooperated with Interpol and had taken the investigation out of the Italian's hands. Durand had arranged for the arrest warrant to be made in the name of the Swiss Judicial Directorate and sans frontières, or without borders. Police corruption in domestic Italian organised crime was still rife, and they did not want to risk falling foul to a senior police officer with criminal underworld connections. Fortez had also employed a security company. Research into the company in question showed that in addition to providing alarms, CCTV, and panic buttons, they had a uniformed security team, covert bodyguards and a rapid response unit. The company boasted that their personnel were all ex-soldiers and had served in Afghanistan. They were also licenced to carry firearms. Getting Fortez away from Lake Como and into Switzerland would be better all round for everyone. They had not recorded Milo Noventa's involvement, recording instead that they had used the man's digital identity because of his former working arrangements with Fortez. They had sanitised their presence in Switzerland and as far as the Swiss police would be concerned, the joint Interpol-MI5 operation required a Swiss judicial connexion for the arrest of Fortez.

Caroline had cleared the empty food boxes away and taken her coffee out onto the veranda. She could see a sliver of moonlight gleaming on the still waters of the lake. There was a chill in the spring air, and she buttoned up her coat and eased herself down into the cane chair. She let out a gentle groan, the pins in her leg aggravated by the past few days.

"You shouldn't be here," Sally-Anne Thorpe said from behind her.

"Give it a rest..." Caroline replied tiresomely without looking up. "Don't you ever stop? Tell me, have you been single for long?"

Thorpe ignored her quip and instead said, "You're clearly not fit for duty." She paused, stepped around the low coffee table, and stood at the rail, watching the same view of the moonlight on the water. "You could put your fellow teammates at risk."

"Not a chance."

"You can barely sit without it causing you significant pain," Thorpe replied.

"I've overdone it, that's all. I need Giuseppe Fortez out of the picture."

"Because your judgement is clouded. It's understandable, the man has a contract out on your partner, but that's still no reason for you to be here."

"Alex is on a mission, he isn't able to put a stop to this himself." Caroline paused. "And he's operational, therefore out of contact. When he returns, he may well have let down his guard. The Security Service owe him a duty of care. In my book, that extends to putting an end to Fortez and his contract. If we don't, then Alex will stop Fortez when he finds out…"

"By killing him? Because that seems to be the man's answer to everything. It's just as well he's out of the picture, then."

Caroline sipped her coffee and rested back in the chair. She knew she wasn't fit for duty – she'd never intended to return – but she was damned if she could take being lectured anymore. "You did well today," she said.

Thorpe, clearly caught off guard by her response, frowned. "Meaning?"

"At Milo Noventa's place."

"Meaning?"

Caroline shrugged. "Meaning, you were there for the team."

"I merely advised the best way to get rid of Dave's DNA in a compromising situation," she replied guardedly.

"Oh, I didn't take it like that," Caroline sipped another mouthful of coffee. It was cooling quickly, the night air chilling rapidly. "I thought you took over, used your specialist skills and experience and ordered us to sanitise the crime scene." She shrugged. "Naturally, we did what you told us to, after all, Neil Ramsay bought you in as an expert in your field and we all look to you for the legal angle. Just to stay the right side of the law, that is." She paused, looking quizzically at the ex-detective. "I must admit, I was surprised by the turn of events…"

"Are you serious?" Thorpe stared at her coldly, failing to hide her anger.

"It's strange how things can be remembered. Especially in tribunals or a court of law." Caroline shrugged again and smiled. "Or forgotten. It pays to stay on the right side of people. Especially those with whom you work."

Thorpe shook her head as she chuckled quietly. "We really should start again," she commented flatly. "But I suspect it's probably too late for us."

"Never say never," Caroline replied breezily, then looked up at her. "Okay, maybe we should. If you want to start over, then perhaps you could do me a favour?"

"Okay…" Thorpe replied warily.

"You're right," she said flatly. "I'm not up to fitness, and I have overdone it somewhat. I brought along just one crutch to save face. And I walked unaided far too soon. I am in pain, and yes it could affect my judgement. I need some seriously strong pain killers, which I would appreciate you getting for me from a pharmacy. I have also arranged for another crutch to be sent out and it's arriving tomorrow at the post office in Menaggio at around ten-AM. It will need signing for, but if you could get it for me, I would really appreciate it. I don't want to make a fuss and I guess, if you could get it and I simply have it to use, then I won't lose face in front of the others." She shrugged. "I'd really appreciate your help, and discretion."

Sally-Anne Thorpe looked back at the sliver of moonlight and said, "Alright, I'd be glad to help."

"Thank you," Caroline replied sincerely. She eased herself out of the chair and picked up the empty cup. "I'm going to my room now," she said. "It's too cold out here to sit watching the view, beautiful as it is." She shuffled across the veranda, taking easier steps once she loosened up. She looked back and said, "Thanks, once again, Sally-Anne…"

Chapter Thirty-Six

Barents Sea

King had woken to a thick blanket of fog outside the porthole window of his room, the outside lights from the deck creating an orange hue in the darkness. Grainger had collected him at five-AM and together with Rashid, they had taken a quick breakfast of scrambled eggs, with toast and bacon and some strong tea in the refectory, where food seemed to be served around the clock. They had then taken a medium-sized rib to one of the salvage ships moored to a buoy a mile from the rigs. Grainger had explained that when the conditions were calm enough to moor, they always did so with a one-mile safety buffer. It made sense, given that so many people remained on the rigs. In rougher weather, the boats pulled clear and headed back to Longyearbyen port, and the seven rigs would be self-sufficient until the conditions were once again favourable. It was a world, an existence King had never given a thought to. Naturally, he had seen footage or pictures of the rough seas lashing at the oil rigs of the North Sea but had never thought any more about it. He had heard of Aurora before the meeting with Mereweather and the man's eccentric father but did not know the scale of the green energy company's research.

"Here, drink this…" Grainger placed two cups of coffee down in front of King and Rashid. "We'll be at the site soon." He sat down beside them at the fixed table. Everything was fixed. The tables, the chairs and the cupboard doors all had thick rubber bands and hooks holding them closed.

King nodded thanks, although he wasn't a coffee drinker. Rashid sipped from his gratefully. "So, how do we work this?" King asked.

"I've told them that I intend on testing the submersible while the rest of the salvage teams get assembled and organised back at the rigs. It's my company's submersible, and it cost ten-million quid, so they'll have to accept my terms because the next useable submersible is still a week away. We have to return with some data… film, confirmation of depth, water temperature etc. Technically we're a reconnaissance party."

"Your company?" Rashid asked.

"Yes. I work for a company called Total Marine Solutions based in Southampton, but we have been subcontracted by Aurora and that's why I'm here. I'm actually one of four partners in the company, but I'm in the habit of saying I work for them, it's far simpler really."

"And embedded by the Security Service…" King added quietly, although they were on their own in the small galley. "You're a rather busy bloke."

Grainger smiled. "It's nice to be in demand." He paused. "I'm helping Simon, keeping my ear to the ground, or the sea that is. Some people in government are not taken in by all of Aurora's green energy claims, and then of course, there is the question of start-up capital. As in, there's no trail…"

King nodded. "Okay, so what about today? How far can we take this?"

Grainger leaned forwards conspiratorially. "We can use today as a recce if you like. But that puts the emphasis on tomorrow. It has got to be done then. If it all looks good when we get down there, and you have time, I would suggest getting on with it. How long will it take you?"

King shrugged. "There's a lot of weight, so it will mean multiple trips between the two vessels. I'm not entirely sure what I'll find, either. Simon told you about the circumstances in which the submarine lost contact, didn't he?"

"Simon is Simon. In that he says little, infers less and admits to nothing."

King nodded. He felt it only fair to put the man in the picture. "Alright. There was a person put on board, and we suspect she was infected with a virus."

"Well, that changes a few things…"

"Just wait," King interrupted. "The experts down at Porton Down…"

"Hold on, Porton Down?" Grainger interrupted. "So, this isn't like Covid or Flu, this is a biological weapon of some sort…"

King shrugged. "All I can say is the experts at Porton Down assure us that the virus is not airborne. It certainly is an airborne pathogen, but only from a live source. Outside of test conditions and without a live host, the virus dies quickly." King paused. "It won't be pleasant, though. There will be signs of gruesome deaths."

"Well, I have to remain on the controls of the submersible, so it's all down to you." Grainger nodded. "But tell me. Did these experts ever consider that without communication and with a system failure, the submarine could still have survivors?"

"Survivors?" Rashid commented.

"Yes," said Grainger turning to him. "This is a nuclear submarine. If it rested on the bottom of the ocean, with the reactor still functioning, then water, air and power systems for the lights, heating and air-conditioning would still be functioning. The scrubbers may clog with mud on the seabed, but it's a possibility…"

"Shit…" King shook his head. "No, the Royal Navy will have considered all of that, surely?"

"Yes, but the Royal Navy think their submarine is going to be salvaged by hippy marine engineers and towed to the Faroe Islands." Rashid paused. "What if the crew are still alive?"

King shook his head. "The virus would mean that they did not survive," he said emphatically. "We saw the footage from the facility, saw what the effects were on the test subjects."

"Test subjects?" Grainger asked.

"Better you don't know," replied King curtly. "Shit, I thought this was a demolition mission, I hadn't given the thought to the possibility of there being survivors…"

"We can tap on the hull when we get down there using the retractable hands," said Grainger. "It's proof positive. If we hear anything back, then you'll know."

"And that presents a whole new set of problems…" said King.

Rashid shrugged. "Not really. The mission to destroy the submarine can't go ahead. Simple as that." He stared at King. "Can it?" he asked edgily.

"Of course not," King replied. "But if that virus spread…"

"From what I saw of it, if the virus took hold, there being survivors would not be an issue." Rashid paused. "It either spread and everybody died, or the submarine sank because of another issue. That scenario means there could still be survivors. In theory."

"I suppose," King sat back in the chair and frowned. "What a crappy mission," he announced. "Blowing one of our own submarines to kingdom come and destroying all chances of families getting their loved one's bodies back because MI5 and MI6 need to cover their tracks. Because the world, fresh off a pandemic doesn't need to hear that a far worse one could have been released, or still could be in the future."

"It's a bit late now for a crisis of morality," said Rashid.

Grainger smiled. "Sir Galahad once told us that when you work in the shadows and lie to the public for a living, the lies only ever get larger and the shadows only ever get darker…"

"I'm beginning to think Sir Galahad is a very wise man," said King.

Grainger looked up as the boat's engines reversed and cut out. Anchor chains rattled forward and aft. "Anyway, we're here now. So, in a few hours, you're going to find out what the hell happened to that submarine, and the poor souls onboard."

Chapter Thirty-Seven

Lake Como, Italy

"Any problems?"

"No," Sally-Ann Thorpe replied. "Why, should there have been?"

Caroline went to get out of the chair but winced. She looked up at Thorpe somewhat dejectedly. "You wouldn't unwrap it, would you?"

Thorpe looked at her for a moment. She could see that Caroline was suffering and looked thoroughly exhausted. She shook her head somewhat unsympathetically and said, "No, I'll do it in a moment." She rummaged through her tote handbag and said, "Here, take two of these." She passed Caroline a box of tablets, then fetched her a glass of water. "They're the strongest they would do over the counter. Paracetamol and Codeine, take two every four hours."

Caroline took the box and opened it, taking out two of the capsules and swallowing them down with the glass of water. "Thanks," she said quietly.

"You shouldn't be here," Thorpe said,

taking hold of the large box and using her thumbnail to break the tape seal. "I understand why you're doing this, but just look at you. You can barely get out of a chair, now."

"I'll be better with the second crutch."

Thorpe shook her head. "I'll meet with Fortez." She ran her thumbnail down the seal and placed the box back down on the table.

"No offence, but you don't talk the talk. Not in this game, at least." Caroline shook her head. "Fortez thinks he's meeting with an ex-soldier who runs a team of ex-special forces mercenaries."

"You're taking Dave with you. He can talk the talk for me."

Caroline watched Thorpe undo the box. She worked at the joins of tape with her thumbnail. She must have caught under the nail with a sharp piece of tape or card because she sucked on her thumb, before using her nail again on the join. "I have a pair of nail scissors in my bag," she offered.

"No, I'm fine," Thorpe replied irritably. She finally got the lid of the box open and reached inside for the crutch. "Gosh, it's heavier than I expected."

"That's why I don't like using them…" Caroline shrugged. "That and the fact I have always been so active. I guess it's just vanity, really."

"It's necessary! Just use them, and you will heal more quickly. Christ, you're like my nan! When she broke her hip, she just kept rushing her recovery, you're no different," she beamed a rare smile and Caroline could see that she was in fact quite pretty, underneath her normal, if somewhat austere façade.

"Are you calling me an old lady?" Caroline grinned. "I suppose I have rushed it a bit, I'm just fed up with how slow the process has been, that's all," she said, then added, "And thanks for doing this."

"Don't mention it." Sally-Ann pulled the crutch out of the box with both hands and placed it beside Caroline's chair.

Caroline yawned, then looked up as Ramsay entered the living room.

"Finally getting along, then?"

Caroline smiled. "It's these painkillers she got me. I think she substituted them with horse tranquilisers…"

"Hah!" Sally-Ann laughed. "Now there's a thought!"

Chapter Thirty-Eight

200 miles south of the Polar Icecap, Barents Sea

"Sir, she's back," the sonar operator announced. "Due east, two-thousand metres and turning towards us."

Commander McClure nodded. They had just retrieved the communication buoy and the Virginia class submarine's cutting-edge 'periscope-less' camera. Instead of the classic periscope and fold-down double handles associated with military submarines, the Virginia had a retractable camera that used 3-D imaging, infrared and laser-distancing. The picture was both crisp and clear and could be viewed on various monitors. The sea ice was still abundant but becoming thinner with every mile further south they travelled. The captain had contacted Washington on the direct link made possible by the communications buoy and reported the confrontation. His orders were not to use torpedoes unless fired upon. The standard 'do not fire unless fired upon' protocol that had dogged every soldier, sailor and airman in the theatre of operation for the past sixty years.

"Sir, this is a direct act of aggression!" Lieutenant-Commander Jacobs protested, albeit quietly a foot away from the man's ear.

"You read the transcript just like I did," McClure replied somewhat tersely. "We have a job to do, and we need to do it. So, we need to get out of here…" He paused. "Maintain course, silent running, dive to two hundred feet, speed to four knots." The nerve-wracking and inconvenient truth was that to run silent, speed had to be greatly reduced, thus inhibiting their ability to change course quickly and potentially make themselves a sitting duck to the enemy. He waited for the quiet confirmations and realised he was subconsciously rubbing the St. Christopher medallion which hung around his neck next to his dog tags. He stopped at once, checking that the buttons of his shirt were secure. He glanced at his second in command, but the man hadn't appeared to notice. "With any luck, we'll pass directly beneath her. Ready anti-ship missiles."

"Anti-ship? Will they detonate under water? I didn't think they would, I haven't seen any data for such an action."

The submarine was equipped with an array of weapons from ground assault cruise missiles to anti-ship missiles and torpedoes. Torpedoes were launched in the water and travelled through the water to their target, while anti-ship missiles were fired either underwater or on the surface and travelled through the air to their target.

"Let's see, shall we? The transcript said not to fire our torpedoes unless fired upon." He paused. "And anti-ship missiles, and I'm sure you'll agree with this XO, are not torpedoes. This boat isn't going away. The Russian skipper is belligerent, and I have one-hundred and twenty-eight lives to consider."

"But if the missiles don't detonate…"

"Then they'll give the bloody Russians something to think about, won't they?"

They still had two torpedoes loaded in opposite tubes, and the countermeasures had been replenished. The crew were maintaining their silent running orders, but everyone was wearing an expression of worry and anticipation. The tension was high, and the atmosphere seemed like a touchable, pliable entity. The men were perspiring, for although the submarine was operating in waters of around -1.8°c (seawater freezing at -2°c), the heat from the crew's bodies, the electrical devices, and operating systems, as well as the kitchen galley meant that air-conditioning would normally be in use, but with the silent running orders this was not a possibility. Sweat was visible at the men's armpits and the small of their backs, and the temperature added to the tension.

"One-thousand metres, coming right at us. She should clear us by one hundred feet," the sonar operator said quietly.

"If she fires, I want both Barracuda torpedoes launched, then a hard to starboard, full-speed and dive to three hundred." McClure paused. "Confirm intent."

"Roger, hard to port, vent and dive, full-speed," replied the helmsman.

"Two barracuda, check," replied the WEPS.

"Ease speed to eight knots," McClure said, and the submarine noticeably slowed.

"So, this is it," Jacobs murmured. "Our Virginia class against Russia's newest hunter-killer. So far, I think we're winning…"

"How so, XO?"

"Well, they're still heading for us, no change in speed. Our equipment is obviously superior to theirs."

"XO, there are half the crew members on that Russian boat. Sixty-eight to our one-hundred and twenty-eight. Which tells me they have equipment and tech we don't yet have, nor understand..."

"Torpedo! Torpedo! Torpedo!" the WEPS exclaimed. "Eight hundred metres!"

"Evasive action!" the commander shouted.

"Torpedoes away!" the WEPS confirmed.

"Enemy sub breaking hard to our starboard!" the sonar operator shouted.

"Helmsman, new orders! Hard to starboard! Dive one hundred! Full power!"

"They were assuming we didn't have torpedoes already in the tubes and are taking evasive action themselves..."

"And now we'll go right underneath her..." Commander McClure gripped the rail tightly as the vessel dived, turned, and accelerated hard. There was an almighty explosion and the submarine buffeted as the shockwave engulfed them.

"Direct hit! Enemy torpedo destroyed!" the sonar operator exclaimed.

"Where's the sub?" McClure shouted.

"Same course, passing over us in five seconds!"

"Self-destruct the second torpedo and ready three ship attack missiles. Fire in... three... two... one... away!"

There was a hissing sound and all at once, all three vertical tubes sent waterborne air attack missiles directly above them. The sound they made impacting on the enemy submarine's hull sounded like cannon fire and every man felt the vibration in their chest as the Virginia class shook with the impacts.

"Three hits, Commander!" the sonar operator said triumphantly. "Multiple alarms sounding, and they are surfacing rapidly.

"Maintain course, level at three hundred, bring speed back to twenty knots," Commander McClure ordered. "Monitor for an SOS..."

"Aye, aye, skipper."

The ship attack missiles were designed to be fired and home in on either pre-entered coordinates, or laser guided by air support or ground troops, who would 'paint' the target with a laser for the missile to lock onto. The missiles could be controlled via the communication links, which were sent to the surface with the communication buoy, but in this case, the missiles were launched without targeting, meaning that they would not arm the warheads, and would have self-destructed after a two-thousand-foot vertical climb. The system had been designed for emergency ice breaking, should the submarine not have enough power and momentum to break through polar ice in the event of mechanical failure. The Russian submarine would have undoubtedly suffered damaged in the triple attack, the seams rupturing from the impact creating serious flooding inside and would likely have to be evacuated if a support vessel could not be reached in time and moored to.

"They are taking on water, Sir. Venting the ballast tanks and sending out an SOS to all vessels in the vicinity." The sonar operator paused. "There is no other shipping nearby…"

"Launch the communication buoy," McClure said quietly. He turned to Jacobs and said, "Get Washington on the line…"

Chapter Thirty-Nine

Barents Sea

The lights cut a swathe in the ocean darkness, occasionally lighting up darting shoals of fish and jellyfish with their long tendrils wafting lazily and snagging shrimp and tiny crustacea in a web of stinging death. King heard his own breathing, shallow and unsteady, but he knew it was down to nerves and adrenaline at what had to be done next. Grainger had made docking the submarine sound easy, but he knew that in practice it would be anything but. The docking collar would need a good, smooth fit. All very well in theory, but they did not yet know if the submarine had sustained damage that would make a secure fit an unrealistic option. And then the water had to be pumped out under a pressurised seal. King would then have to get the hatch open, another two escape hatches below that, and if the British submarine was full of water, then the geyser which could erupt would give Old Faithful a run for its money and the seal would be broken. To save Grainger from this fate, he would first have to lock one of the hatches above him. It was as simple as that. Once they docked, King's next move would be one of life or death.

They found negative buoyancy halfway down, at around three-hundred and sixty metres. Grainger checked the display and air mix. "Doesn't hurt to slow descent and get adjusted at this depth."

"How far down can this thing go?" asked King. There was the sound of metal flexing, the rivets tightening under pressure. The sound was both eerie and worrying. Grainger did not seem unduly bothered, and the fact relaxed King, if only a little.

"We've done work at five thousand metres, so it's signed off to that depth. The oceans aren't the deepest around here. Six hundred metres mainly, with trenches of up to three thousand metres. To the north in the Arctic are some of the deepest waters on the planet. Of course, the Mariana Trench off the Philippines gets the record, at least that we know of, but the North Atlantic and Arctic Ocean can get bloody deep. Twenty-two thousand feet under the icecap and thirty-thousand feet in parts of the Atlantic Ocean. That's jumbo jet cruising altitude and certainly higher in terms of direct measurement than Mount Everest. Imagine putting Mount Everest, everything from peak to sea level into the ocean and not being able to see its summit."

King glanced at his watch. On the face it showed that it was rated to 1000ft or 300m. He'd always marvelled at that fact and wondered if it would work at that depth, then supposed he would find out soon enough if the docking procedure didn't go according to plan.

The submersible craft was more robot than vehicle. An umbilical cord made up of a cluster of tubes fed a clean air supply down from the support boat, along with their power supply and communication cable. Onboard, air tanks and a separate electric motor meant they could take control and make it back to the surface in the event of the umbilical cluster being severed. Rashid had remained on deck and had asked to be involved in the electric winching process, not least so he could keep an eye on the crew and provide them both with top-side security and with it, the peace of mind that he had their backs. With foreign agents in the mix, nothing was out of the question. King was seated directly behind Grainger, who was naturally at the controls and seated within the bubble, which was made up of three bulbous Perspex windows, which looked in appearance like a giant old-fashioned deep-sea diving helmet. Grainger used what looked like a bicycle handlebar to control the direction of the submersible, with a throttle lever for the electric motor. Compressed air vented from the external bladders at regular intervals to provide the sink they needed, and compressed air tanks would be siphoned into the external bladders to create float. Unlike the military submarines, the craft did not take on water for ballast.

Behind King the bags of explosives and equipment he needed filled the cramped space, and below him the hatch he would need to open and close behind him. Beneath the hatch was the diving chamber and external hatch. King was desperately trying to remember the procedures Grainger had told him on the way down, because Grainger would have to remain at the controls and make subtle adjustments for movement and any current that they encountered, although he assured King that it was never rough at depth and the currents in the Barents were worse nearer the coast where several oceanic currents met the Gulf Stream and gave a conveyer belt ride into the Northern Sea Route.

Grainger started the submersible on its descent once more. King could feel the pressure in his ears and was grateful for the brief pause. Outside two curious sharks cruised slowly past the bubble windows. Each shark was around eight feet in length and swam effortlessly. Their grey bodies with white underbellies were uncannily close in appearance to Great Whites. "Porbeagles grow larger here than in the South Pacific," said Grainger. "Usually around ten feet in length as opposed to approximately six. The waters are extremely rich in plankton here. Which provides food at the beginning of the food chain, going all the way up. This is the issue with ocean health, it all starts with plankton. Plenty of that and everything benefits. Even the quality of the air on the surface."

King nodded, transfixed on the two sharks. He had thought they were Great Whites but now felt foolish and didn't tell Grainger his first thoughts. He wondered if Madeleine would ever see her coveted Greenland sharks this closely. All at once, the two sharks thrashed their tails and were gone. Several squid replaced the sharks, and a shoal of glistening fish blocked their vision entirely as they were engulfed in silver and blue, reflecting in the powerful lights like disco balls. The shoal was immense and stayed with them for most of their descent. They disappeared as suddenly as they arrived, and the silhouette of a large rock was visible at the end of the light's range ahead of them.

"That's strange," said Grainger. He controlled their descent and powered forwards. The seabed looked muddy and devoid of life. There were perfect skeletons of fish reflecting white in the lights, then as they progressed perhaps a dozen metres, King could see thick blankets of crabs travelling across the seabed like lines of traffic. An army of seabed cleaners on their march to pick another carcass clean.

"What's strange?"

"That's the submarine ahead." He checked the laminated notes clipped to a piece of string within easy reach. "We're bang-on for coordinates and depth, but the outline is all wrong…"

King squinted against the light. There was no real colour, just the thick brown sludge of the seabed and the black void of the ocean beyond the beams of light. He frowned, taking in the sight of the submarine as it came slowly into view. He could make out the conning tower and the thick, bulbous prow, the elongated tail. "It's too big," he said. "It's almost as if…"

"It's carrying another sub…"

"Shit…" King caught hold of Grainger's shoulder and said, "Don't go any closer!"

"Why?" Grainger frowned. He pulled back and the lights moved with the slight change of course from his sudden movement. Then, answering his own question he said, "Oh my god, there's a smaller submarine attached…"

King stared, transfixed on the submarine piggy-backing the British vessel. "Reverse back, come in on another course, directly from behind."

Grainger did as King told him, and the powerful lights swept across the black void, then picked up another submarine suspended in empty space over a hundred metres away. It was utterly buoyant with no movement, part of it suspended over the ridge, with the stern above the void. "Christ almighty…" he said quietly.

"That's a small reconnaissance vessel that has docked the Astute-class," said King. "The bigger sub looks like a Russian diesel Kilo-class. The Iranians have another name for it, if indeed it is them, but I'm willing to bet that our Iranian friend has been their eyes and their ears and contacted them with the coordinates, and now their operation is underway…"

"Look!" Grainger pointed. "There are clamps on the deck of the larger sub, that smaller one must have hitched a ride."

King nodded. "Keep back and dim the lights. Military submarines don't have windows like this one, windows can't cope with depth charges or torpedoes, but that smaller sub will have cameras for sure. Launching from and docking to that large submarine will necessitate the need for cameras, so they could very well see us right now."

Grainger killed the lights and switched to a red beam that barely reached the large submarine but gave them an ambient light from which they could make out the hulk of the British vessel.

"That smaller sub, do you think it would be large enough to ferry cruise missiles between the two?"

Grainger considered this for a moment and shrugged. "That would depend upon the size of the missiles. How big are they?"

"About fifteen feet long and as wide as this…" King made a ring with his arms until his fingertips touched."

Grainger thought for a moment then said, "Two at a time, perhaps. It would be a tight squeeze, but I think it would be feasible. Time consuming, certainly." He paused. "How many do they have on board?"

"At least thirty."

"Can they do a lot of damage?"

"They flatten large buildings. Like the bunker busters you will have seen during the Gulf War footage on the news," King replied. "But there has been a development…"

"I don't like the sound of this."

"Continued Russian belligerence dictated that the cruise missiles were armed with American nuclear warheads. They are what is known as dial-a-yield, so can be adjusted to flatten say a military base, or at maximum yield, then a town of small city."

"And the Iranians don't yet have nuclear weapons," Grainger said sardonically. "But I guess they do, now…"

"Not if I can help it," replied King. "Get us back to the surface."

"It's going to take an hour," he replied. "The pressure can't be ignored."

The longest hour of my life... King thought.

Chapter Forty

Lake Como, Italy

Sally-Anne Thorpe looked at the monitor and frowned, shaking her head incredulously. Captain Durand looked up at her from his seat, his expression quizzical. Neil Ramsay shrugged when she caught his eye.

"You've gone ahead and made arrangements for the meet?" she asked, taken aback.

"Fortez knows he's meeting a woman," Durand frowned. "You knew that."

Thorpe nodded as she straightened up and looked at Ramsay. "I could have gone in her place."

"Caroline met with Noventa, it was the natural progression of the operation for her to arrange to meet Fortez," replied Ramsay somewhat curtly, as was his manner.

"But we've monitored the email accounts and he did not make further contact until he typed what we told him to say."

"We did not monitor Noventa's mobile phone between the café and his home. If he spoke with Fortez, then he could have described

Caroline to him." Ramsay paused. "Caroline is comfortable with doing it. I don't see a problem."

"And when was this decided?"

Ramsay shrugged. "We had a conversation this morning while you were out. I trust Caroline and she knows what to do. You're an investigator and legal expert, Sally-Anne. You've never been undercover. It doesn't state so in your file, at least."

Thorpe spun around as Caroline entered and said, "Is this down to you? You send me out for your medical supplies, and then work on everybody here?"

"We had a chat," said Caroline shrugging off the woman's accusing manner. "I thought you were only too happy to help me earlier…"

"Bullshit!" snapped Thorpe. "You set this up! You got me to collect the painkillers and your bloody walking stick while you manipulated the rest of the team!"

"Firstly, it's a crutch, not a bloody walking stick…"

"And secondly?" she fumed.

"Secondly, can I assume the honeymoon is now over?"

"Piss off, you conniving little bitch!" Thorpe snapped.

"Sticks and stones, luv…"

"Ladies…" Neil Ramsay stepped forwards and made himself a buffer between the two women. "Let's not lose focus. Caroline is more than capable of getting Fortez to admit everything for the recording. The camera is in place, then once we have everything we need, Sally-Anne, you can make the arrest with Captain Durand." He paused. "Durand, you will read the man his rights using your position with Interpol Special Operations, before we take him across the Swiss border."

"Sure thing," the Frenchman said, his amiability suggesting he had tried to lighten the mood.

"See?" Caroline said, staring directly into Thorpe's eyes and giving her nowhere to go. "You can have the official glory, while I do the dirty work and take all the risks. You should be more than happy with that…"

Chapter Forty-One

CIA Headquarters
Langley, Virginia

Robert Lefkowitz wiped his brow with the clean handkerchief and went to tuck it into his pocket, but the nurse reached around and took it from him, leaving a clean one on the table in front of him. The drip had been removed and both men opposite seemed relieved, as if experiencing the man's relief on his behalf, but Lefkowitz knew it was just that the treatment was a reminder of their own mortality and it had made them uncomfortable. Fools. They worked in an agency where death was merely part and parcel of what they did, but still they had not become used to the idea that death had neither prejudice nor mercy. The inevitability of time was something they still thought they could disregard. Lefkowitz was no longer scared of death. He would welcome it when he was ready, but not before. There were matters to attend to, cases to close. Only when he had secured his legacy would he give up the fight.

"Their orders should still stand," Admiral Casey argued. "The Russian submarine fired upon them. Multiple times. They were bested, and now they should live or die with the consequences."

"The operation is still active," Becker agreed.

Lefkowitz shook his head. "This Russian situation is a gift," he said. "The world will know that Russia attacked a US submarine on routine patrol in international waters. The US submarine defeated the Russian threat by utilising a non-lethal counterattack, then rescued the Russian crew…"

"But the Russians attacked us, Sir!" Admiral Casey countered belligerently.

"And if our sub leaves and the Russian crew perishes, then we will have committed our own act of war…" Lefkowitz turned to Becker and asked, "What of our agent?"

Becker checked the notes in front of him. "His mission relies upon our submarine. He's on his own up there and there are hostile forces on location, as well as friendlies."

"Friendlies?" Lefkowitz frowned.

"There are at least two British agents up there." Becker paused. "Our asset reports that one is known to us. The MI5 link in the Standing affair…"

"Do you think they can handle it? Tidy up their own mess?"

"They generally tend to get the job done, Sir, yes."

Lefkowitz nodded, then looked at Admiral Casey and said, "Admiral, with respect, the cat and mouse affair with the Russians has affected our deadline. Our asset is in limbo. But we can come out of this clean and leave the Russians with dirt on their faces. The world will hear about Russia's aggression, but it will also see that the US showed restraint. Not only bringing superior military tactics to hand, but the merciful action of reacting in a way not learned in The Naval Academy at Annapolis, but by a submarine captain trying to avoid all-out war. This slaps Russia across the face far more than a protracted standoff of firepower and display of military might. And the people left in no doubt of Russia's part in US vote rigging, leaked documents and communications tampering will see that they are a viable threat. The millennials and post boomers and snowflakes of the world who only get their information from social media need a wake-up call. Perhaps this will be it. Russia has the firepower to blow us off the map, so now they may take the threat seriously." He paused, reached for the clean handkerchief, and dabbed his brow again. The colour, what little remained, had drained from his cheeks. "Russia will be left knowing it fell short, their tech-laden new submarine was not a match for our own, and the worst of it all is they will have to thank us for saving their crew. Look at the Kursk in two-thousand, and the fiasco of them turning down specialist help from other nations, only to botch the rescue and cost the lives of all one hundred and eighteen souls on board."

Admiral Casey stared at his hands, looking up slowly. He glanced at Becker, who nodded. "Okay, Director, you make a compelling case." He paused. "Tell your agent to make alternative travel arrangements." He stood up and gathered the papers in front of him, packing them into a leather documents case.

"I'll get word to your asset," Becker said. "Who is he?"

"He's my man, Becker…" Lefkowitz coughed several times, covering his mouth with the handkerchief. The nurse stepped around him to offer him some assistance, but was curtly waved away as he said, "I'll do it…" A good agent was hard to find but keeping one alive required a short chain of command. Lefkowitz had learned this lesson from bitter experience, and even in his twilight tenure of the agency, he would not lengthen the links in the chain at any cost. "Gentlemen, I think we have the result we need. Perhaps not the one we expected or hoped for, but one that will play into our hands all the same."

Chapter Forty-Two

200 miles south of the Polar Icecap, Barents Sea

Commander JT McClure watched the Russian submarine through the array of monitors. The cutting-edge electronic periscope, known as a photonics mast, relayed the vessel in HD, with a monitor using thermal imaging so powerful that the crew were visible inside the metal hulk, brighter shades of orange denoting the clusters of men as they looked to their captain for what they should do next. Another monitor viewed the vessel in x10 magnification and McClure could dial it all the way to x50 if he so wished.

"She's listing badly, Sir." Lieutenant-Commander Jacobs paused. "Do we pull alongside and tether to her?"

McClure wanted to help, but he was damned if he would risk the lives of his crew and the seaworthiness of his vessel. If the Russian submarine went down suddenly, it could pull them with her. He checked the distance and their heading and said, "Get some Survival Systems into torpedo tubes one, two, three and four and release when ready." McClure paused, looking at his commander. "Get an eight-man security crew ready to go top-side. Full armaments."

Jacobs nodded, "Sir, I understand, but the Russians will have men on deck armed with Kalashnikovs and pistols before we do. Probably a heavy machine gun as well…"

There was a rush of air as the pods containing life-rafts, lifejackets and emergency heat packs and rations were discharged under compressed air at over 500 psi, enough to launch them close to eighty-metres away before they floated to the surface. If McClure's calculations were correct, as well as some dead reckoning, the pods should open on the surface close enough to the Russian submarine for the deck crew to retrieve with hook lines.

McClure nodded, then said, "Then perhaps they will need a demonstration…"

"The Cyclops?"

"Forbes has reported that the US Navy are developing a high energy laser for our Virginia class boats, maybe the Russians should have a glimpse of the future. They have reported that nothing under the waves can match the

Yasen-class submarine, and I think we've already dispelled that rumour…"

"Two for two, Boss?"

"Yes. But get that security detail ready to get on deck ASAP." McClure turned to the helmsman and said, "Get us broadside to their stern, fifty-metres out and hold depth." He paused. "Launch the Cyclops, regenerate five-hundred kilowatts from the reactor and wait-out. Radio operator, contact the Russians on the emergency channel…"

"Cyclops ready, Sir," the WEPS announced nervously. He had fired the nuclear-powered regenerative laser system only a few times in exercises. Ships, aircraft, and high value coastal targets were the targets of the Cyclops – the laser capable for frying circuit boards and communication systems in fractions of a second, or incinerating sections of metals such as engines or communication masts - but submarines were not considered targets because the laser system only worked above water, fired from the refractor which had been built into the multi-function photonics mast.

"Russian submarine reached, Sir. The captain has sent word to Russia that we have committed an act of war and that they will defend their vessel at any cost…"

"Relay my sympathy that he was bested in a fair engagement, inform him that we have black box data that will show that they fired first and completely unprovoked." He paused. "And that we will assist them in any way possible. However, we would like to inform him that he is taking on water, that we have sent survival systems to aid him, and that we will be surfacing imminently."

The communications officer relayed the commander's words, then made shorthand notes as he listened to the message, which again would come through the Russian submarine's communications officer, and never from the commanding officer. "Sir, the Russian captain said he will fire upon any submerged vessel, and that he does not require our assistance."

"Tell the Russian captain that his weapons will be useless against our own."

"Sir, he has asked to inform you that he has men deployed on the deck and they have a twelve-point-seven-millimetre heavy machine gun loaded with armour-piercing rounds, that would suggest otherwise…"

"WEPS, can we see the machine gun?"

"Yes, Sir."

"Melt it…"

"Yes, Sir!"

Commander McClure focussed the camera using the mousepad on the display monitor and studied the two men lying on the deck, their large-brimmed sailor's caps with ribbon tallies tied around were not the most intimidating, but he knew submariners to be a tough bunch the world over. He watched as the WEPS counted down and fired. The two submariners looked confused, then scared and suddenly leapt up from their position, one sliding overboard into the icy water. The other looked as if he contemplated leaping in, too, as the machine gun and deck area underneath it reached 1000°c in a matter of seconds and the ammunition cooked off and fired away like a string of firecrackers. The machine gun continued to heat up, glowing red, before buckling and bending and the deck around the weapon started to glow red. The remaining submariner ran for the conning tower and skidded over the wet casing, where sailors aimed their Kalashnikovs at an unseen, unheard threat.

"Tell the Russian captain that we can cook his entire vessel and everything inside if we so choose. Tell him we are surfacing and offering him assistance, and that I suggest he accepts it graciously. Just one shot fired upon us and we will sink his vessel and send both himself and his crew to the bottom of the ocean…"

Chapter Forty-Three

Barents Sea

They were heading back to the Aurora rigs at full speed. The bow of the working boat was crashing down on the gentle swell and cascading huge plumes of icy water over the deck.

"We may have an issue when we get there," said Grainger ominously. "This swell is small, but it's building steadily. If they haven't already pulled in the pontoons, then they most likely soon will."

"Where does that leave us?" King asked, his eyes on the distant rigs ahead. Slight mounds on the grey horizon that could have been boats had they not known the course and distance.

"The RIBs will run between them for a while. But it's not a taxi service, we're talking emergencies or people caught on the wrong rigs. The RIBs will at least run until the swells hit three or four feet, but if the sea becomes choppy, then forget it. We'll be rig-bound for the foreseeable future." He paused. "There is a helicopter on Rig Three, the main admin rig, but it will only fly for casualty evacuations to Spitsbergen or special circumstances."

"Shit!" King snapped. He paced to the port-side window but more for the distraction, returning having not even looked outside. "Okay," he said decisively. "I need to find someone on one of the rigs. Rig Two, I think. A Swedish girl, or woman... her name is Madeleine. I don't know her surname. She has just got assigned to the marine biologists studying pods of orcas."

"Orcas?"

"Yes," King replied tersely. "Make the call, get somebody to find her and then get her on the line, Grainger. We don't have much time..."

***

Hormuzd Shirazi did not have much time either. He had the coordinates and the ETA. It would require a leap of faith, but faith was the one thing he had. Unwavering, resolute. Faith was his constant.

He had packed his kit in the duffle bag and changed into his cold weather gear. He was not a fan of the water, so wore a lightweight CO_2 inflatable life vest over his jacket. It was the type that inflated upon full water submersion, or by a toggle which could be activated by the wearer. He had assembled the lightweight AR-15 rifle complete with folding stock and a shortened fourteen-inch barrel. He had smuggled the stripped weapon into Spitsbergen inside an empty diving bottle with a false section in the bottom. The weapon, and others like it, had been taken from Israeli commandos who had been killed in a failed attempt to assassinate Iran's top nuclear scientist. The irony that the assault rifle – made by the Americans and used by their lap dogs in the Middle East - was being used in an operation to arm Iran with nuclear weapons was not lost on Shirazi, nor indeed on the intelligence chief who had hand-picked him for the mission. Shirazi had regretted missing the British agent at the storage depot, and unashamedly missing him again a second time on the rig because of the kafir protecting him. But now, he was of no consequence because his mission would soon be over. The submarine commander and his crew would soon complete their task and rendezvous with him, where they would return to Iran and the glory that awaited them. Heroes of the people of Iran and of the Supreme Leader – the Grand Ayatollah. And, of course, the almighty Allah.

***

Madeleine looked down at them pensively as they disembarked the work boat and climbed the ladder from the inflatable pontoon to the first deck of the rig. Grainger had been correct in his prediction that the linking pontoons would be unshackled, deflated, and stored in each rig. The swell was only running at three feet or so, but King could see that walking a kilometre along the links of inflatable pontoons would be a hazardous affair. Another foot or more of swell and Grainger had been adamant that the docking pontoon would be lifted, too.

"I have what you asked for, but I'll probably lose my position in the research team when they find out," she said tersely. "Now, tell me what the hell this is about."

King smiled. "You won't lose your job, I'll see to that," he replied. "Now, show me how to use it."

"It's not as simple as that!" she scoffed. "I…" She stopped as an alarm sounded above them.

"That's curious," Grainger said. "That's

the security alarm."

"Is that rare?" Rashid asked.

"I've only ever heard it in practice. Even when things have kicked off between love rivals or gotten out of hand after long periods of separation or being couped up together, it's usually been sorted out internally. We have a security team, but it's run like an internal fire team and made up of volunteers. Only in the security team's case, they are theoretically only called upon when there is a direct threat to life." Grainger walked past them and lifted the hatch on a red box. He retrieved the telephone receiver and started to talk.

King turned to Madeleine. "You were saying?"

"Right, yes. The codes need entering into the software before and after they are initiated…" She looked at King, who was staring at something behind her. "What now?"

King watched the RIB power away from the second rig. It was barely a spec at a thousand metres distant, but it left a clean, white wake in the greyness of the ocean, and the bright red of the craft was framed not only by the grey water, but of the mirror-image sky. A fleeting red speck in a monochrome backdrop. "Where the hell is that going to? There's nothing out there…"

"There's been a fatal stabbing," Grainger said gravely as he returned. "The suspect has stolen…"

"A RIB and fled the rig?" King interrupted.

"Yes, how did you know?"

King pointed behind him and Grainger turned and stared. "Oh, that's vexing…" He turned back to King and said, "A security party is being assembled, but all the other RIBs on Rig Two have been slashed or punctured."

"It's the Iranian," said Rashid. "It has to be."

"But where can he hope to go?" Grainger trailed off. "Oh…"

"Exactly," King said flatly.

"Would someone just tell me what the hell is going on?" Madeleine exclaimed.

King turned to Grainger. "What's the fastest boat on this rig?"

"The rescue RIB. Twin one-fifty engines, thirty-foot long."

"What type of craft is the one fleeing?"

"Sixteen-foot with a single one-hundred horsepower four-stroke Evinrude engine. All of the engines are Evinrude. It was a sponsorship deal."

King nodded, calculating the disparity in engines versus the lightweight advantage of the smaller RIB. The rescue RIB would have the advantage, but after the weight they would be taking with them was allowed for, it would not be an easy race. He turned to Rashid. "Did you get a rifle in Svalbard?"

"Of course. It's the law. Not many places can say that."

"Is it on this rig?"

"I'm on it," he replied, seeing where King was going, and sprinted across the grating to the stairwell.

"Grainger, I want that rescue RIB."

"And I'm on that..." Grainger went back to the telephone and picked up the receiver.

"Are you ever going to tell me what's going on?" Madeleine protested.

King pushed past her and stood at the edge of the deck. He signalled for the skipper, who ducked outside of the wheelhouse and frowned up at him. "Change of plan, I need my equipment!" King turned back to Madeleine. "Just be ready to move. And are you sure that's all the kit you need?"

"Of course." She paused. "I only need to…" She frowned as she realised that King was no longer looking at her, nor paying attention. "What?"

"Grainger! Who is on the second RIB?" He pointed at a flash of red tracking down the fading wake of the first craft.

Grainger put down the phone. "Nobody knows. It came in from Rig Three, moored briefly at Rig Two, then took off after the first RIB. The rescue RIB is now cleared for launch."

"Cleared for launch?" King said, then watched a mechanical arm lowering on the other side of the platform. He ran around the gangway and watched as the craft was lowered from the centre of the rig. He looked back as Rashid ran from the stairwell breathlessly. He had a rifle in his hands, the same standard Browning A-Bolt .30-06 model that King had rented back at the gun shop back in Longyearbyen. "Get my equipment," he snapped at nobody in particular, but all three ran back to the mooring and heaved the bags back to him. King took out the Leatherman knife he had purchased at the gun shop in Longyearbyen and worked his way among the row of RIBs which were all hauled out for storage. He pulled out the anchors and the six-feet lengths of chain and sliced through the ropes attaching them with the razor-sharp blade. He tossed the anchors onto the galvanised steel grating floor and shouted for Grainger when he returned with one of the bags to get the rescue RIB ready for launch. "Rashid get my equipment aboard! Madeleine, load those anchors!" King shouted as he heaved the last of the anchors at her feet, then turned to watch the two boats, but could no longer see the first. He estimated the second RIB to be five-hundred metres distant.

Grainger started the engines and detached the craft from the automatic mechanical arm. He used a little throttle to square the boat to the bottom of the ladder, then feathered the throttle to match the swells, and keep the boat steady. Rashid dropped the first heavy bag into the centre of the boat, then climbed the ladder to fetch the second bag. The RIB was essentially a solid fibreglass hulled craft with inflatable sides that were multi-chambered to withstand several punctures, the advantages of the design giving rigidity and lightness, as well as rendering it unsinkable. The second bag was dropped beside the first and Rashid climbed the rest of the way down the ladder. Madeleine looked at King with uncertainty.

"Go on!" he shouted. "We don't have much time!"

Madeleine shouldered her bag and caught hold of the ladder. "But I still don't know what we're doing!" She shook her head and hurried down, where Rashid caught hold of her and steadied her into the boat.

King slid down the ladder, clutching the sides with his hands and clamping his feet on either side. He landed heavily and shouted to Grainger. "Here, give me the controls," he snapped. He pushed the throttle forwards and the engines roared into life, the bow coming up steeply. "Rashid, get ready on the rifle!"

"On it," Rashid replied, loading the Browning magazine with three bullets. He worked the bolt, checked the safety, and ejected the magazine to load another and give him four bullets at his disposal. The small magazine capacity was an unfamiliar trait compared to the rifles he used and trained with, but he reflected that the rifle had been designed for hunting and not for combat. "Who's in the second boat?"

"I have a suspicion, but I'm not certain. But if the first boat is being driven by the

Iranian, then I think we can be sure how he's getting home…"

"And if it isn't?"

King thought of the tiny reconnaissance submarine docked on top of the British submarine. He had known that returning to the rig carried its risks. There had been nothing more he could have done down there. He couldn't have dived at that depth and he certainly wouldn't have been able to get on board the Iranian vessel. Capturing Shirazi had been his first thought, but if the Iranian was supporting the submarine from the surface, then he would need a ticket out of there. But had Shirazi fled because King and Grainger had been seen? The reconnaissance craft would undoubtedly be equipped with cameras and certainly would have been able to fire upon them, and if the hunter-killer fired upon them in the submersible, or upon the support boat, then they would give themselves away and risk a full-scale military retaliation. No, the Iranian submarine commander would have calculated the time it would take them to return to the Aurora rigs and by then, they could alert their asset and he could head for the rendezvous. Which meant the Iranian submarine was close.

"We just have to hope it is," replied King. "They wouldn't steal the missiles or the warheads and risk leaving their asset behind. It would be too risky. He could be captured and interrogated before they made it through the Northern Sea Route and by then, the Yanks could hunt them on the other side from their bases in Alaska. No, Hormuzd Shirazi is on that first boat for certain."

"Then who the hell is on that second RIB?" Rashid settled the rifle on the edge of the control panel and squinted through the monochrome hue ahead. "Friend or foe?"

King said nothing.

Friend or foe, indeed.

Chapter Forty-Four

Hormuzd Shirazi glanced behind him and saw the RIB gaining on him. He was not well-versed with boats and he had found that the bow was riding too high to cope with the speed. Each time he neared full throttle, the bow rode so high that the engine almost immersed itself in the freezing water. He worked the throttle forwards gently and again, the bow pointed skywards. He looked for something heavy to shift into the forward third portion of the boat, but there was nothing substantial. Instead, he slowed the boat down, engaged neutral and drifted while he picked up the AR-15 and shouldered it. The scope was a x4 magnification, and he could see the man behind the control console. He did not recognise him, but he had just killed a man to steal the boat and he suspected there would soon be more people on the way.

Shirazi fired three shots and the pursuing craft veered to the right. He tracked and fired another four rounds. He could not see if he hit the boat, but he didn't see any plumes of water indicating a miss. The boat veered again and this time Shirazi fired six or seven shots at the engine, allowing several inches for travel. He got his answer to whether he had hit as the boat's engine pitch changed and black smoke started billowing skywards. Shirazi dropped the rifle onto the deck near his feet and checked the coordinates on the GPS handset before working the throttle again. He was so nearly there.

***

King had worked the trim and tilt, adjusting the engine's angle of tilt with the twin propellers' revs and the rescue rib was slicing through the water cleanly, the bow hunkered down as if weighted down and the throttle was at full power. They had been steadily gaining on both boats, but he could now see that one of the craft had stopped with engine trouble.

"Give me the pistol, Rashid," he said. "And get the rifle on the person in the rearward boat."

"Do I take him down?"

"Not yet, mate…" King tucked the Makarov pistol into his pocket, the silencer making it difficult, but he got it in butt first. Not ideal, but it was where he needed it.

He throttled back and kept the RIB in a position where Rashid had a clean arc of fire and wouldn't be firing across their own bow. They were one-hundred metres out, and even with the rifle's open sights, Rashid wouldn't need a second bullet.

"Hands in the air!" King shouted and the man complied, carefully but confidently. "Don't move a muscle, my friend doesn't miss!"

"You'll be buying me flowers next," Rashid murmured quietly.

"Prat…" King said under his breath and eased the RIB forward, making steering and throttle adjustments with the swell to keep Rashid and the rifle on target. He looked at the man, studied his features. Apart from having him down as American and assuming him to be CIA back on Spitsbergen, there was something familiar about him. As if seeing him gave him an easy sense of Déjà vu.

"I was gaining on him, but he hit my engine," the man commented, giving a shrug.

"Who are you?" King asked. "You broke into my room back at the hotel in Longyearbyen. Had yourself a good nose about. But you didn't spot my camera."

"Right." He shrugged. "I guess those are the breaks in this game…"

"So, who the hell are you, then?"

"My name's Newman."

"That's what you said on the boat, but I don't believe you."

"It's true. David Newman. Cover is simpler when it's the truth." He paused. "I guess you could say we're on the same side."

"That's doubtful…"

Newman shrugged. "Most of the time, anyway."

"Is the man in the other boat Shirazi?" King asked impatiently.

"He's Iranian, but I didn't have a name. He killed a member of the Aurora crew and stole the boat. Where he's heading, there could only ever be one method of picking him up. Which doesn't bode well for you…"

"Meaning?"

"Well, they've obviously got what they came for. And judging by your little war party, you know it, too."

King stared at him. He did not like the man's eyes, nor his confidence. He supposed he reminded him of himself. The man was certainly not to be underestimated. "What's your exfil?"

Newman lowered his hands and Rashid fired into the control panel mere inches from his arm. Newman hurriedly shot both hands back into the air and Rashid had already worked the bolt. "Jesus!" he glared back at them. "It was meant to be one of our own subs. But they're all tied up milking the glory out of a little skirmish with a Russian submarine north of here. Seems like the hunter became the hunted and was then promptly rescued by their former prey. Washington has a tremendous victory on so many levels and will be using it for years."

"I haven't seen the news," King replied sardonically.

"I have your pistol," Newman said agreeably. "Whatever happened back at the yard with all the shipping containers between you and the Iranian, I was going to get you to hospital, but got out of there when the cops showed up. I thought the pistol might complicate matters for you."

"That was definitely him then?" King stared at Newman coldly. "Thanks," he replied without emotion.

"I'm reaching for it now…" He lowered his hands and slowly pulled the compact Beretta out from his pocket. He tossed it to King, who caught it in his left hand, his right still on the wheel. Rashid's aim did not waver. "I'll come with you to lend a hand…"

King shook his head and hammered the throttle forwards. Newman was left staggering for balance as his boat rocked wildly in their wake .

"Good call," Rashid said. "I don't trust that guy."

"I know that man," King replied. "But I just can't figure out from where or when."

"It'll come to you."

King nodded. That was what he was worried about, but at least the man was behind him now. Ahead, the RIB was still a speck of red in the monochrome, but King was at full throttle and had the trim and tilt working well, the bow slicing cleanly through the slick water.

Chapter Forty-Five

Shirazi struggled to reload the AR-15 and keep the RIB on course. The bow was riding high – he did not know that the trim and tilt lever altered the angle of the engine planes and brought the front of the boat down, allowing the boat to 'plane' smoothly – and he was fighting the attitude of the tiny craft and unable to use full throttle. When he turned, he could see a boat behind him. A thousand metres ahead of him, the Tareq-class submarine was surfacing. Commander Keshmiri Pezhman had been adamant that the vessel would only remain surfaced for five minutes. He needed to make the rendezvous, or he would die at sea. There was no returning to the Aurora rigs, no chance of being captured. He would gladly serve his country, the great Ayatollah, and the almighty Allah, and he would readily die for the holy trinity that was all three. However, he had been assured that in the event of his capture during the course of his mission, then his family and extended family would be arrested and would never be seen again. Such was the sensitivity of the mission, there really was only one way out for him and the head of the Iranian Secret

Service, The Ministry of Intelligence of the Islamic Republic of Iran, had personally given him the means to do so – a two-shot .32 calibre Derringer pistol, small enough to sit in the palm of his hand, which he had smuggled into Norway and Svalbard in the same cut-out diving tank that he had used to smuggle the AR-15 assault rifle.

Shirazi surveyed the ocean ahead and watched the submarine break the monotony of the horizon, a sliver of black separating the greyness of both sea and sky. The vessel rose slowly, steadily from the water, becoming larger with every twenty or thirty metres of travel. He did not hear the gunshot above the whine of the engine, but he felt the sting of hot copper and his left leg gave out completely. He struggled to remain balanced in the unsteady craft and the wave of pain shot through him, the epicentre of which was his left hip and buttock, although the nerve endings from his knee to the small of his back pulsed as if he had been electrocuted.

He released the steering wheel and struggled to pick up the rifle. Using just one hand he wielded it clumsily behind him and rattled off a dozen rounds in the direction of the approaching boat. He had merely glanced at the wound, but he already knew he was finished. A large calibre weapon with expanding hunting ammunition. He would need a trauma team and a hospital to work on him, and without that, he did not have long.

This is it. This was how it ends… thought Shirazi. Well, so be it and so shall I be unto Him… He pulled the throttle control backwards and mouthed, Allahu akbar, silently.

God is great…

Chapter Forty-Six

"You'll never make the shot! Not with open sights," King had said sharply. "I'll get you closer!"

The rifle had recoiled sharply as Rashid had squeezed the trigger. They were still four-hundred metres distant and travelling at thirty-five knots in a three-foot swell, and the young former SAS officer had still made the shot. Shirazi had jerked and slumped and clambered back to his feet, holding the rifle in his right hand.

"Who says?" Rashid smiled as he worked the bolt, took up aim again and waited for another shot.

"Smart arse…" King turned to Grainger and jerked his head for the man to come to him. "Can you take the wheel?"

"Certainly." Grainger stepped into King's position and ducked his head as bullets sprayed near them from Shirazi's AR-15. "Are you hit?" King asked, taking hold of the Beretta, and checking the magazine and breech.

"I… I don't think so…" He glanced down, patted his arms and sides. "No, all good!"

Madeleine was hunkered down on the deck near the twin engines. She looked pale. King asked if she was ok, and she nodded. King said, "Madeleine, get your kit ready to deploy." She nodded and opened the case she was clutching. King turned his eyes back to the boat.

"I can take him down now for sure," said Rashid. "We're close enough for me to aim at his back, dead-centre…" He ducked as Shirazi fired wildly, but the bullets tracked a long way in front of them and to the side. "Say the word and I'll take him down…"

King watched the submarine ahead of them. They were now only two-hundred metres from Shirazi, and the man had killed his engine and was drifting. "Slow down," he said to Grainger. "Approach at five knots, no more." Grainger nodded and throttled back. "Come hard to port," said King. "Then pull hard to starboard so Rashid remains on target. I'm going to board him."

King tore off his jacket for ease of movement. The Makarov tumbled out of his pocket and he tapped Rashid to make him aware, then placed the weapon at his feet so he would have a rapid-fire option once he'd fired the rifle. King shivered against the cold. Shirazi was only fifty metres away now and fumbling with the rifle. Ahead of them, the submarine had fully surfaced.

"Shirazi!" King hollered. "Put the weapon down and place your hands on your head!" The man continued loading the magazine with 5.56mm ammunition from his pocket. "Drop the weapon!" King grit his teeth in frustration. Beside him was one of the best snipers he'd ever encountered, and the Iranian had until he raised the weapon to live, but King wanted what the man knew. "Shirazi, it's over!" The Iranian inserted the magazine and put his hand on the charging handle.

But he didn't get to pull it backwards...

The .30-06 rifle jumped in Rashid's hands and Shirazi fell out of sight into the hull of the RIB.

"Grainger, get alongside!" King shouted and got ready to leap across.

The RIB nudged the other boat, Grainger pulled the throttle backwards all the way into reverse, then back into neutral as the boat lurched to a complete stop. King leapt into the boat and aimed down at the Iranian, kicking the assault rifle aside. He kept the weapon on him, but Shirazi merely smirked back at him. There was a trickle of blood at the corner of his mouth, and he was already looking pallid, or perhaps it was the Azerbaijan blood in him.

Shirazi coughed and spittle and blood speckled his chin. "The crew had died a horrible death, a sickness of some kind, apparently…"

King nodded. "Then there's a chance the crew on your sub will be infected. I'm glad you lot got there first. You've probably saved my life."

"You're bluffing…" Shirazi replied weakly. "You know nothing of it. You're just a foot soldier. Anyway, you're too late," he sneered. "The submarine will dive inside a minute and the next thing you will know about the warheads is when one explodes in a city of our choosing. Hopefully, your city, with you and your loved ones in it…"

King ignored him. "Where are they taking the warheads?" He glared down at him, the pistol firm and steady in his hands. "Tell me!"

Shirazi smiled. "To Tehran, of course…" He coughed again. "And some will go to our friends in the DPRK. The world is changing and soon, you and the Great Satan that is the United States will no longer assert their dominance on the rest of us… "

"North Korea?" King frowned. "They aren't your friends…"

Shirazi smiled then coughed again. This time, a steady gush of blood left his mouth and when he spoke again, it was a gargle. "The… enemy… of… my… enemy…" He coughed, then rasped. "… is… my… friend…"

King looked at the submarine. He had no idea how many warheads the Iranians had taken aboard, but he knew he could never afford to let them get away. He looked back at Shirazi, but the man was holding something, trying to get the dexterity back into his freezing, dying fingers. King saw enough to recognise two small hexagonal barrels, and he shot Shirazi in the forehead and turned for the other RIB.

"Get us to that sub!" he shouted at Grainger. "Madeleine, are you ready?"

"All set!"

The RIB sliced through the water, gently lifting as it drove head on into the rolling swells. King watched the submarine ahead. A figure appeared at the top of the conning tower, head and shoulders above the rim. He could see them using binoculars. The figure disappeared and King knew what would happen next.

"She's going to dive!" he shouted, turning to Madeleine. "What do I do?"

Madeleine staggered unsteadily forwards, clutching onto the seats for support. She held out the tubular device approximately the size of a can of deodorant. It was made from clear hardened plastic and inside, King could see a processor, coloured bulbs, and a tangle of wires. What looked like a series of SIM cards were inserted into a cartridge and a long trail of fibreoptic cable dangled down at least eighteen inches. At the other end of the tube a ring pin had been threaded with metal clips. "It's designed to be inserted into the flesh at the base of a shark or whale's dorsal fin," she shouted in King's ear. "I have just finished substituting the barb for metal ring ties. Not that you've actually told me, but I kind of figured out what you're up to. The tracking unit has been tested to one thousand metres and has a battery life of two weeks."

"How deep can it go without losing a signal?" King asked as he started to strip off his clothes.

"The animal has to surface for the data to be collated. That's water temperature, the animal's heartbeat, distance travelled etc…"

"It's not a bloody animal!" King interrupted tersely.

"I know!" Madeleine snapped right back. "The data will not download, but the unit will emit a signal constantly. The control receiver will pick up the GPS signal and show on the map on the laptop." She paused, throwing what looked like a buoy into the water, but instead of floating it sank out of sight and Madeleine ran the end of a cable into a small, black unit, then plugged the unit into her laptop using a USB cable. She gathered some length and wound it round one of the heavy-duty rubber cleats so that the USB would not pull out of the unit of the laptop. She looked back at King as he tore off his trousers and stood in just a pair of black boxers. Her eyes had briefly focused on his taut muscles but lingered on the scar. King had been shot in the stomach and the surgery to remove the bullet and stop the internal bleeding had left his stomach looking as if a shark had bitten him almost in half but spat him back out. At his shoulder and right pectoral muscle there was a track of scars from bullet holes. She looked back at him, a little shaken and tried to regain composure. "The receiver is in the water and picking up the signal. There is a second's delay for every one-hundred metres in depth and an additional delay for speed. The tracker is designed for use with sharks and whales, not submarines travelling at thirty knots."

"More like twenty-two for this model," King said, starting to shiver. The air temperature was -8°c and the water temperature was just above the -2°c mark. He looked back at the submarine, now just one-hundred metres distant and almost half submerged. "Get with Grainger and work out approximate figures for delays given depth and speed information. I'm supposing that if you receive the signal and we know the time between transmissions, depth and speed can be calculated?" He paused, smiling nervously, or he could have been shivering. "I think you and Grainger will be better placed to calculate that, rather than Rashid or myself. Get those degrees, Master's and PHDs working…" He took the tracker unit from her and looked back at the submarine, now almost completely submerged except for the top third of the conning tower. The water looked like it was boiling, but it was merely the expelled air creating bubbles as the ballast tanks were expunged and water was sucked inside. He took a series of deep breaths to psych himself up and said, "Okay, Grainger. Get me right on her!"

King knew what to expect as he dived outwards from the moving boat, but the pain was far worse than he had anticipated. He had taken short breaths enabling him to hyperventilate on the approach, readying his lungs for as much breath as he could load them with, and to thoroughly oxygenate his internal organs for the extreme drop in temperature. He couldn't afford to lose time on the surface, fighting for breath or acclimatising to the searing cold in vain. He was in a fight for survival. He needed to enter the water and swim downwards, but as much as he needed the air inside him to feed his heart and lungs, he was too buoyant and fighting against simple physics. He blew out about half his breath, the bubbles temporarily blinding his vision, and powered downward with all his strength. At eight feet he caught hold of the hatch wheel in the conning tower and gripped for all he was worth. The speed of the submarine's descent was terrific, and it was all he could do to hold on. He needed to equalise the pressure in his ears by clenching his nose and blowing until the pressure inside his ears popped, but as soon as he achieved this, he was needing to equalise again. He had underestimated the light factor, too. The clean quality of the water meant that visibility was good, but the light at twenty feet and counting was getting darker with every foot travelled. King equalised again, his head feeling light and his lungs fighting for breath. He could not feel his hands or fingers and as he threaded the metal clip through the hatch, he could barely see to snap the clip together. Without feeling, he heard the metallic click in the water, echoing in his ears. The tracker was in place and he pushed off hard and stroked for the surface. Only now, with his lungs devoid of air, he had no buoyancy, and every stroke was an extreme effort, and every second was a second more than he felt he could be there. With ten feet to go, he could no longer fight the desire to snatch a breath, and with that, he started to black out.

King didn't see the bubbles or the figure swimming down to him, and nor did he feel the hands upon him, the desperate kicks to get him back to the surface. He didn't feel the hands pulling at him, nor the firm rubber side of the boat. Rashid struggled in after him, pulling himself in as Madeleine and Grainger heaved on King's limp arms, but he took what he thought would be his final breath and pictured Caroline, the image rushing to him more clearly as he took in precious air and the saltwater kiss of death never came…

King looked up, confused. He had expected the breath to be his last. He was shivering and became aware of painful touch as both Madeleine and Grainger pulled on layers of clothing and put on Grainger's own warmed pair of gloves as they turned their attention to assisting Rashid with dressing him. King stared up at the grey sky. He was shivering less, but he felt drunk and what he felt was an existential experience – a visitor to his own body and a voyeur to the scene around him. He closed his eyes, the image of Caroline coming to him more clearly. She was laughing, her hair blowing in the wind atop a cliff, the sea shining behind her. He had been a fool to leave her in her fragile state, recuperating from her ordeal. How could she ever forgive him? She was vulnerable and needed protecting and looking after.

Chapter Forty-Seven

Lake Como, Italy

"You don't look how I expected," said Fortez, gesturing her ahead of him.

Caroline was dressed in a white linen dress with a thin, grey cashmere cardigan and white linen gloves. She wore a white, silk headscarf and it was contrasted greatly by her oversized black Gucci sunglasses. Big Dave had commented that she looked like Audrey Hepburn and that she should perhaps travel by Vespa. She had told him that the crutches might hamper that. She placed the foot of the crutches carefully on the gravel pathway and started out ahead of him. "Don't let the crutches fool you," she replied. "Injuries are an unfortunate part of the business we're in. I will soon be healed, and the mark will soon be dead."

"No, I wasn't referring to your injuries, just that you look so beautiful and elegant. It's difficult to imagine you in such a role." He paused. "And Milo Noventa told me you are part of a formidable team," Fortez said. "And yet you show up alone. Rather reckless, given the business you are in and the obvious injury."

He nodded for the guard to stay with them. The man had earlier searched Caroline professionally from ankle to crotch to breasts and under her arms. There was nowhere she could be concealing a weapon in her outfit, and he had allowed Caroline to see the Beretta 92FS in the holster on his right hip for good measure. "I assume your partner is nearby?"

"I don't have a partner," she replied. "I employ ex-soldiers, just like your rent-a-muscle here. But mine are undoubtedly a far more professional breed."

"The security agency only employs ex-soldiers with combat experience," Fortez corrected her, smiling at the guard, and sharing a condescending expression with him like the lady had meant no offence. "I am well-protected, am I not, Marco?"

"Sì, Signor Fortez," the guard answered ruefully.

Caroline smiled and nodded, pausing at the top of the terrace to admire the view. "Yes, but with respect an Italian ex-solider is not up to the same standard as an ex-British soldier, and certainly not up to the standards and experience of the SAS or SBS, and those are my team's credentials. And believe me, you will need a

team like mine, given the calibre of your target."
She paused, staring at both men. "Think what
you like, but I'm right and unless you're both
deranged, you know it, too. And yes, I have
someone nearby."

"How much has Milo Noventa told you?"
Fortez asked, annoyance in his tone. He turned
to the loitering guard and waved him away, but
the man only walked a dozen paces and stood
facing them with his back to the lake and his
hand near the 9mm pistol.

"Not the target's name, just that they
work for the British intelligence services and that
the man killed your sons. Or one of them at least
and was responsible for the death of the other."

"Killed him like a dog..." Fortez said
coldly.

Caroline nodded. She didn't know how
much Fortez had discovered about his son's
death, but it involved being injured by a gunshot
and going down in a light aircraft. Hardly a
dog's death, but since Fortez had elected not to
attend the inquest he had probably built up a
picture in his grieving mind. She did her best to
pull out the chair at the table, and Fortez walked
around the table and helped her. "Thank you,"
she said, attempting to rest both crutches against

the round table, but they slipped and so she rested them carefully on the table instead.

He nodded like it was nothing and took his own seat. "I have arranged for coffee and amaretto biscotti," he said.

"Thank you."

"I am surprised you came alone," he said. "No wires or weapons. I'd have expected more in your line of work."

"You should have expected less," she replied. "It was pretty obvious that I would be subject to a search. And if I turned up here armed, what would that prove? That I work in a dangerous business? You already know that much, otherwise why else would I be here?"

Fortez smiled. "Why else indeed…" He looked over to the villa where a traditionally dressed maid in her thirties stepped outside with a serving tray. "Ah, coffee!" He waited until the maid had silently placed the tray on the table, then smiled as he took the silver pot and poured the coffee into both demitasse cups. "Sugar?"

Caroline shook her head. "Nor cream, thank you" she said.

"Your injuries," he ventured. "An accident perhaps?"

"Of sorts," she replied.

He looked at her crutches on the table, at her white linen gloves. "Your hands are injured as well?"

"No," she replied. "But the crutches have given me bad blisters and they are rather unsightly."

Giuseppe Fortez nodded. "So, to the point. The target. Noventa did not tell you the target's name?"

"No."

"But he told you what the man is, who he works for?"

"Yes."

"But Noventa is dead, surely?"

Caroline looked at him curiously. "Why would you think that?"

***

"She's blown! Get her out of there!" Durand said urgently.

"And where the hell is Dave? He's meant to be with her..." Thorpe stood up abruptly, staring at the screen.

"Wait…" Ramsay watched the monitor. Big Dave had rigged the camera on the neighbour's property and Durand had given Caroline a working watch with a microphone built in. It was larger than she was used to wearing, but it was the fashion for many women to wear men's stainless steel diving watches on a loose strap. "Let's see where he's going with this…"

"You can't be serious?" Sally-Ann Thorpe asked incredulously. She dialled on her phone and said, "Dave, where the hell are you?"

"She wanted to go in alone. You know what she's like…"

"Damn it! Are you close enough to get her out?"

"Sure. What's going down?"

"She may be blown…"

"She said she'd give me a signal if the meeting takes a wrong turn. I trust her, so I'll wait until I hear it."

"Hear it?"

"Going now, I need to keep my phone line clear…"

"He's hung up on me." Thorpe grimaced. "Bloody hell! I knew she wasn't the best person for the task. And she's not fit enough to move if she has to!"

***

"I live here in relative exile," Fortez pontificated upon his fate and continued, "I am a lesson to others. My sons died, my empire was weakened, and I was spared. Like a stud horse who cannot service the mares, I am left to grow old and fat and ignored." He shrugged. "But I can live with that. I can live without seeing the wives of my sons, and their children. Because I play the long game. I will amass strength and when my enemies least expect it, I will strike. Perhaps it will be someone else who does the killing, or perhaps, eventually, it will be me. But the killing will be done and the people who stood by idly and watched my fall from grace will pay. If not with their lives, then with their wallets and the threat of the spectre of death at their shoulders."

Caroline nodded. "Well, perhaps when I complete this contract, you will bear my organisation in mind for some repeat business."

Fortez nodded and smiled sagely. "So, if Noventa is dead, why are you here? And what's more, did you have anything to do with it?"

"Noventa was greedy. Tell me, how did you know?"

Fortez shrugged. "People talk," he replied. "I have people everywhere."

"Well, I'm here for the contract," she replied looking perplexed. "You still want it fulfilled, don't you?"

Fortez ignored her question, instead focusing his gaze on the lake. "My son, Gennaro was a hothead. But he knew enough about the man he went to England to kill. He put enough pressure on the man's boss to learn some key facts, and he learned of the man's weaknesses. He also learned all about the woman in the man's life. A colleague. Wounded terribly. Broken arm, two broken legs… one so badly that she would have been left with multiple operations and months of physiotherapy and recuperation ahead of her. He also had a picture of the man and his woman. He uploaded it into his cloud before he died and while my computer expert was hiding funds and losing money trails, he retrieved this photo." Fortez paused, took his eyes away from the glorious view of the lake and stared directly into her hazel eyes. "And now that young lady sits in front of me, unarmed and with a head full of vengeance…"

***

"La merde!" Durand shook his head. "We need to call the police!"

"I'm on it," Thorpe said and dialled 113, Italy's national police emergency number. She walked away from the others as she spoke.

Ramsay took out his phone and called Big Dave, then cursed as he failed to get through. He tried again, but still there was no connection. On the third attempt he cursed loudly and threw the phone into the chair beside him. He then thought better of it and dialled again.

"The police are on the way," Thorpe announced as she hurried back to the screen. "I just hope they can get there in time…"

***

Caroline smiled. She was quite calm and confident and held the man's stare. "You are an intelligent and resourceful man, Signor Fortez. And you know all about retribution, and how it eats you up, gnaws away at your insides. But once someone makes up their mind to kill you, you can't simply let it go. They will find a way.

You decided that my fiancé could not go on living, and you will never let it go…"

"And you're here to implore me to lift the contract? I must admit, it was a bold move on your behalf." Fortez laughed raucously. "You may be a fool, young lady. But you have a big set of balls!" He made a gesture with his hands as if they were wrapped around an imaginary pineapple each. "Enormous!"

Caroline shrugged, unperturbed. She was looking him directly in his eyes and her tone was unwavering. "So?"

Fortez continued to laugh as he placed both hands flat on the table. When he ceased laughing, he looked at her quite seriously, his fingers drumming slowly and impatiently on the table. "No, my dear, I will not be lifting the contract. In fact, as we speak, colleagues of Marco's are on the way here to take you away." He looked at the bodyguard, who sneered back at Caroline. "So, you will soon see how effective Italian ex-soldiers can be. And after that, perhaps the contract will be served to these same mercenaries. Perhaps I should have looked closer to home and not used that slimy snake oil salesman Milo Noventa? But he was the expert in the dark web, and that was where I was advised to go for anonymity… for all the good that has done me. Now that my boys are dead, and my empire has crumbled, maybe the old-fashioned way is the best way, after all? In the old days, you just held onto a man's wife and child and told him he'd get them back after they killed the person you had a grievance with. The job got done, and you were up to your eyes in alibis when the hit was carried out. If it went wrong, you slept safely in your bed. It was a win-win affair."

"From a man like yourself, I'd have expected no less."

Fortez smiled. "What did you hope to achieve? To get near enough to me to kill me?" He paused. "You were searched. My guard enjoyed it. His hands on your soft skin, lingering between your legs, at your wonderfully pert breasts. I certainly believe there was no weapon hidden there…" he laughed. "Perhaps I should check for myself…"

"You really are a loathsome man. Your son died having taken a fifteen-year-old girl hostage. That's the same age as your eldest granddaughter." She smiled when she saw the flicker of annoyance, or perhaps concern in the old man's eyes. "Yes, I know all about your family. But tell me, what sort of man condones this action? You sit there like you have this self-righteous higher authority when you are in fact nothing but a crooked businessman who has profited from spreading fear and reaping the success of others. Your sons did this, too. But they branched out into drugs and weapons and sex trafficking… things that cause people great pain and anguish… and you sit there, staring out on this beautiful view with thoughts of murder and head full of lies and retribution. An old man, not long for this world, who is practically a prisoner in his own home, because he has been neutered by his opposition and spared only to be humiliated further. Whose last thoughts are bitter and twisted and vengeful." She paused. "Your sons were killed because they took a wrong path. And you have trodden that same path for far too long."

Fortez smiled, but it was mirthless and thin, and his eyes bore nothing but contempt into her own. "The time for talking is over…"

"I couldn't agree more," Caroline replied. She placed her hand on the nearest of her crutches and moved it a few inches until the rubber foot lined up just above the man's ample stomach, then she twisted the handle. There was a colossal gunshot and a fist-sized hole appeared in the man's sternum. He grunted, his eyes wide and his mouth open in surprise and disbelief. And then the wound started to bleed like a hose with the tap turned on halfway. She pushed out her chair and aimed the crutch at the bodyguard. "Easy... put your right hand on your head!" She shouted. "Take out the gun with your left hand. Fingertips only. Toss it towards me..."

The bodyguard stared at the dying man, his eyes transfixed on the open wound. Behind the blood and mess of shredded flesh and bone, the remains of the man's heart, speckled with holes from the lead shot, was still beating and pumping blood outside his chest. The heart gradually stopped after a few more beats and Fortez tensed, then slumped in the chair. The guard complied with her orders and the Beretta clattered at her feet. Relieved she had fooled the guard - the custom weapon could only fire one shot - she picked up the pistol, flicked off the safety and shot the man in his right leg. He fell to the gravel screaming and clutching his shattered kneecap. Caroline thought it payback for the revolting way he had placed his hands on her intimate areas, and she turned and placed the crutch on the table. King's weapon contact in London, who he only ever referred to as 'The Man', had sleeved a 24 inch, 12-bore smooth barrel inside the crutch and a simple spring-powered pin and cap assembly in the handle of the crutch would fire a single 12-bore shotgun cartridge filled with number five shot. A twelfth of a pound of lead balls, two-hundred and twenty in number, fired at fourteen-hundred feet per second at a distance of just eight inches. It was a one shot, one time deal. Reloading would require complete disassembly of the weapon with specialist tools. 'The Man' had texted Caroline with the plans and instructions on releasing the safety and firing the weapon, which she had promptly memorised before deleting the series of messages.

Caroline picked up the other crutch and stood up from the chair. She could hear a helicopter in the distance and when she looked for the direction of the sound, she could see a Robinson R44 coming in fast and low across the water. On the other side of the villa sirens approached from nearby Navale where the *Guardia di Finanza-Comando* were based, but they did not get discernibly closer. Caroline imagined

Big Dave pulling the lorry he had 'borrowed' across the road and tossing the keys over a hedge as he walked calmly away, blocking the traffic in both directions. It would be enough to hold up the police until the chopper put down safely on the lower terrace.

Caroline made her way down the steps, using the crutches, although the heavier adapted one slid on the stones, the rubber cap somewhere inside Fortez with almost two ounces of lead shot behind it. She watched Flymo pull up vertically, then bank the helicopter hard, the tail spinning around so he could put down with the left-side doors facing her. He couldn't simply fly in straight and steady – it wasn't in the ex-army pilot's nature - but the man had style and lived up to his nickname. Like the lawnmower of the same name, nothing could hover lower than a helicopter with Flymo on the stick.

Caroline tossed the pistol off the cliff and into the lake, then hobbled the last few feet to the helicopter, the rotor wash billowing up her headscarf and her mousey blonde hair across her face. She opened the door and slid onto the seat, removing the headscarf completely and smoothing her hair back before putting on the headset and shutting out the terrific noise of the spinning rotor blades.

"Your taxi to Switzerland awaits, Miss Darby," Flymo joked playfully. The helicopter lifted and set forward before she got the harness on, dropping down off the edge of the cliff, where he settled it at fifty feet and powered out across the water.

"I'm certainly pleased to see you," she commented with relief. The gunshot had alerted Big Dave and he had made the call to Flymo, who had been flying a lazy circle a couple of miles to the south. She had spent most of her savings on hiring the helicopter in Switzerland, but Flymo had been glad to travel out and provide his services free of charge. He had fastened some white tape over part of the registration to corrupt the numbers and would land and remove it once they were out of Italy. She would not meet back with the team, her flight from Geneva to London was scheduled to leave in just over three hours and she already had a connecting flight booked for Poole in Dorset. Giuseppe Fortez had been a killer. From the moment Ramsay had told her about the contract on King, she knew there was only one way it could be settled. She imagined the team in disarray. Big Dave had known her intention from the start and had collaborated with her throughout, and right now he would be heading south in a hired Fiat where he had a flight booked from Pisa to Dusseldorf and planned to lie low for a week or so. Caroline had asked him what was waiting for him in Dusseldorf, and he had simply told her that he had never tried curried bratwurst, fast becoming the national dish. He hadn't decided whether he would return to London and continue to work with MI5, although he had doubted that would be an option after her handiwork at the villa.

Caroline was sure that Neil Ramsay would come around. They had been through a lot together. Captain Durand would be on the same page and likely help concoct a story with Ramsay when they got clear and had time to revaluate. Milo Noventa would be the link between them, and it wouldn't be a stretch for the investigating officers to think that whoever killed Noventa had killed Fortez, and that it concerned dark web dealings or payback for a mafia boss' earlier life. Ramsay would be capable of leaving the relevant traces for an investigating team to discover. Which just left

Sally-Anne Thorpe. Caroline knew that Thorpe would not condone what she had done. There was too much police officer in her for that. Part of her imagined the woman on a personal vendetta, blowing the whistle on MI5 and outing rogue agents such as Caroline. But it wouldn't be that easy for her. And Caroline was damned if she would make it so. She glanced at the pair of crutches beside her. "Did you bring the box?" she asked.

"Yes, it's in the back. I've got the parcel tape and bag you asked for as well," Flymo replied as he gained height and headed for the alpine range of snow-capped mountains ahead of them.

Caroline smiled. Big Dave had met with Flymo further south on the lake and handed him the original box the crutch had been sent in. Thorpe's DNA and fingerprints were on the crutch as well as the box, and especially the tape she had used her nail on to cut a slit in whilst opening the box. The woman had thought in helping Caroline unpack it, she had taken up the offering of an olive branch, but Caroline had been in the game long enough to remain a step or two ahead. She'd give Thorpe a call when she landed and let her know that the weapon used in an assassination had her prints and DNA all over it, and that the box had her prints on, too. CCTV at the post office would show Thorpe collecting the parcel, while the CCTV at Fortez' villa would show a woman of athletic build - the same height, weight and build as Thorpe - the colour of her hair hidden by a headscarf. Pertinent to these facts, Caroline had not handled either the weapon or the box without the thin pair of linen gloves she now wore. Once they landed at Geneva, she would slip the box in a parcel bag and seal it, and then Flymo would take it to the storage facility just outside the airport and store it in the locker she had paid for and would continue to pay for monthly on her credit card. Just twenty euros a month for complete peace of mind.

Chapter Forty-Eight

Barents Sea

The feeling was slowly coming back to him, his limbs burning as they warmed and his lungs feeling as though he'd been hung up and turned into a punchbag. He looked at Rashid, resting in the same manner as himself, sitting in the hull of the boat with his back propped up against the bolster of the seat.

"I bloody hate swimming at the best of times," said Rashid.

"I'm going off it a bit as well..." King replied. "Thanks, by the way. That felt a bit too close..." He twisted around, caught hold of the seat and pulled himself up. It seemed to take all of his strength and energy. He took two of the chemical handwarmers that he had bought back in Longyearbyen out of his pocket, snapped them sharply to start the chemical reaction and handed them to Rashid. They were already hot in his hand by the time Rashid gratefully took them from him. "It's come to me, now."

"What has?" Rashid shrugged it off and pulled himself up as well. He tucked the handwarmers inside his jacket and watched as

King snapped two more and tucked them into his inside pockets. He then turned his attention to the case beside him and carefully lifted out the charges and underwater detonation cord. He was warming quickly, the marvellous devices feeling like two hot water bottles inside his jacket.

"That man Newman."

"You know him for sure?"

King nodded. "Last year, the whole Cole thing, the fallout from the Willard Standing affair. That guy was with Rachel Beam in the CCTV taken from the service station. He slotted Cole and then he killed her, too. A nice tidy end for the CIA to get us all back on side again."

Rashid nodded. "What are you going to do?"

King shrugged. "I set Beam up good and proper to get to Standing, but she shouldn't have been killed over it. Newman must have fooled her into helping him get to me, but in fact he was hunting Cole all along to draw a line under the tit-for-tat between us and the CIA."

"He doesn't have an engine, he's not going anywhere." Rashid shrugged. "The ocean is a dangerous place, especially at these temperatures."

"We'll see. I don't particularly want to spark another thing between us and the CIA again, but I don't like the way that man Newman works."

"Some would say the same about you, my friend," Rashid paused. "You aren't exactly subtle."

"We have a clear signal," Madeleine announced. "One-hundred and fifty metres depth, twenty-knots and heading North-East."

Grainger looked at the depth finder on the console. "We have an undulated seabed and two-hundred metres of depth in total. That's why the sub's kept to that depth. I know that three miles north-east of here, the depth goes way down. There's a deep channel that funnels various currents, including the Gulfstream into a tremendous current through the Northern Sea Route."

"How deep does it get?" asked King pensively.

"Beyond the scope of that tracking device," Grainger replied glibly. "Whatever you're going to do, you've got less than three miles to do it in…"

Rashid picked up a charge and studied it. It was heavy, five kilogrammes and the size of a family-sized cereal box. "These are not standard," he commented.

"They have been prepared by Royal Ordnance. The wrapping is waterproof and the det cord is for underwater demolition use," King informed him. "The charges have a non-return rubber seal through which to feed an RDX detonator and cord."

"Initiation?"

"Electronic timers. They have a waterproof housing but unless we get the calculations right, then we could miss by a hundred metres or more."

"The anchors are approximately five kilos in weight," said Madeleine. "Grainger and I have worked out sink rate of those, adding five kilos will be relatively simple to calculate. It's more to do with mass than weight when calculating how something sinks." She took out her smartphone and opened the calculator app. "The charge should reach one hundred and fifty metres depth in thirty-seven seconds. So, if you want to hit the sub travelling at twenty knots, we need to get approximately three-hundred and twelve metres ahead of it. But if we can be sure of reaching it at a speed of thirty knots, then we need to be in the ballpark of five hundred metres, which allows for the submarine's speed of travel."

"Approximately and ballpark?" King asked incredulously, as he attached the detonator cord to the RDX detonator and pushed it through the rubber seal.

"Give or take," she replied. But it's a large vessel, longer than a jumbo jet, and the variables are better for a shorter distance as it will still land on top of it, whereas if you drop too early, it will miss, and the submarine will sail over the charge." Madeleine paused. "Is the underside of a submarine softer or harder than the top of the hull?"

"I wish I knew," King replied lamely. "I was briefed to attach the charges to the side as there is a seam and it's the weakest spot. The idea being that it split open like a peeled banana."

"You were always going to blow it up?" she asked. "Why?"

King shrugged. "Not this one, another… It's complicated…"

"Hardly," she retorted. "You were sent to blow up your own submarine? Jesus, this is why I steer clear of politics."

"It would be better for you if you could forget you heard anything and don't ask anything else," Rashid replied, giving her a wink.

"Great…" she sighed, exasperated.

King taped each charge to an anchor with the lengths of Velcro from his kit, then wrapped the chain around and tucked the loose end of chain through itself to make a knot. Rashid followed suit, and they attached the electronic timers, setting the first three to thirty-three, thirty-five and thirty-seven seconds, respectively.

"The only problem I can see is that after the first explosion, they'll change their course," said King.

"Really? That's the only problem you envisage?" Rashid countered in good humour. "They could zig-zag, adjust their depth or speed." He paused. "Or of course, just send a bloody torpedo or two up to us to round off a pretty shitty day…"

"Okay, well all of that, then," King shrugged. "It sounded better in my head."

"What if the nuclear reactor is damaged?" Madeleine asked.

"It's a diesel submarine," King replied. "It works by a diesel generator system charging an electric motor. Even if it was a nuclear-powered sub, it would still only meltdown, it would never explode."

"Tell that to the crew of the Kursk," Madeleine replied.

"Perhaps our subs are better than the Russian's subs."

"But the warheads, then?" she protested.

"They wouldn't explode either, not even in the event of them being blown up directly. The thermonuclear detonation can only initiate in a three-stage process."

"Well, as a committed marine biologist, I'm not comfortable with blowing up a submarine in a UNESCO World Heritage environmental zone." She paused. "But I'm guessing from all of this, there isn't much choice?"

"The Iranians have stolen some British cruise missiles, or at the very least, the warheads inside. Those missiles are armed with illegally installed dial-a-yield nuclear warheads. Believe it or not, treaties and conventions dictate the way in which nuclear weapons can be used. The Iranian threat with those warheads in their possession is bad enough, but they're about to drop a few off to North Korea when they get the chance, so no. Nothing else is springing to mind." King picked up the first charge and said to Grainger, "Okay, so to get us approximately three hundred and twelve metres ahead of the submarine when we drop the charges, we need to get five-hundred metres ahead of a blip on Madeleine's laptop."

Grainger shook his head. "The GPS doesn't make such small calculations," he said. "I won't know if we're four-hundred or approaching five-hundred metres ahead."

"Shit..." King frowned, looking at the screen.

"What about these buoys?" Rashid suggested. "They're about the size of a man's head. Drop them out one at a time, and I'll tell you if we're five hundred metres away." He shrugged and looked confidently at King. "I can do it."

"You'll barely be able to see them without a scope."

"They're brightly coloured and the sea and sky are grey. I can do it."

King looked at the buoys, then back at his

friend. He knew that if anyone could judge that sort of distance, then it would be Rashid. "Do it…" He looked at Grainger. "Are we over them now?"

"Yes."

King turned to Rashid. "Drop the buoy!" He then looked to Grainger. "Hit it! Thirty knots!"

Madeleine kept her eyes on the screen. "Keep on that course," she said. "No change…"

King readied the first charge. It seemed like an age for the boat to get a five-hundred metre advantage, but Rashid raised his arm and lowered it quickly as if starting a race.

"Five-hundred!" Rashid shouted.

King tossed out the first charge. He bent down and picked up another, then dropped it as he had the first. "Keep on this heading but slow to fifteen knots," he told Grainger.

"Why not drop another?" asked Madeleine, not taking her eyes off the screen.

"We might be wrong. We only have four more and it's going to take at least two to damage that hull, and they're going to have to get pretty damned close."

The explosions came one after another. Even at a depth of one-hundred and fifty metres, two large plumes of water cascaded high into the air, spraying them with a fine, icy cold mist.

"Bang on!" Madeleine exclaimed. "Right on top of the beacon!"

"It's impossible to know if it has been damaged!" Rashid shouted. "We need to hit them again!"

"Only a mile until they enter the channel and then they can dive!" Grainger exclaimed.

"And they'll know that," said King. "But they need to escape, and they need to use the Northern Sea Route. They won't risk deviating. Once they hit the channel they'll go deep. But they will stay on course." He paused. "So, we do it again, with everything we've got!"

"But if we miss…" Rashid started.

"Then we bloody well miss!" King snapped. "We need to stop that sub, and we can only do it if we unload on them." He paused, glancing at Madeleine. "What's the beacon telling us?"

"They're on the same course, speed is increasing to twenty-five knots," Madeleine replied.

"Grainger, get to thirty-five knots, continue on the same heading. Rashid launch a buoy and you'd better pray you've got your eye in…" King readied the other charges. He still had the one set for thirty-seven seconds, and he shrugged as he set the next two for the same time and the other three for thirty-five, thirty and twenty-six seconds, respectively. Like spreading bets on a roulette table. The science of blind luck. "Madeleine, how's the course?"

"The same."

"The channel is fast approaching…" Grainger informed them.

"I reckon we're four hundred metres from the buoy." Rashid paused. "Four-twenty…"

"Course?" King asked.

"Steady," replied Madeleine.

"Four-forty…"

"Let's give them five-fifty to account for their increase in speed," King looked at Rashid and shrugged. "It's worth a shot."

"Approaching five hundred…" Rashid said, squinting at the buoy. He raised his hand. "Five-fifty!" He dropped his hand as if launching two drag racers off the line, then threw himself across the boat to help lift the charges for King.

King armed the first charge and tossed it over the side. He took the rest of the charges from Rashid, repeated the process three more times then stood up, breathless from the cold, the exertion and adrenalin. "Slow down to ten knots and keep the course steady…" he said to Grainger.

"We need to," Grainger replied. "We've barely got enough fuel to get back to the rigs…" Grainger was cut off by the first explosion, which was quickly followed by the second. Plumes of water spewed into the air like geysers. But the third charge sounded hollow and rumbled, the surface bubbling rather than sending up a plume of spray. The fourth charge exploded, again sounding hollow and was followed by a muffled 'thud', which reverberated through them and strangely, without rocking the boat.

King said, "Kill the revs…" He paused. "Explosions take the path of least resistance, no plumes would indicate two direct hits…" He stared at the ocean's surface, where large pockets of air bubbled up and popped on the surface, each one the size of a beachball. He turned his eyes to Madeleine's laptop, but there was no 'blip' displaying the submarine. Which could merely have meant the tracker had been destroyed. He looked at the GPS and made a note of the coordinates. When he looked back at the surface there were a few lifejackets floating, empty plastic bottles and strangely, a metal teapot with its lid still fastened in place.

"We got it!" Madeleine exclaimed. "I can't believe we got it!"

"So, it would seem," Grainger said somewhat subduedly.

"Forgive me if I don't cheer," Rashid commented, his voice seeming to echo in the stillness.

King watched the jetsam rolling in the gentle swell. The lifejackets afloat, while their loose straps drifted lazily beneath the surface like the tendrils of a shoal of yellow jellyfish. Calming and serene. "Hollowest victory I've ever had…" he said quietly.

Chapter Forty-Nine

London

Whether it was because he had experienced such a brutally cold climate, or whether it was because spring had finally sprung in London, he did not know. But it was evident that the sun was bright and hot on his face and the breeze blowing up the Thames was warm and smelled of the distant estuary and sea. The azure sky had given the river a mirror-like sheen and the buildings on the South Bank reflected clearly on the river's surface. The people of London were not generally known to be a friendly bunch, but today, as joggers, dogwalkers, and mothers pushing prams met head-on with commuters jostling their way to work at the tail end of the rush hour, there seemed a little more tolerance in the air than perhaps there would have been if the wind had blown cold and the clear sky above had scudded with dark rainclouds and the Thames had flowed brown and choppy and slick.

King knew that events were not going to run smoothly. Simon Mereweather had declined an office meeting. From his experience, a 'meeting without coffee' was one thing, but to be denied access to the entire building was quite another. The survival instinct in King had kicked in and he had procured a small automatic with a suppressor from his usual contact. He'd wanted a quick service and had received it. A text and a reply, a dead drop for the cash and another dead drop for the package to be retrieved. As usual, the weapon was clean – meaning no crimes had been committed with it – and King would have no doubts about its reliability.

The time and place had been arranged, but King had arrived an hour and a half early and before the rush hour had begun. He had used the time and the cover of people and traffic to survey the area. He hadn't spotted anybody, but that wasn't to mean he was in the clear. As he had recently started to do, he checked regularly for common drones – simple toy and craft shop models could now perform surveillance beyond MI5's wildest dreams ten years ago. Capable of hovering perfectly and film from a great distance in full HD, they were difficult to spot and practically impossible to destroy.

King had watched Simon Mereweather take a seat on a park bench opposite a statue of a lion. King had only recently discovered that London had ten thousand of them. Some on bridges, some on pavements, but many secreted around the city in the most unlikely of places. Many were in long-forgotten walled gardens. Sometimes King felt like one of those lions – caged and under constraint. Soon to be forgotten.

A woman in activewear stopped and placed her foot on the other side of the bench and fastened her trainer. She jogged on the spot while she checked her messages on her phone or changed her playlist. She turned and jogged away, and Mereweather never looked up from his paper.

King walked a lazy circle around the area, then zoned in on the bench and sat down.

"You're late," Mereweather said without looking up. "Happy I'm alone?"

"I don't mess about, Simon. There's a crosshair on you," he lied. "So, this had better be a friendly meeting…"

Mereweather folded his paper and placed it between them. His expression made it clear that he wasn't sure if King was bluffing, and to confirm this, he glanced around wondering where the best place for a sniper to view him from would be. "I sent you up there to destroy a British submarine," he said uneasily. "You failed. The submarine will now almost certainly be raised and handed over to the Royal Navy at the Faroe Islands. What terrible secrets are on that vessel will soon be discovered. We are in talks with the Admiralty to cobble together a story about a leak in the nuclear reactor. Under those circumstances, Aurora will likely back off and the Royal Navy can assume control, even within a UNESCO World Heritage area."

"Good," replied King curtly. "The families may never be reunited with their loved ones remains, but at least they'll have a story with an ending and a memorial."

"We are struggling for the general public's support of nuclear-powered submarines and the huge cost implications maintaining and developing them. Now we have been placed in a position where we will be forced to fake their unreliability. The public's support for an expensive nuclear weapons program has waned, too. Which brings me on to my next point…"

"I'll save you the trouble," King interrupted. "If you want me gone, then I'm gone. But that sub shouldn't have been carrying nuclear warheads. And we shouldn't have done half the things that we have over the years. So that's the pieces on the board, and it's a stalemate. Make your move Simon, but be prepared to be taken…"

Mereweather smiled. "I admire you, King. You have no limits, no boundaries you won't cross."

"For the right reasons," King said sharply. "I've done everything within my power to win the fight for this country."

"It's more than that," Mereweather replied. "You can't lose. Or at least, you don't know how to. You must walk into a situation with great confidence, which I suppose has come from winning at what you do." He paused and reached into his inside pocket but froze when he saw the muzzle of the suppressor poking out from King's worn leather jacket. "Jesus…"

"Nice and slowly now, Simon."

Mereweather breathed out a deep sigh and chuckled. "You make me nervous." He pulled out his hand, which was holding a dark blue velvet coated box. "You saved the day by destroying that Iranian submarine. I can't emphasise enough how those warheads in the wrong hands would have been a catastrophe beyond the worst recesses of our imagination. If Iran and the DPRK got their hands on those, then all bets would be off."

"They will get them eventually."

"No doubt."

"But not today."

"No." Mereweather paused. "In the report that you emailed from Spitsbergen, you mentioned an American agent. What became of him?" He absentmindedly thumbed the soft velvet covering the box, grateful for the tactile distraction.

King shrugged. "When we returned to his boat, he wasn't there."

"You said he was, in your opinion, the man who killed Cole last year. And by that token, he killed the Secret Service agent Rachel Beam as well."

"I reckon."

"So, the CIA sent a man, but he simply disappeared?"

"Into thin air."

"Right…" Mereweather said dubiously. "I suppose he could have met with another US submarine in the area?"

"That would be my bet."

"Did you kill him, King?"

"No."

"But he simply disappeared…"

"Trust me, we'll cross paths with that man again," King replied.

Mereweather nodded, finally accepting King's version of events. "The world's media has gone crazy over the story of two duelling submarines under the ice. Washington will be bolstered for years from the way that worked out for them." He opened the velvet case and showed King the medal inside. It was a cross with a medallion in the centre and bore the inscription For Gallantry around it. It shone brightly and had been crafted from highly polished silver and attached with a dark blue ribbon. "It's registered as an operative of the Security Service, awarded in a secret ceremony."

King frowned. "I thought I was getting fired…"

"No. Far from it. When the PM heard what had happened, or at least the salient facts, he insisted on awarding you the George Cross. It's the highest order for bravery in the British Isles and awarded to both civilian and military personnel alike. That said, I do want you to lie low for a while. There's an external review imminently on behalf of the Joint Intelligence

Services and Whitehall and it would be better all-round if…"

"If all the loose cannons were off deck?" King interjected.

"Indeed."

"I could do with a rest," said King. "And I want to spend time helping Caroline to rehabilitate. She will have been lost without me recently."

Mereweather cleared his throat nervously and looked away momentarily. "You haven't spoken to her?"

"We don't when the other is operational. I'm driving back down to Dorset when we're done here."

Mereweather sighed. "We've let her go, Alex."

"What? You fire her before giving her the chance to rehabilitate fully?" He snapped the medal box shut, shaking his head.

"It's not like that." Mereweather paused. "While you have been away Caroline has been assisting with a mission. Giuseppe Fortez put out a contract on you. Interpol intercepted it and brought it to us, Ramsay put together a team and when he informed Caroline of the threat, for her own security, she insisted on accompanying them."

"So why did you let her go?"

"Because she was insistent."

"I mean, why did you fire her?"

"She killed him."

"What?"

"She used the team as a stalking horse to get near Fortez and then she killed him. Ended the threat to your life right there and then. She escaped in a helicopter that she hired privately in Switzerland." Mereweather paused. "We think Dave Lomu was in on it, but he's disappeared. A shame really, because we really would like to talk to him about brokering the deal which saw Fortez put a million euros in Caroline's bank account before the meeting. One of those half-now, and half when the job is done arrangements. That's the bloody gem right there. The rest of the team were not present when that happened. We're not even sure if the broker, a man called Milo Noventa was forced to put the money into her account by Big Dave, before he allegedly came at him with a knife and was killed in the ensuing struggle. It's a mess."

King shrugged. "This is all news to me."

"Quite."

"Sounds like you need a talk with Big Dave."

"I will. Soon enough."

"Who else knows about the money?"

"Dave Lomu and Caroline for sure. Ramsay, because he's accountable."

"And does Fortez want it back?"

"In case you weren't listening, the man's dead."

"Then, I fail to see the problem."

"The problem is Caroline went rogue."

"You said that about me, not so long ago…"

"There seems to be a pattern emerging," Mereweather sneered. "And Leroy Wilkinson, AKA Flymo seems the most likely contender as her private pilot, as the company which hired the helicopter didn't supply a pilot and will not divulge any further information without just about every official channel being taken and without every requisition document known to man being double-stamped."

"That's the Swiss for you…"

"That's it? You hear that your fiancée killed a man, hasn't declared a million euros that was used to entrap a man searching for a contract killer and that's all you've got?"

"She loves me. I'd do the same for her and already have done." King shrugged. "Fortez was a bad man in a dangerous game. If you want to dance, you've got to pay the band…"

"We'll need the million back."

King shrugged. "I don't see how you think it was yours in the first place."

"King…"

"I'm quite sure it's illegal to run an entrapment operation in the way it seems to have been done. Neil Ramsay should have known better than that. And what about the top detective, Sally-Anne Thorpe? She knows the laws regarding entrapment." King paused. "And it sounds as if Caroline was fired from a job she loves, right in the middle of her rehabilitation on sick leave. Surely you wouldn't have allowed her on an operation in her condition?"

Mereweather stared at him, waiting for the punchline but it never came. He shook his head indignantly and said, "I didn't want to fire Caroline, but she gave me no choice."

"And how did she take it?"

Mereweather laughed. "Well, that's Caroline for you. She said, Well, a bullet only does the job it was intended for after it's been fired, maybe it will be the same for me…"

King smiled and stood up. "You know, Simon, I think she's probably right on that count…" He left Mereweather sitting in the shade, the early morning sun warming his face with golden light as he started across Westminster Bridge. In his right pocket the small automatic pistol weighed down his jacket and when he was clear of the couple who were walking towards him, he tossed it over the side and into the muddy depths of the Thames. He took the case out from his other pocket and opened it, the medal glinting up at him. For Gallantry… King thought of the things he had done, the terrible things he had been asked to do and the lives he had taken for his country. The image of the floating lifejackets paused in front of him a moment too long, and he tossed the open box into the water. He watched for a moment as the box floated and the medal glistened in the sunlight, before the box slowly filled with water and started to swirl in the current, and then it was gone. On its way into the murky depths. Another secret lost forever.

Authors Note

Hi – thanks for reading and I hope you enjoyed reading the story as much as I enjoyed writing it! Did you know you can sign up to my mailing lists for news of promotions, giveaways, and new releases? Head to www.apbateman.com to find out more.

I will undoubtedly be hard at work on another thriller as you read this and appreciate your support. If you have time to leave a short review or rating on Amazon, that would be great!

I hope to entertain you again soon!

A P Bateman

Acknowledgments

This novel required some technical data outside my 'wheelhouse', to use a common naval expression. Weapons, tactics, food, drink, vehicles and gruesome fights have never been a problem for my imagination, but the inner workings of submarines, communications and general naval procedures was something quite new for this author.

For their help with US Navy terminology and submarine protocols I would like to thank Richard Ashmore, Rick Nigh and John Bickford.

For her wealth of Royal Navy knowledge from submarines, navigation and communications, ops room knowledge and proof-reading skills, a special mention goes to Jacqueline Beard without whom certain segments of this story would not have seemed so real.

Any mistakes are my own.

The Alex King Series
The Contract Man
Lies and Retribution
Shadows of Good Friday
The Five
Reaper
Stormbound
Breakout
From the Shadows
Rogue
The Asset
Last Man Standing
Hunter Killer

The Rob Stone Series
The Ares Virus
The Town
The Island

Standalone Novels
Hell's Mouth
Unforgotten

**Further details of these titles can be found at
www.apbateman.com**

Printed in Great Britain
by Amazon

14872859R00233